LEGACY ACCEPTED

TAMAR SLOAN

JESS CONNORS
PUBLISHING

To Heidi
For helping me believe
xoxo

"This is where we met."

I turn to Hunter, finding his copper gaze glowing as he watches me. "I thought you might recognize it."

"How could I not?"

Turning on the spot, I take in the tundra. The promise of winter is more like a pledge around these parts. Snow already rests in pockets that used to be puddles, waiting to join with the higher peaks that are already white. You know it's only a matter of time before everything's coated in marshmallow.

Hunter rubs the back of his head, gaze a little rueful. "Well, the first time wasn't long ago."

It never stops to amaze me that this strong, powerful Were, the one who's been an Alpha for two years, who's made choices I don't know I could make, is still uncertain, almost shy, with me. I step forward as I smile. "It was the most vivid dream I've ever had."

Hunter's reciprocating smile is slower...warmer...sexier. "Well, I was dreaming with my eyes wide open."

Another step and I'm just where I want to be—in his circle of warmth. "You were pretty surprised."

"Ah, bedazzled would probably be more accurate." He tucks a hair behind my ear. "You, on the other hand, took it all in your stride."

My hand grasps his, bringing it to my lips so I can kiss it. Hunter's eyes flare copper fire in response. "I knew this was where I was meant to be."

With a soft groan, the one that always seems to be connected straight to my heart, Hunter's head leans down. My eyes close and my breath evaporates as his lips touch mine.

Love fills me, starting from somewhere deep within, meeting the matching fountain of feeling that's pouring into me. I push up, wanting, no, needing more. Then, just like I knew it would, it transforms into something hotter.

Something that has me pulling closer, hands rising to find his dark hair. My fingers spear in, holding the strands like they're a lifeline. Hunter's arms wrap around me, crushing us together so all of me is plastered against all of him.

It's my turn to groan, a sound of pure passion that seems to only tighten the arms I hope will hold me forever. Then hands are moving, tongues are roving. Desire and a sense of rightness are all I feel.

Hunter pulls back, breathing like he's just crossed the expanse of tundra. "You are one amazing girl, Ava Phelan."

I lick my lips, loving the taste of our kisses. "I'm your amazing girl, Hunter Rendell."

Hunter blinks, and for the briefest of seconds, his breath hitches. Then he smiles all slow and warm. "You're everything I've ever dreamed of."

I laugh at his words, but I don't miss the blink and the hitch. I may be the child of the Prophecy, the golden wolf that Hunter saw long before I knew she existed, but I'm not sure Hunter knows his importance in whatever this Legacy is.

Without Hunter I wouldn't have shifted; without Hunter, I wouldn't have discovered who I am.

But more so, without Hunter, the thread that is my lifeline would shrivel up and die.

I'd be nothing but the mixed-blood girl I was afraid I was.

He steps back, grasping my hand. "Come on, let's get this over and done with."

Sighing, I let him pull me forward. It feels like there's never enough time to glory in what we have. It's so startling and new, but so familiar and known. We've spent two weeks literally making our dreams come true. Just like we did in the nights I was asleep, we've run and reveled, sat and reflected.

It's the passion that was the surprise. A pleasant one. Actually, a freaking amazing one. One look from this Were and I'm pretty sure I'll never be cold out here. A fire has been banked and it's waiting for the oxygen that will feed it.

And that essential element is Hunter.

It's only a matter of time before he realizes I'm only something when I'm with him.

As we head back to the quad, I pause, pulling Hunter to a stop. I look at the rock formation to our left. "This is where Sakari set up her den."

Hunter's hand tenses in mine. "Yeah, it was."

I stare as the memories come. "She was all curled up, ready to give birth." I look up at Hunter. "You were so proud."

"That litter was going to mean so much."

Was...I saw those pups the following night. I frown. And I never saw them again. My hand tightens around Hunter's. "They didn't make it, did they?"

Hunter's lips are a tense line. "No, we lost them that night."

"Oh, Hunter."

I wrap myself around him. He's had so much loss in such a short period of time. Each death would be another arrow that stabs straight into the wound of the previous one. I wish they were hurts I could heal.

His hands come up to rub my arms. "Losing them meant we had no choice but try Dawn's captive breeding program." He sighs. "It was probably inevitable anyway."

I look up, knowing I'll find pain in his eyes. "You made the choice that will save these animals."

Something shifts through the copper depths, but with another blink, it's gone. "We're going to find out soon enough."

Stepping back, this time I pull us toward the quad bike. "Yes, you will." I glance over my shoulder. "I already know."

Back at the bike, I finally pause, realizing something that has reality intruding. "The first time we met—I was sleeping at the center at the time. It was cut short because Achak was born."

Which brings me back to why we're here. We've captured the last of the arctic wolves, all three of them. They're now safely held within the walls of Resolve—our own captive breeding center.

But now it's time to bring Achak in.

Hunter's arm slides around me, sending shivers skipping across my skin. "I know this is hard."

I rest my head against him, breathing in the scent that comforts one moment, kindles something completely different in another. "Like you said, as the snow creeps in, he's going to be a sitting duck. His red and grey fur is going to stick out a mile in the white landscape."

His chest rises and falls with a sigh. "Yeah. Doesn't make it any easier though."

It's been two weeks of no poachers and no Furious.

Furious is an unknown entity, but no-one is naive enough to assume the poachers are no longer an issue. Which is why we're bringing the wolves in—it's the only way we can make sure they stay safe.

I climb on the metal steed that has taken us to all ends of the tundra. Hunter tells me that in a couple of months it will become a Skid-doo. A part of me is excited to see the depth of snow that can accumulate here—I'm sure it's magnificent. The other part has no idea how my newly acquired Were body will cope with it. Will I be just as warm as the others? Or will my watered-down heritage still have an impact?

As I settle behind Hunter on the quad, shuffling forward so I'm wrapped around him as snugly as possible, I mentally flick the concerns away. Hunter's glance over his shoulder means they flutter away without a second thought. The promise in those eyes holds enough heat to melt the polar ice caps.

Hunter accelerates, heading further north, and I tap into the thread that connects me to Achak. Before I shifted I could trace them, but now...now they're like tapping into a live-wire. A glowing, moving river of energy that tells me so much. I discover the layers that make us all—the distinctions and diversity that makes us each an individual. Next are the feelings we all experience in various shades. But then there's the essence of the being that I'm tapping into—an essence that's exactly the same as mine. It's the universal energy that connects us all.

I lean forward, talking into Hunter's ear. "I wish you could see this."

He squeezes my knee. "That's why you're the child of the Prophecy."

He powers forward, following the direction that I point. I sense the thread strengthening already. "He's not far."

"I doubt he ever was."

Hunter knows I have a deep bond with Achak. After raising him because his mother was poisoned, his wild soul called to me. It was his strength that gave him courage and determination, something I always respected.

As Achak appears at the top of a hill, I smile. "He reminds me of you."

Hunter pulls to a stop. "Big and hairy?"

I roll my eyes, the smile growing. "Fierce and protective."

Shaking his head, Hunter climbs off the bike, and I'm not sure which part he's denying. I don't say any more, knowing this isn't the time.

Achak stops where he is, a lone wolf at the tip of the gently rolling hill. My heart lightens at seeing him, just as the breeze gusts his grey coat—the one that means he'll never camouflage when this world is white. I swallow as I wonder how I'm going to communicate to him that we need to bring him in. Achak's spirit isn't designed for captivity.

Standing beside Hunter, I watch Achak watch us. He was the one who saved Hunter's life...by killing the poacher who was about to shoot again. A human body that's never been found. It reminds me that whatever is looming is far more unknown and violent than I'd ever imagined.

That I'm not sure I'm ready for.

Hunter's hand slips around mine, like he knows I need a reminder I'm not alone. I squeeze his fingers, tapping into their strength. "I'll go talk to him."

Hunter's gaze is sharp as he releases my hand, the intensity telling me to keep safe. Despite all the unknowns of how Achak is going to greet me, despite saying that I'd go alone, he nods. "You got this."

With a deep breath, I release Hunter's hand and start walking up the hill. The magnificent wolf who I raised watches me approach, showing no signs of movement. He's not running away, but I also expected him to be a little happier to see me. Glancing back at Hunter, I noticed he's taken a few steps forward.

The unexpected stillness rams home that Achak has killed

a human. He's wilder than I was willing to admit, but at the same time, he's shown the lengths he would go to for those he considers his pack. Is it because Furious was once in his blood?

Could still be?

That frightening thought reminds me why I'm here. A deadly virus we still don't understand. Determined poachers who are more coordinated than we realized.

The undeniable truth is, wolves have never been more at risk of extinction.

I slow as I come closer. Achak is sitting, watching me, and I'm not sure what that means. I tap into the thread, trying to sense how he feels. The happiness that trickles through makes me smile—he knows who I am.

Shaking my head, I take him in. "I can't believe you followed me all the way here, Achak."

Achak looks at me like he doesn't understand why I'm surprised. When I take another step though, the happiness dims. Instead, wariness comes through loud and clear.

I stop, the smile I could feel in my chest disappearing. Is this because I left? Is it because of what happened with the poacher? I hold out my hand. "Thank you, Achak. He," I glance over my shoulder at Hunter, "holds my heart."

If it wasn't for this silent, still wolf that I've known since a cub, Hunter would probably be dead.

I send my gratitude through our connection, knowing he may not understand it, but he'd know it's a peace offering. Considering what I'm about to do, it's the least I can give him. I feel Achak's impulse to step forward and close the distance between us. It's a flash of the Achak I know.

But he doesn't. Like he's made a decision, his body tenses, becoming even more resolute. His canine eyes gaze straight at me. He's trying to tell me something, but I don't know what it is.

Please let him come with me. Taking in Achak against his will isn't something I want to have to do.

As I take a step forward though, Achak takes a step back.

I gasp, because the movement has him standing---and revealing what he'd been hiding.

Achak's been injured, his hind leg is a mat of dark red, the soil where he was just resting spotted with the thick liquid.

The wind gusts again and I hear Hunter move. He must've smelled the copper tang on the breeze. I don't look away from Achak though, knowing I need to keep our link. "You need to come with us, old friend. It's for your own safety."

And if that wound was caused by a poacher, then the need just became more urgent.

When I take another step, meaning there are only a few feet between us, Achak retreats again, letting out a bark.

He's telling me to stay back.

Except I can't.

"Please...No one will hurt you," I whisper, letting him know through our connection that I'm not a threat. That I want what's best for him.

But it doesn't matter. For some reason, Achak doesn't want what I'm offering. Maybe he remembers that the last time we saw each other, he was in a cage, but for some reason, I don't think so. Is it because he's injured?

"I can help you."

Our thread pulses, and I feel his flash of pain. This wound isn't new, and it's been causing him discomfort. And yet he didn't come looking for me.

My heart aches as I realize something has changed...and I don't know what.

I'm wondering if I should shift when Achak lets out another bark. One I recognize as goodbye.

"No!" I reach out again, like I can hold him here.

Achak can't leave. He has to come with us.

As if he knows exactly what I'm thinking, Achak turns and breaks into a lope, one marked by a pronounced limp. He doesn't look back as he trots over the ridge we're standing on. Turning, he goes to head back down the opposite side of the hill, going back out to the wilds of the tundra.

The crack of the tranquilizer gun makes me jump, even though I was expecting it. Achak yelps and rears as the dart impales his hind leg and I wince. This isn't how it was supposed to be.

Achak breaks into a run and I feel his pain flare. It stings my eyes and I'm glad to find Hunter by my side. I grasp his arm as he pulls me in close. "He didn't want to come."

"I got that impression." We watch as Achak pauses to look back at us, and I know I'm imagining the feeling of betrayal he throws at me, but it hurts nonetheless.

"He's injured, Hunter."

"I know, that's why I got the tranquilizer. We can't afford for him to keep disagreeing." He looks down at me. "Looks like he got a taste for the tundra."

And didn't want to leave. I'd banked on that. Achak coming back into captivity was never going to be something he agreed to readily.

But I'd hoped our connection was still strong enough for him to trust me.

"Do you think...do you think it was a poacher?"

Hunter sighs. "I hope not. Although that would explain why he's so shy and standoffish with you."

Achak's grey body grows smaller and smaller as he desperately creates distance between us. I close my eyes for the briefest moment, willing the moisture to dry up. The wolf I raised and loved is hurting, and more than just physically. Except I don't know why.

Please, let this be the right thing to do.

Hunter drops a kiss on my forehead and I let the comforting brush reach all the way to my heart. "This way you can heal him, and we can keep him safe."

I nod, knowing what Hunter is saying is true. The skills I've discovered since shifting are still our secret. I know they won't be for much longer, but Hunter understood that I want to see if I can understand them a little more before the world of Were knows.

I step back, not really wanting to let him go. "Come on, we'll need to be there once he's unconscious."

We climb on the quad but I don't need the threads to follow Achak. The scent of blood, the sporadic drops of red, lead us both to his unconscious form.

Just like the others, we'll load his body into the cage on the trailer. Just like the others, he'll wake back at Resolve, surrounded by chain-link fence.

Except it will be nothing like the others.

I raised Achak. I know him.

I asked him if he wanted this.

And he said no.

D awn peels the gloves off her hands as she exits the cage holding Achak. "The wound doesn't look recent. No sign of infection."

That's because I spent some time healing it before we brought him back. I've heard my mother describe the signs of infection enough times to know the redness and swelling weren't a good thing. But a few moments of tapping into our thread and magnifying our inbuilt capacity to heal, and the wound shrank and paled. I know I need to share these skills I've discovered, what I've become, soon. But I reach behind me for Hunter's hand—having a little more time before whatever responsibilities the golden wolf will have isn't too much to ask for is it?

Hunter steps forward and our fingers intertwine. "A gunshot wound?"

Dawn's Fae green eyes tense. "Unfortunately, yes. He must've managed to get away." She throws the gloves into a nearby bin. "He was lucky."

"Which means the poachers are still around. It's a good thing we brought them all in."

Achak's legs stretch as consciousness starts to return. My chest tightens as I wonder whether he'll think the same thing when he realizes he's woken up in captivity. Again.

Dawn lifts the vials of blood she collected while checking Achak's wound. "This may give us some answers."

I stare at the thick, red liquid. Achak is the only wolf who's been cured of Furious, and maybe that blood sample can explain why. I'm not sure what those results are going to mean for him.

Hunter nods. "KJ's been looking forward to getting his hands on that."

Dawn smiles as she heads down the hall. "Well, he's going to have to wait a little longer. This vial has a date with some Petri dishes." She pauses at the turn to the lab. "Ava, you still right to do the check on Sakari with me in about half an hour?"

"Sure. I'll be there."

Once she's gone, I sink into Hunter, needing his warmth even though I'm not cold. "Achak isn't going to like this."

Hunter's arms cocoon around me. "He may be like me. Happy to be anywhere you are."

I breathe in his wild, wonderful scent as I finally manage a smile. "Maybe you could have a talk with him."

There's a canine groan as Achak's body moves. His eyes open, groggy and unfocused, but I know that won't last for long. He's about to register his surroundings.

His nostrils flare as that dialed-up sense of smell gathers information. In a flash, his eyes open wide and he struggles to sit up. Even though his body isn't ready, he pushes himself up. First on his front paws, then on his hind legs.

Stepping forward, I lace my fingers through the wire. Achak will have to spend a few days inside before we can put him in one of the enclosures. We need to make sure the wound heals cleanly.

And Dawn may want more blood from the sole survivor of Furious.

"Hello, friend."

Achak spins at the sound of my voice and I see the recognition in his eyes, I feel it in our connection. Except there's no greeting. No flashes of happiness at seeing me. He lets out a bark, then heads straight for the wall. In the space of a breath, he frantically runs the perimeter of the kennel-sized cage. Seeing there's no way out, he runs back the other way. I gasp when he slams against the wire in his frenzy.

"Achak! Please, stop."

He does as I say, but only to head to the gate that leads outside. He begins to scratch and scrabble at the ground, futilely digging at the concrete floor.

"Man," Hunter breathes. "He really does want out. Did he do this last time?"

I shake my head. "No. Achak never liked captivity, but it's never been like this."

Hunter squeezes my shoulder. "He'll get used to it. And in a couple of days, he'll be out in an enclosure."

"I hope so."

I reach out through the thread that connects me so deeply to Achak. I try to send him reassurance, but I hit a wall of desperate fury. I frown. For some reason, he really doesn't want to be here.

I look up at Hunter, not voicing the fear that has germinated like a weed. Is this because of Furious?

Hunter cups my face, his copper gaze intense. "He only did what he did to save you. You know him."

I nod slowly. Hunter's right. Achak may be wild, but his soul is gentle. He's everything wolves stand for—loving, protective, loyal. This is just a shock for him. I rest my forehead on Hunter's chest. "I wish I could help him."

"You have to tell yourself you already are."

I nod again, not looking up, noticing that Achak's frantic scrabbling has stopped. Hunter's had to make these choices, which means I can too...because he's by my side. Looking over, Achak's laid down beside the gate that leads outside. He stares at me, a silent question you don't need a connection to decipher. Achak wants out.

"As soon as I can," I whisper.

Hunter squeezes my arms, then turns me towards the door. "Why don't you give the health check a miss? Maybe grab yourself a Mocha Munch muffin."

That almost has me smiling, despite it all. "I can't believe your mother made those for me."

"Unless Riley has eaten them all again."

"Surely that's not physically possible." This is the third batch. "But it doesn't matter. I can't miss the health check. They always go smoother when I'm there." I stop midway down the hall, wide eyes looking up at Hunter. "Plus, today is the first ultrasound."

Hunter scratches the back of his head. "Oh yeah. There's no way you'll miss that."

I tug on his hand, but Hunter doesn't move. He shakes his head. "I'll be in the comms room with KJ."

Like he has been every time so far. He says it's better to have less people there, to keep it as stress-free as possible for Sakari. I know he's right, but I wish it's something we could do together. Sakari's bond with Hunter is just as strong as mine, probably stronger.

With a kiss that I wish could be longer, we head down the hall in opposite directions.

By the time I get there, Dawn already has the chunk of meat sitting on the large set of scales within Sakari's enclosure. Seeing as we already know its exact weight, once Sakari climbs on to eat it, we're able to monitor her weight gain.

Dawn looks up with a smile as I approach. "She's just smelled it."

She's right. Sakari is coming out of her den. Glorious and white, she stretches at the mouth of her home. This is where she'll give birth to her litter of pups. The only litter of arctic wolves we know exists.

So much rests on their unborn shoulders. Possibly the future of their subspecies.

Sakari sees me and trots over to say hello. I squat down so I can scratch behind her ears through the wire. She leans into my fingers, seeking more pressure. I smile. "You're looking great, girl."

The greetings done, Sakari heads for the scales. Trotting past Dawn, she steps up, then sits down. The chunk of meat is gone in one mouthful.

My eyebrows shoot up. "Whoa, she must be hungry."

Dawn nods, her own eyebrows raised. "I'd better be quick."

She leans forward, eyes scanning the digital reading, then quickly jots down what she sees. I walk over, curious as to how she's going.

Dawn does a last scribble with a flourish. "She's gaining weight, which is wonderful. Even a little quicker than we would expect."

Relief has me relaxing. "That's great news." I look up at the camera angled down at Sakari's enclosure, giving a thumbs up. Hunter and KJ can hear everything we're saying thanks to the upgrade KJ made to the cameras. Not only can they hear us, there's even a speaker system if they want to answer.

Sakari wobbles a little as she steps down. "Will the sedative be enough?"

Dawn watches the female wolf closely. "I hope so. I didn't quite allow for that much weight gain, but it should be fine."

Sakari takes a couple of steps in the direction of her den,

wobbles again, and sits down. Now we wait ten minutes for the sedative to take effect.

Dawn steps back and leans against the back wall. "How's Achak?"

I sigh. "I haven't seen him object to captivity with that much ferocity before."

"He's been in the wild far longer than a cage. It would be hard for him to be back."

"I know." I just hoped that our connection would make it that bit easier for him.

"The blood tests will probably give us some answers."

I nod, knowing we need them, but also finding it hard not to be nervous about it.

"Ava." Dawn steps forward and her hand comes to rest on my shoulder. "I want you to understand there's a possibility that Furious—"

The door opens and Hunter strides in. "I thought you might want to know that Achak's settled right down."

I wipe the surprise off my face. "Ah, thanks."

Hunter glances at Dawn, a frown on his face. "There's no sign of any concerns."

Dawn straightens with a smile. "That's great news."

At least I'm not surprised when KJ joins us. He slips through the door, tugging down his beanie sheepishly. "We figured this was an important one to sit in on."

I raise a brow. Or Hunter just went all protective on me so I didn't have to hear what Dawn was about to say.

Not that he needed to. The moment I agreed to bring Achak in, I knew he'd be scrutinized. That someone might suggest he's still rabid. But I know my wolf, and he's not a threat to anyone.

And the promise I made stands—no one will hurt Achak while he's here.

Hunter being here tells me I'm not alone in upholding that

pledge. I look at the guy who's the reason my heart beats. "He knows he has friends here."

Hunter nods, face serious. "Damn straight."

KJ clears his throat. "Not meaning to interrupt whatever y'all are obviously committing your lives to, but I wouldn't mind knowing how those pups are going."

Dawn grabs the bulky bag by her feet and heads to the gate. "I know the feeling, KJ."

Sakari is asleep where she laid down, her big body breathing evenly. I follow Dawn in and we kneel on the compacted earth beside her. Dawn does the usual check—gently tapping the corner of Sakari's eye to make sure she's not under too deep, checking her teeth, then pulling the stethoscope out to listen to her heart.

She nods once she's done and turns to get out the ultrasound machine. It's a compact, portable one I've seen her use back in Jacksonville. While she's doing that I spear my fingers into Sakari's thick fur while I dive deep into our connection.

I sense her relaxation, feel the rhythm of her breaths. Sakari's lifeforce, like all of them, is so beautiful. Warmth connects us as I find the motes that make up everything that is life and follow them. They swirl and twirl through the fibers between us and I have to stop myself from smiling.

I'm vaguely aware of Dawn pushing some buttons and pressing a small, rounded probe against Sakari's belly. I stay still, realizing that modern medicine is trying to see what I already can. Dawn focuses on the grainy, grey image that appears on the small screen. I can't really tell what's on there, but it doesn't matter.

As Sakari pulls in a breath I head a little deeper. All of a sudden, I feel them.

"There's three!" Although Dawn's voice is hushed, it's full of the wonder I'm feeling.

Behind me, I hear a high five as Hunter and KJ celebrate the news.

Yep, there's three. Three heartbeats tripping through the thread, singing a song of promise and possibilities.

"Goodness, they're bigger than I expected."

Dawn's brow furrows as she moves the implement around. A similar feeling starts to bloom in my chest. There's something about these babies...

It's like they're familiar. Like there's a part I already know.

My hand jerks back a bit. It must be because I've shifted. I've never tapped into a pregnant animal, let alone since I've developed the sense of detail I now see. But still, there was something that hadn't felt...usual...

As I return fully to the physical world, my fingers finally register what I hadn't noticed below Sakari's thick fur. My hands move over Sakari's ribcage and I feel each and every one of them.

"She's very thin."

I hear KJ and Hunter step closer to the wire. When I look up, I find Hunter's gaze on me, even more intense than usual. He would've known I was tapping into the threads, so I'm not surprised he was watching me. But for some reason, he looks like he's holding his breath.

KJ frowns. "I thought you said she's put on weight."

Dawn puts away the ultrasound machine. "She has." She reaches over to feel what I just did. Beneath the thick white coat, Sakari's ribs are a noticeable corrugation of bumps. "Ava's right, though. She's lost condition."

Hunter is still watching me, not saying a thing. What is his gaze trying to communicate?

KJ rubs his forehead. "It must be the pups." He looks up at Hunter. "Maybe they're older than we calculated?"

Hunter finally tears his gaze from me. "Maybe..."

Dawn picks up her clipboard, scanning her notes. "It's the only logical explanation why the pups are bigger than anticipated."

KJ's hand drops as his grin reappears. "That sly Zephyr. Didn't waste any time, from the looks of things."

Hunter looks away, staring at Sakari's sleeping form. "We'll have to increase her food allocation."

Dawn pushes herself up. "Good idea." She dusts her hands on her pants, looking down at me with a smile. "Looks like these three guys will be arriving sooner than we expected."

I stand too. "That's exciting news."

Except when I look over at Hunter, excited isn't the word I'd use. He looks...nervous.

It must be because of how important this litter is. Three pups. One litter and the remaining number of arctic wolves has almost doubled.

And Hunter has seen the loss of so many wolf lives...

With a last glance at Sakari, I leave the enclosure. The sedative will wear off shortly and she'll head back to her den. Right now, I can feel that Hunter needs me.

KJ heads for the door, grasping Hunter's shoulder on his way. "This is going to be a good thing."

Hunter seems to tense, his gaze lasered on KJ. "They need to be born before we can say that."

I slip my arm around his waist. Yep, he's worried about this litter, especially after Sakari lost the pups two years ago. "They have a dedicated team looking after them. There's nothing we won't do to make sure they survive."

KJ arches a brow at Hunter. "Exactly."

With a sigh, Hunter looks down at me. He pulls up a smile. "Exactly."

Dawn strides past, patting my arm on the way, the bag slung over her other shoulder. "They're off to a great start."

Once KJ and Dawn are gone, I wrap my other arm around his waist, bringing myself to stand straight before him. "We won't let anything happen to them."

Hunter's eyes close as he brings his forehead down to rest on mine. "Ava..."

Cupping his handsome face, I gently pull up until his gaze is level with mine. "We got this. Our love is as old as this Legacy. There's nothing that can conquer that."

"Ava."

This time my name is said as a prayer. His mouth descends on mine, his arms wrap around me like I'm a lifeline.

There are cameras everywhere here, but I don't care. Hunter and I personified loved-up-couple the moment we admitted our feelings, the others have got to be used to it by now. I open myself up, loving that I can take as much as I give.

As our love is reaffirmed, as passion tugs deep within, I kiss Hunter. I show him what we are together. What we have.

And what we will be when he finally believes.

"So, when Hunter and Ava take things to the next level, they, like, really take it to the next level."

Yanking off my beanie, I scratch my head, sighing as I shove it back on. What about seeing those two on camera makes me feel envious and uneasy at the same time?

Well lookee here, they've actually come up for air.

Dawn smiles as she glances at the screen. "They're very intense."

I stretch my arms out, grinning. "Hunter was born intense."

Dawn lifts a vial from the centrifuge machine, holding up the red liquid. Her gentle face is full of excitement. "They're ready."

I rub my hands together. This is finally happening. "You look for antibodies, I look for virus particles?"

Dawn grins. "Deal."

Dawn slides the tube into a holder and we each grab a dropper. I suck up a globule of the complicated liquid and watch as it drops onto the small glass slide. Technically, blood's mostly a mix of water, salt, and protein. But you look beyond that, and you see how much more it is. It transports, it regulates, and it protects, twenty-four-seven. It's the lifeforce of any sentient being. You literally can't live without it.

But more than that, it carries the blueprints that connect you to your ancestry, whether you like it or not.

Sliding the small glass rectangle onto the microscope platform, anticipation is like soda in my belly. Achak's blood could hold a whole heap of answers to Furious and what we're up against. If he still has traces of the virus in his system, I can start studying the molecular bastard.

And hopefully, learn how to nuke it before it wreaks any more damage.

Dawn's sitting further down the bench at her own microscope, her slide already waiting to be studied.

She pauses. "That's wonderful news about Sakari, isn't it?"

My gut clenches. "Yeah. Once we get some more calories into her, she'll be right back on track."

"A lot is riding on that litter."

I study Dawn—her pale grey hair tied back in a braid, the ageless skin that talks of wisdom and maturity. There are things the Fae figured out way before Weres or humans even thought it could be a thing. Can I tell her about what Sakari is carrying? That everything she's taught me gave me the tools to splice and blend our DNA with that of wolf embryos. More than that, it's the fact that she believed in me that meant I had the courage to try it.

I open my mouth, but something stops me, just like it has all the times before, and I hate that. How can I not trust the woman who's been the closest thing I have to a mother? And she's a freaking Fae elder, for sheep's sake!

"Is everything okay, KJ?"

I smile, working hard to maintain eye contact. "Sure. This is all pretty intense, that's all."

Her returning smile is so full of warmth, it lights her whole face. "You haven't backed away from that yet."

Damn right, I haven't.

I look back at the microscope, knowing this moment could be pivotal. "So, what's our hypothesis?"

Dawn looks down at her own glorified magnifying glass. "That the therapeutic vaccine can work."

That's certainly been the question. Other wolves have been infected with Furious, but despite the vaccine, none survived. Which doesn't make sense. What is it about Achak that makes him so special?

"Well, only one way to find out."

I lean over, adjusting the zoom until the image comes into focus. The blood cells, a collection of hundreds of little red circles that look like frog spawn, sit in suspended animation. Just like Dawn taught me, I quickly label the plasma, the red blood cells, the white blood cells. Frowning, I shift the slide left then right. This isn't what I was expecting to see.

Clicking to a stronger lens, I go through the routine again. This time they're bigger, you can see their doughnut shape, their dark pink spongy texture. It confirms what I saw a moment ago.

I lean back, looking up to find Dawn frowning down at her microscope too.

Nervousness is making my whole body feel tight. "You seeing what I'm seeing?"

"I think so." She looks up. "It's all perfectly normal."

Dammit. I shove my chair back. "There's no trace of Furious."

"So, no particles?"

"It's like I'm looking at a healthy wolf's blood. Surely there're antibodies though? Even traces of them?"

Dawn's already shaking her head. "I'll take another sample,

but there weren't any here." Her tone says exactly what she's expecting to find on the next one.

I slide back, taking another look in the hope that I missed something. But it all looks healthy and average. I could be looking at any of the wolves' blood right now.

Dawn's voice gives rise to the logical answer. "Maybe he never had Furious..." She stares straight ahead. "That would explain why he was cured." She puts the last word into bunny ears. "He wasn't infected to begin with."

No. My mind rebels against the suggestion. Everything Ava described points to Furious.

Dawn sighs. "Our lack of adequate equipment doesn't help."

I hold up my hand. "Don't start with that again."

A hint of smile sparks in her eyes. "I was just saying. An electron microscope sure would come in handy."

I arch a brow. "Like the ones you have back on the mainland?"

"Exactly."

It's Dawn's tenacity to this cause that first drew me to her when normally I'd shy away from anything to do with the mainland. Just like Hunter, I'd found someone who was willing to put in the never-ending hours needed to get results. But when it comes to talking about the mainland, and the lab where that electron microscope can be found, well, that tenacity is a little less appreciated...

"Do you remember what I said the first time you suggested that?" I ask.

The smile breaks free. "That you'd rather sit for a family portrait."

The equivalent of riding a slow train to hell. "Enough said."

Dawn stands, stretching her back. "I'm going to grab a cup of tea before I get the next slide ready. Did you want anything?"

I shake my head. "Nah, I'm all good."

Dawn pauses at the door. "Maybe we should keep this between us for now, until we know for sure?"

Keep it secret? I glance at Dawn—this is the first time she's ever suggested something like that.

"I just think that until we have something concrete, there's no point worrying everyone."

I nod, figuring it makes sense. Isn't that one of the reasons I'm keeping Sakari's litter a secret?

I tug down my beanie, staring at the microscope. It doesn't make sense that Achak didn't have Furious, no matter what the bloodwork says. He almost killed the girl who raised him, for sheep's sake. We're talking Ava, child of the Prime Prophecy, the most gorgeous soul, probably the only one who can reach past Hunter's self-hatred, Ava.

Then how is he still alive? I frown, remembering what Dawn said to me once. Grabbing the slide, I head back to the centrifuge machine. Maybe I'm asking the wrong questions.

Dawn pauses as she walks past me to the door. "That's what I like about you, KJ. You think outside the square and you don't give up." She squeezes my shoulder as she passes me. "It's exactly what this fight needs."

4

HUNTER

"We need to tell her."

KJ doesn't lift his head from the microscope, but I don't bother repeating myself. As much as he likes to pretend he's not Were, I could have whispered it and he would have heard.

The silence in the lab stretches out, but that's fine by me. We have some big stuff to sort out.

KJ leans to the side, jotting something down on the page beside him. I cross my arms and lean against the bench. He knows I'm waiting.

He goes back to looking over the microscope, fiddling with a knob on the side.

I shuffle a little, letting him know I'm making myself comfortable.

KJ sighs but doesn't look up. "We've been over this."

Yes, we certainly have. I tell KJ this can't be kept a secret. KJ points out that this is a lot to lump onto a new relationship. I remember that no one knows Ava is the golden wolf and we've done some pretty impressive dream-teleportation for two years.

As I go to argue, KJ points out that we don't know how she would take it.

That I could jeopardize everything with her.

We finish on a stalemate—because he knows she's the one thing I can't bear to lose.

But that was before the ultrasound. "We know exactly when Sakari conceived, because you artificially inseminated her."

The fiddling pauses for a second.

I take a step closer. "They're growing faster than they should, KJ."

KJ pushes back in frustration, his angry gaze coming up to connect with mine. "And you reckon Riley is tenacious."

I shrug. "The words I use are 'stupidly stubborn', actually."

"Well, it seems like it's a dominant trait in your family."

A couple more steps and I'm beside him. I lean back against the table, crossing my arms. "You met my dad, so I don't know why you're surprised."

KJ brings his hands up to rub his face. "Nothing seems to surprise me anymore."

Well, I got one hell of a shock this morning. "Weres grow faster in-utero, KJ."

KJ sighs as he rubs his eyes. "I know."

"That's not a good thing."

"I know."

"I need you to explain this to me. They're only meant to have wolf genes."

KJ explodes to his feet. "Have a look around, Hunter. Does this look like a professional genetics lab to you? I did the best I could with what I had."

My arms fall to my side, suddenly feeling too heavy to hold up. "You mean..." I shake my head, trying to grasp what that means. "KJ, what if...?"

KJ's fingers spear beneath his beanie, pushing it up from its usual low-brow position. "I don't know what it means. I did everything I could. I used genetic probes. I isolated the genes with as much precision as I could. But there was always a risk."

A risk? What sort of risk? But I don't ask the question—I'm not really sure what the question would be. And if I can't finish the question, KJ won't be able to answer it. This is quickly getting out of control. "I'm not keeping this from Ava. Dawn needs to know too."

KJ is in front of me in an instant. "No! They're Fae, they'd never understand."

"KJ, Ava is..." The one probably more connected to wolves than we are. "She isn't going to like it, but we can't keep this from her."

But KJ is already shaking his head. "And what if they don't understand, Hunter? What if they don't want these pups to be born?"

I suck air in only to find it gets stuck in my tight chest.

"Then we lose our last hope."

Like we were in a boxing ring, and he just dealt the knock-out blow, I reel back. Ava would never...

"Sakari may not see this pregnancy to term. The pups could be stillborn. They may not make it past their first week. You want to risk everything with Ava, for me to lose Dawn, the one who finally gave me a way to fix all this, on an if?"

The pieces of this puzzle, the way forward, are a whirlpool in my mind. I can't keep hold of anything long enough to be able to make a decision. Ava and the Legacy, Dawn and her determination, KJ and his drive for redemption. Me and my twisted heart desperately trying to make it something deserving of Ava.

KJ's arms fall to his side. "We started this, Hunter. We see it through."

I step back, and then back again, needing some space. We

just went through a round, and bruises were dealt to both sides, and still came out at a stalemate.

Heading to the door, I almost wish I'd never come in. The squeak of KJ's seat as he returns to the microscope scrapes across my ears. I'm almost out when the last sucker-punch hits me. It has everything tightening enough to hurt. I turn to see him leaning back over like we never spoke.

"The only problem is, KJ, we don't know what we've started."

I shut the door before he can respond, knowing he probably won't anyway.

The comms room is emptier than the lab was, but I know that won't last for long. It's almost evening, which means time to head home. I check the roster, seeing that it's Riley's turn to stay at Resolve. I make a mental note to make sure Josh is in the car on the way home. The permanent-texting is fine between her and Ava's cousin, but all night alone out here? I don't think so.

The screens flicker up on the wall, some cycling through the three or four cameras they're connected to, others fixed on the more important areas. Dawn is outside the remaining three wolves' enclosure. She's pacing, a phone held tensely against her ear. It seems we're all on edge.

Riley and Josh are patrolling the enclosures. Both wearing t-shirts and jeans, they hold hands and chat and smile. Although the wolf in me wants to go all protective on my little sister, Josh seems like a good guy. And ultimately, any promise of love at the moment is a good thing.

KJ is back to bonding with his microscope. His drive to fix this legacy has always been a personal one. He's decided he's solely responsible for the hatred humans feel toward wolves, which isn't logical...or fair, but nothing has really felt fair since this all started. My jaw is tense as I look away. I don't know who I've betrayed more by making the decision about the genetically engineered pups. My kind, or the future I desperately want with Ava.

I'm scanning for the one person who can make me believe this may turn out okay when the door opens behind me. It's probably her—she always seems to know when I need her.

But the body who comes through isn't Ava. It's tall and male with the strong physique of a Were.

I straighten. "Gareth."

The man who was my father's best-friend nods. Gareth is tall, taller than my dad, and leaner. His dark hair has always been a little too long, his light grey eyes more piercing than I would like.

"Hunter." He takes two steps in and stops. Actually, I'm surprised he's come in this far considering how my pack feels about the captive breeding program. "How's Ruth and Riley?"

"Mom is loving more people to fuss over back at home, and Riley, well..." I think of how inseparable her and Josh have become. "She's been busy too."

"That's good to hear."

I'd ask the same of Gareth, but he doesn't have any family. Every pack has their confirmed bachelor, the one guy who never seemed to have found his mate. For the Rendell's, that's Gareth.

I wait, knowing this isn't a social call.

Gareth crosses his arms. "The pack are worried."

So they should be. "We all are, Gareth. We're facing some serious threats."

"And we don't think captive breeding is the way to solve this. It's not natural to have wild animals in cages."

My fists clench. This isn't something I haven't heard before.

"Your father wouldn't have—"

And we're done here. "I didn't see you step up as Alpha, Gareth."

Gareth's frown is ferocious, but I don't regret my words.

When my father was shot, the pack grieved, but no one was willing to take over the reins until I was old enough to at least shave regularly. Every one of them knew some hard decisions would need to be made.

Moving forward, my frustration matches his. "There are very few arctic wolves left and we're doing everything we can to make sure they survive."

"You've lost just as many in this," Gareth's arms wave to encompass the concrete around us, "tomb than we did out there. If Furious hits again, you'll wipe them out in one sweep."

I hate that he's right, but I don't let Gareth's words have any air time. "We leave them out there and the poachers have their target practice."

Silence dominates as we both pull back. I hadn't realized how wound up I'd become.

Gareth huffs. "This isn't the answer, Hunter. This was never what the Rendells are about."

I raise my brows. "Doing what needs to be done to protect the wolves?"

Jeez, I'm starting to sound like KJ.

Gareth looks away, his head shaking slowly. I'd like to think he's shaking up his own unquestioned beliefs, but I know he's far more likely rejecting my words just because that's what they've always done.

The screens capture his attention and he straightens, taking it all in—the desks, the computers, the intensive surveillance system. Yes Gareth, this isn't some barely-thought-out project. Gareth looks at them long enough for the images to scroll through their various cameras.

He frowns. "Who's that?"

I don't need to look up to know who he's talking about, but I turn around anyway. There's only one person here that grabs you like that and doesn't let go.

"That's Ava." My light and my heart. "Ava Phelan."

Gareth grunts and I wonder which part of Ava's reputation is most salient in his mind. The fact that she's the child of the Prime Prophecy? Or the fact that no one believes she can shift? It's only a matter of time before they all know she's not just everything I've ever wanted, but she's everything we all need.

"And that wolf." He steps closer. "It's a grey wolf."

"Ava raised him. He followed her here." I wait, curious what he'll make of that.

"From the mainland?"

I shrug. "My guess is he snuck on one of the cargo ferries."

Gareth enters the room fully so he can stand before the bank of screens. Achak is back to pacing the perimeter of his small cage. Ava is sitting on the other side of the fence, not talking, not moving. I'm one of the few people who know she's tapping into the threads she sees. She'd be trying to reassure Achak without crowding him, her unique recipe of compassion and patience weaving its magic.

My chest swells with pride as I watch. As much as I want to shout it over the tundra, I don't mention my relationship with Ava. She hasn't told her parents, and therefore her pack, about us. I get why—the ramifications are significant—but part of me wants to give Gareth another reason to shut the hell up.

Although, there's always the possibility that it'll be better for no one to know...

"That poor animal."

What?

Gareth turns to me, anger a bubbling cauldron in his eyes. "This is exactly what the pack is saying, Hunter. You're caging these animals against their will. That's not the way of Weres."

Achak is still pacing, very much playing the caged animal. If I start telling Gareth this isn't typical, that Achak was born in captivity, that a wolf wouldn't follow anyone if they weren't willing to risk imprisonment, then he'll think I'm trying to justify the choices I've made.

And I did enough of that two years ago.

"Have you ever had to make a tough decision, Gareth? One where your heart went one way and your brain the other, and who freaking knows where the right choice lay?"

He pulls back, like I just punched him in the gut. I'll take that as a yes.

"And how did the decision sit with you?"

Gareth turns away, frowning, but it's not the victory I was looking for. He heads for the door. "All I'm saying is that this isn't the solution, keeping them in cages."

He shuts the door behind him and it feels like I just went through the same chest-crushing conversation I had with KJ... which ended with the same result—a stalemate.

This time when I look up at the screens, they're empty. The wolves are in their dens, and the others would be packing up to go home. Actually, I think I need a break from this place tonight.

When Ava walks in, I pull in a deep breath. It's like everything brightens when she's in my orbit. I know without a doubt, that just like she's my beacon of hope, that is what she'll be for everyone impacted by this Legacy.

Which is why I'll do anything to keep her safe.

She frowns when she's in front of me. "Is everything okay?"

I want to touch, but for some reason, I hold back. Ava's love, her very essence, is so honest and pure. What is she doing with someone like me? "One of the Rendell pack just stopped by. He thought he'd remind me of how my pack feels about Resolve."

Ava slips her arms around my waist, curling into me. "Oh, Hunter. They just don't understand."

Her touch is a balm to the ache in my chest, and I can't help but fold around her. I bury my face in her gossamer hair, breathing in deeply.

She looks up, a smile sparkling in her green eyes. "You know this just shows how strong you are? Who else could have stood up for what they felt was right at a time like that? You were sixteen Hunter, and you'd just lost your dad."

Only Ava could look at it like that. Like a guy in need of salvation from this angel, I kiss her. I try to show her what her belief in me, misplaced as it is, means. I pour my soul into the places we connect.

And Ava takes it all. She pushes up on her toes, no longer giving me reassurance, now seeking something more. The knowledge that I can give it to her explodes through me like a firework. I pull her in tight, hands moving down her length, molding all of her to all of me.

She part sighs, half groans. It's a sound of surrender and victory all in one. It's a sound that has my heart smiling and my soul soaring. With this amazing girl, miracles will happen.

We pull back, holding each other close. I stroke a strand of her pale hair back from her face. "You have me believing, Ava."

She plants a butterfly kiss on my lips. "I never knew it was possible until I met you."

If a camera was on us now, I wonder if it would capture the amount of emotion I'm feeling. I haven't heard anything good today, but just a few minutes with this girl, and I start believing in unicorns.

Ava steps back, hand sliding down my arm to grasp my hand. "Let's go see what your mom has made us for dinner."

I chuckle. "You know we didn't have any vegetarian cookbooks in our house before you came?"

She grins. "Riley mentioned that, but used a totally different tone."

"You mean Josh hasn't informed her of the health benefits of such a diet?"

Ava giggles and the sound is a melody in a laugh. "I'm not sure they get around to talking that much."

Heading for the door, I glance back over my shoulder. Resolve seems quiet, reminding me of a sleeping beast.

Maybe one that's waiting.

For now, I'll wait too. Right now, I have Ava, and that's far more than I could dream of.

And I'll protect her, and Resolve, for as long as I take breath.

5

HUNTER

"I don't think I've ever had a soufflé before." Ava is patting her flat belly as we stand outside the bedroom door.

I grin. "Do you think double-baked is just a fancy term for warmed-up?"

She mock glares at me. "Personally, I don't care. It was delicious."

"Even Riley didn't complain about that one."

Ava opens the door and I lean against the doorjamb. This is a routine I've come to savor. "Good night."

"Well, they used to be."

I frown. This isn't how it usually goes. "You're not sleeping well?"

Ava's unfocused gaze stares up at the ceiling. "I used to have the most amazing dreams."

Relief has every muscle relaxing. "They would never compare to what I saw out on the tundra some nights."

"Luckily, now my days are even better."

She pulls me down for a kiss. Our goodnight kisses stay chaste for a reason, but man, it's getting tough to do that. There's a deeply primal part of me wanting to stake a claim on this girl.

It doesn't help that it feels like she's doing everything she can to leave a mark of her own.

We separate, breathing a little faster.

I step back. "I love you, Ava."

She slides further into the room, her kiss-swollen lips smiling. "Hopefully as much as I love you, Hunter."

I turn and head down the hall, figuring I might as well unstack the dishwasher before I go to bed. My buzzing body isn't going to be settling down anytime soon.

"Hunter?"

I turn, wondering about the change in routine again. "Yeah?"

"Are you sure it's okay for me to use your room? I don't mind giving it back."

Shaking my head, I smile. "I barely used it anyway, so it was a logical choice." I throw a little heat into my smile as I turn to face her. "We could share..."

Ava's cheeks heat up, just like I knew they would. "Hunter! Your mother would...would—"

"Wonder if you're really a princess?"

She glares at me. "You know I hate that. I'm talking about probably embarrassing her in her own home. "

"Is that the only reason stopping you?" I tease.

Ava angles her head and the length of her hair slides to the side. Tapping her lips, she looks at me. Suddenly, I'm feeling a little flushed myself. "Well, there is one other reason..."

I swallow, my mind jumping to a few painful conclusions. "Oh?"

Her chin drops. "I'm pretty sure I wouldn't be acting like a princess."

Oh.

My heart stutters. My mind blanks. My legs forget they were heading somewhere.

Ava's Fae green eyes twinkle. There's a glint of mirth, but

also a healthy gleam of passion. She's teasing me, testing me, but also letting me know she's half-serious. All of the above are everything I need right now.

Are everything I'll ever need.

"Ava."

"Yes?" Man, I like that breathy tone.

I take another step down the hall, more to bolster my own self-control than anything. "Every now and again, Mom goes away for a night..."

Ava's eyes widen, and I think I've finally leveled the playing field, but then her smile grows too. It grows so slowly and so sensually and is so full of promise that I happily concede defeat. Every gauntlet that's laid down for this girl is just another challenge for her to accept. I love that our passion is one of the ones she wants to step up to.

With a wave and a look filled with untapped potential, Ava disappears into my room. I grin, and grin hard, as I finally find the ability to move again.

I've unstacked the dishwasher, swept the kitchen, and folded the laundry before I've dialed-down enough to climb into bed. Although bed is a fairly loose term for what I have.

The trundle that's wheeled out into the lounge each night was made in a torture chamber. It's a good thing I don't sleep much. Too many nights patrolling the tundra for the past two years has meant my body clock has decided sleep is overrated.

Tucking my hands behind my head, I stretch out until my feet hang off the end of the metal framed contraption. Staring at the ceiling, I admit I miss being out there. There's the hidden power, the isolation, the promise of peace that somehow lives in the air. It's there that I met Ava as the golden wolf, it's there that we finally learned we could have what only seemed possible in dreams.

But with all the wolves now at Resolve, there's no need to

run over the soil and snow. Instead, I get to stare at the light-fitting that Mom made me dust three times before Ava arrived. The flower-shaped glass dome isn't even attractive, but I think someone gave it to my parents as a wedding present.

I recognize the footsteps the moment I hear them. Riley couldn't tiptoe even if she was trying to sneak some Mocha Munch in for a midnight snack, and Mom has a slightly uneven gait from an accident in her teens.

So why is Ava creeping around at a time like this?

I sit up as she stands in the doorway to the lounge. "I can't sleep."

"Me either." Between my demons, missing the tundra, and her sexy teasing, I never stood a chance. But what would keep Ava awake?

She comes in and sits on the edge of the trundle bed, eyes raking over my naked chest. It creaks loud enough for us both to freeze. After a few moments of confirmed silence, she leans forward. "I miss running with my white wolf."

I yank in a breath. We haven't run in what feels like ages...

Ava's smile glints in the dark. "Wanna play tag?"

WE PUSH the quad out of the carport and most of the way down the street. Were strength certainly comes in handy when you're trying to sneak out to the tundra with your girl. Our smiles are full of anticipation as we climb on the moment we're far enough away from the house.

The autumn landscape at this time of the night is cold. The wind whips your face with enough sting to let you know you're alive. Behind me, Ava is curled around my back, sharing warmth and probably not realizing how much it raises my body temperature.

Once we're past the town, she pushes up to whisper in my ear. "Faster."

My grin feels like it stretches from horizon to horizon. Was it really only a few weeks ago that she said the same thing to me? "Your wish. My command."

I accelerate, the cold making me squint, the rush making me smile. Ava's arms tense around my waist, her excitement matching my own. I've spent so many nights on this tundra, it's like I'm back with an old friend. Killing the lights, I let my Were sight do its thing, loving the workout for my reflexes. Ava gasps, and I wouldn't have thought it was possible, but my grin grows.

Ava has only been full Were for a short period. The heightened senses are all so new to her. Right now, she'd be seeing what I do—a landscape looking like it's built of shades of moonshine and shadows. It's like it's in stark relief but muted all at the same time.

We reach the place we met and I cut the engine. When the last of the roar dies, the silence is absolute. It's like even the wind doesn't want to make any noise. We climb off and stand, face to face, letting the anticipation build.

I try for some semblance of Alpha-like responsibility. "This isn't something we can do too often." Although the poachers would be gone by now, it's still a risk to run as a wolf.

Ava nods. "We haven't done this for two weeks."

"And we can't be out too long." My mother has worrying stamped into her DNA.

Ava shakes her head. "We won't be." She angles her head. "Although, we'd be home quicker if you talked less."

I grin—cheeky minx. "Shall we shift together?"

"That's my Alpha."

The grin grows as I shake my head. "On three. One. Two—"

In a flash Ava has shifted. Because I wasn't expecting it, I barely get to register the flash of pale skin that would probably have my heart stopping before a glorious, golden wolf is standing before me.

She literally robs me of breath. She's all the shades of heat; from the depth of glowing embers, to the flickers of a wildfire. She's sunset and sunrises all in one.

There's no doubt in my mind that Ava is my mate.

What's more, there's even less doubt that she's the key to this Legacy.

She tilts her head, those familiar wintergreen eyes growing bigger as she raises her brows. My golden girl is waiting.

Well, I'm more than ready.

I let the explosion of a shift overtake me, the freedom erupts through my body. In only seconds, the world is even sharper again, smells and sights are overwhelming for a split-second, all of a sudden, sounds that hadn't existed filtering over my eardrums.

It means Ava is even more beautiful. She steps forward, eyes soft and warm and I fill my lungs with everything that is her. Beauty, power, love. I angle my head down and our foreheads touch. We stand there for long moments, breaths matching, hearts thumping. This is just Ava and me and everything we are together.

Her eyes light up a split second before she moves. It's invigorating to realize I've known her long enough to predict what's coming next. With lightning Were speed she taps her nose against mine, spins around, and streaks away. I wonder whether I should give her a head start, then consider slapping myself if I had hands. This girl is happy to play dirty if it means winning.

I push off the hard soil, injecting as much speed as I can into chasing after her. She glances back, eyes widening as she sees me not far behind, and lets out an excited bark. With a last challenge thrown over her shoulder, she hangs a sharp left. My adrenalin spikes as my heart smiles.

Let's do this.

We power over the patchwork of snow and soil, and I can see how much Ava is loving this. To be honest, I don't think it'll ever get old. She runs faster and faster and I periodically pull in and fall back like a breath. The night is our only witness, the cold no longer noticeable.

Deciding it's time to live up to my name, I gain some speed and reach forward and ever so gently brush her tail with my nose. It's a subtle touch, but I knew she'd feel it. It seems to shiver through her. With a "you're in!" yip I head east—let's see how long I can last. With the grace of someone who's been a Were for much longer, she spins and changes trajectory. I take in the excited, determined gaze and figure I'd better pick up some speed. I don't think this victory is going to last long.

In all fairness though, I want to get caught. If being touched by Ava means losing this game, then that's okay by me. I pretend to play hard to get, but as inevitable as my falling in love with her, she catches me. Her tag is a whole lot more playful—she runs up beside me and bumps me with her shoulder. Her smiling eyes come in close for the briefest of moments and she nudges me with her nose. In a flash, she does an about turn and heads back the way we came.

The excited bark I let out is almost involuntary; so much happiness and pride are pulsing through my body. I slow just a little, wanting to take in the beauty that is Ava in full flight—golden fur rippling, graceful limbs running. We're on a track that countless animals have created, that the wolves once used. The compacted strip will take us back to the quad. I'm going to memorize every second of this moment.

A gust of wind slaps at my face and the smell that whips past my nose has my eyes narrowing. It's a familiar smell...but one that should be alien in this setting, but it's gone before I can place it. I pick up the pace, hoping to smell it again. Ava hears me coming but doesn't accelerate. It looks like someone else is just as happy to be caught.

When I smell it again, I register exactly what it is. It's a scent that has my head lifting and my chest tightening. It's a smell that shouldn't be here anymore. It's the mark of a wolf, but no wolf who has lived here.

Only a few yards away I realize why that smell is here. There's a low bush, an outcropping of rocks. If you squint, you can see where the soil has been disturbed.

Someone has set a trap.

And Ava is running straight towards it.

I run forward, as hard and as fast as I can. In seconds I'm beside her, wishing I had the power of voice. If she doesn't stop or change direction—

She looks up, eyes alight with love and life, but then she sees my urgency. She frowns and slows.

But it's too late. As her long-legged lope takes her straight over the top of the metal-jawed ambush I shove her with my shoulder. Her green eyes flash wide with shock and she has no choice but to honor the laws of physics. My momentum propels her to the side, sailing through the air as she shifts back to human. I don't get to see her land because I hit the ground and the trap snaps shut.

The pain is sharp and immediate as my foot's crushed between the metal jaws. This isn't some captive breeding trap that's designed to not cause injury. As I feel it slice through my flesh and lodge in my bone, I know this was set by someone who didn't care about the agony it would inflict.

I'm yanked to the ground with a clang of the chain. I clench my jaw and every muscle I can find to stop myself from crying out. I need to make sure Ava is okay.

"Hunter!"

She falls to her knees beside me as I lay on the ground. The pain is trying to expand beyond my leg, but I don't let it. It takes all my concentration to keep it contained.

"Don't shift."

I don't think I could if I wanted to.

Her hands flutter over me, looking to see if anything else is hurt. I don't think so, but it's hard to think beyond a foot that feels like it's got a saw wedged in it. We both look down and her gasp tells me she sees the damage too.

Serrated teeth are lodged in white fur, red flesh, and redder blood a bloom around it. The rest of the trap and the ground beneath it match the grisly claret color.

Ava swallows, her eyes looking like they're holding as much pain as mine. "I'm going to have to release the trap."

I nod. It's the only way.

But damn, the thought of more pain isn't appealing.

She shuffles down, face tight as she takes in the train wreck that is my leg. She's looking forward to this as much as I am.

I lay my head on the ground and close my eyes, pretending I'm ready.

"I'm so sorry, Hunter."

There's a click and I swallow. There's a movement and I tense. And then she does it. As much as I want it off, and as much as the release of pressure is welcome, it feels like someone is serrating my flesh again, but this time in slow-mo. Every muscle knots with the agony, and it feels like I'm trying to pull in on myself to make this more manageable.

"It's off." Ava's voice is a comforting breath amongst the maelstrom of pain. "Hold still."

As a wolf, I can't point out that I'm not going anywhere anytime soon.

Ava's hands move back up to my chest and then stop. They sink into my fur, gentle and graceful, as her eyes close.

I've experienced Ava's healing before. It saved my life after the poacher shot me. I can verify it's the most inexplicable, amazing feeling a person could ever experience. There's a warmth that you can't tell whether it's inside or outside. There's light you can't see, but know is there. You know this girl is touching somewhere you forgot you had.

The pain dissipates wave by wave and I relax. It feels like each gash and bruise and rip of my skin is becoming a memory. I can no longer feel where the bone of my leg is, or every fiber that it's attached to. I pull in a breath into lungs that suddenly feel free and easy.

Man, this girl is magic.

Ava sits back, relief sagging her shoulders. The flicker of a smile graces her lips.

I shift back to human, looking down at my leg. It aches and I won't be looking at running a marathon anytime soon, but Were healing will take care of the rest. Ava stands and pushing myself up, I test my weight and find it barely hurts at all.

I look up, wondering how I'm going to say thank you for the second time, when I notice that Ava is cradling her arm. Frowning, I grasp her elbow, seeing the damage the fall caused.

"You kinda surprised me, so I shifted midair." She glances down at her arm. "I didn't land very gracefully."

I stare at the angry, painful graze. "You need to heal yourself."

Ava closes her eyes, that same peaceful, compassionate look overcoming her face. She pulls a deep breath in, then lets it slowly out. Except her shoulders remain tense and after several seconds, nothing seems to have changed. Her eyes flutter open, her brows crinkling with confusion. "I don't think I can."

I blink. "You can't heal yourself?"

She shrugs and then winces. "Looks like that gift is for others only. I suppose I've never tried to tap into my own thread."

"Ava, I'm...I'm so sorry." Guilt slams me in the solar plexus. I've injured her.

Her good arm shoots out so she can touch my cheek. "Hunter, no! You saved me. What would have happened if I'd landed on the trap?"

She would have sustained the injury I did. An injury that neither of us could do anything about. "But…"

She strokes my skin, her hand feeling warm and wonderful. "I'm a Were too now, remember? Finally, I'll get to show off my own Were healing."

The tension in my chest eases a little. "I suppose so…"

She rolls her eyes. "You know so." She stretches her arm back, trying to make a show of being okay. She tries to hide the wince, but I let her know I saw it. She smiles sheepishly. "Maybe you should drive back."

I scoop her up. It's not far to the quad. "Getting you home is a given."

Now nestled in my arms, Ava's mouth has formed a delightful 'oh'. Her eyebrows hike up. "You're going to carry me?"

I start walking, enjoying the weight of her in my arms. "Yup."

"But your leg!"

Is showing no sign of a limp. "Is fine."

"I only hurt my arm. I'm perfectly capable of walking."

My arms tighten a little, bringing her flush against my chest. "I know."

She sighs as her head sinks down, snuggling into my shoulder. "There're times your stubbornness is almost cute."

I smile, knowing she can't see my face. I'm almost tempted to remind her she said that one day.

We've only walked a few yards when Ava speaks again. "Why was there a trap? There aren't any more wolves out here."

I'd been wondering the same thing. "Maybe it was left over from before."

"Maybe they're hoping there's more." She glances up, eyes wide. "Could there be more wolves?"

"I would love for there to be more wolves. But if there were, I'd know about them."

Ava sighs. "It means they aren't finished yet, doesn't it?"

I suppress my own sigh. "Yeah, that's what it looks like." Humans are making sure they get every last wolf.

Pushing away the depressing knowledge that will be waiting for me to face it soon enough, I focus on the girl in my arms. Ava feels warm and soft and relaxed.

She presses her cheek to my chest, eyes closed, face smiling. "I can hear your heart," she murmurs.

My response is nothing but a whisper. "That's because it's yours."

She doesn't open her eyes, she barely moves, but the smile that somehow softens and grows tells me she heard me. Seeing that glow has the exact same effect on my chest.

I want to carry this girl with me for the rest of my life.

When we arrive at the quad, I'm not sure I'm ready to let her go. But getting Ava home so we can tend to her graze is the priority. It doesn't mean I can't hold her against me as I release her, letting her slide down the length of me. Her gasp is directly connected to some fiber deep within me.

Her feet hit the ground and we stay where we are, holding each other close. Ava looks up at me, her wintergreen eyes luminous. "You never cease to amaze me, Hunter. Thank you for saving me."

I tilt my head down until our lips are only inches apart. "This is what I was born for, Ava."

Protecting wolves.

Protecting her.

This kiss is gentle and soft, an affirmation of our feelings, of the potential we keep discovering. Ava pulls back and we fold around each other. As Weres, we technically don't need the body heat to stay warm, but I feel like a sun was just born in my chest.

Ava tucks into my shoulder, obviously not willing to let go yet. "Hunter, we can't tell anyone about this." She waves in the direction of my leg. "We can't explain why you're better."

"I know." Because no one knows about the golden wolf, which means no one has any idea of what Ava's capable of.

I've no doubt she knows that it's going to get harder to hide this. That it's only a matter of time before we have to tell, but I have a feeling that maybe Weres need to know sooner rather than later.

And then Ava will be known as who she truly is—the golden wolf.

The tightening of my arms is unconscious, and Ava snuggles in another inch, because I know the risk is she'll no longer be my golden wolf.

She'll be *the* golden wolf this legacy has been waiting for.

6

SAYEN

"We need more people like you, Sayen."

Standing, I stretch my back, letting the cool breeze wash over the bare shoulders my tank top exposes. These mountains are amazing. So many shades of emerald. Growing up on the Tate ranch had meant falling in love with rolling hills and grass that could grow long enough to tickle your knees. But the pine forests that surround Jacksonville are...something else.

I squat down again, packing away the syringe and vials. Yes, yes we do. "If only humans realized what they're doing."

They're about the only ones who can stop what's coming.

Eden is kneeling over the unconscious wolf by my feet. She brushes his fur, probably working some of her Fae magic as the sedative begins to wear off. Despite being old enough to be a mother, her long dark hair brushes past smooth skin that speaks of ageless beauty. "Some of them do. We just need the others to realize and then this fight is over."

Standing again, I hoist the vet pack, smiling like I mean it. "Your fabulous captive breeding program is a great step in that direction."

The wolf by our feet stirs. Pale shades of grey, she's the last one we've checked today. All the wolves the program has released back into the wild have been tagged so we can find them again. It means when we get some blood samples to see whether the vaccine has remained in their system it's easier and quicker. Follow the beep on the screen until they're in range of the sedative gun.

Simultaneously, we retreat as consciousness comes back to the wolf in stages. The body stretching. The eyes blinking. The struggle to get standing.

Wolves are such beautiful creatures, so beautiful it makes my chest hurt. Being a Were means great responsibility toward these animals. Unfortunately, it's the sacrifices that need to be made to see results that hurt the most.

The wolf stands, shaking off whatever just happened to her whilst she was knocked out. She looks at us both, calm thanks to Eden's presence. My teeth are clenched as the wolf pauses as she takes my measure. Why does this never get easier?

I hold still as she decides what her next step is. Movement would just agitate her right now, and she's had enough invasive procedures thanks to this whole unnatural system. The wolf takes a step toward us, but I hold my position. Even a step back could be seen as a threat. Reaching her decision, she spins and heads for the protection of the tree line. In a flash, her dusk-colored body is gone in search of her pack.

I let out the breath I'd been holding, wishing the strain would go with it.

"You're just so good with them." Eden's smile turns a little sad. "It reminds me of Ava."

She's been mentioning her daughter more often since I arrived a few weeks ago. "You're worried about her, aren't you?"

Eden's surprised green gaze flicks back to mine. "I think that's why you're so good with them, Sayen. You're very intuitive."

Or I know a lot about her family. My smile turning crooked, I shrug. "It's probably the American Indian in me."

Eden brushes my arm as she walks past, heading back to the truck. "Or you have a good heart and they recognize that. You should become a vet."

Not turning to stone from the pain that tightens every muscle is a conscious effort. My passion for animals is what meant Noah and Eden were so happy to have me join the team at the center. Despite being a senior, I know my way around a lab enough to be able to help with the vaccines and the blood testing. Being a Were from a neighboring pack meant an automatic assumption that they could trust me.

No one has asked how I've learned what I have...

"I'll just let Noah know we're heading back." Eden pulls out her phone and walks a few steps away.

"Sure." I move a little further, giving her some privacy. Standing beside the truck, I watch as she smiles into the phone.

What would it have been like if my dad had lived beyond my first year? Would he and Mom have been like those two? Seeing Noah and Eden together at the center is painful. They present as so in love, so dedicated, so...right.

My phone vibrates in my pocket, but I climb into the cab before I read it.

Any news?

I suppress the frown. *You aren't supposed to contact me now.*

I hadn't heard anything.

Why do those words sound like a whine? *Message me tonight.*

So there's news?

Eden is just hanging up as I rapidly type out the last text.

You might want to head to Jacksonville.

She climbs into the driver's seat and I smile at her as I pat the vet pack containing the blood samples. "Let's go see where we're at."

Turning the keys in the ignition, Eden smiles back. "I love your passion, Sayen. It reinforces that there's no way we can lose."

I smile as I look out my window. That's the plan.

My phone vibrates again, but I don't bother to look. He's going to ask a whole heap of questions, even though I never answer them.

Alistair is an idiot.

But it's because he's an idiot that he's useful.

7

AVA

As Josh wipes the antiseptic gauze over my arm, I wince. He peers closely at the graze and I turn away. Who wants to see that stuff at close range?

"It's not deep. It should heal soon enough."

I open my mouth to boast that Were healing will take care of that, but then snap it shut. I haven't shared that I've shifted with Josh, which doesn't sit comfortably—Josh is my cousin, and also my best friend.

Hunter steps in, his gaze catching mine. "That's good news." She arches a brow. "She doesn't stay still for long, does she?"

Josh grins. "Ava decided she was going to save the world when we were six. She hasn't stopped since."

I hop down from the bench I was sitting on, making a point of accidentally elbowing him on the way. "That was after I watched the Care Bears movie and you know it."

Josh deflects my jab, probably because he was expecting it.

Riley steps up to his side. "Maybe it's the preservatives in the Mocha Munch that you keep telling me about, making her all hyped up."

Josh's face lights up. "You've been listening?"

Riley flips her mahogany fringe. "Something about how caramel 262 is going to pickle me from the inside out."

"That's caramel 626." Josh arches a brow. "What did you have for breakfast this morning?"

Riley smiles. "Toast." Then flutters her eyelashes. "And cereal."

Josh snorts as he turns away to wash his hands and I can't help but smile. I have a feeling this battle is going to go on for quite some time.

I head over to Hunter, feeling even the short period when he's not by my side. I slide my hand into his and our fingers interlink. He looks down, his eyes serious as they ask if I'm okay.

I smile, doing a little hair flip myself. In fact, I barely notice the graze, so it seems Were healing is more impressive than I realized.

KJ wheels his chair away from his desk, having been a quiet observer until now. He scratches the narrow space between his brow and beanie. "So, tell me again what happened?"

Hunter rolls his eyes. "This is the last time I'm going over it."

We've already told him twice, so it strikes me that KJ seems to think we've missed something.

"We went for a nighttime walk—"

"Out on the tundra." KJ's tone is full of 'are you mad'?

Hunter glares at KJ. "I've spent a lot of time out there. There're days I miss it."

Huh. That makes sense. Hunter is deeply connected to the tundra. KJ must realize it too, because he gives a 'fair enough' nod.

"And we were mucking around, running about, when I smelled the introduced wolf urine."

"Where were you again?"

Hunter's jaw tenses. "A few miles north."

KJ nods slowly. "That's pretty far out."

"As I was saying," Hunter glares at KJ again, "I smelled it and realized Ava was going to step on it, so I knocked her out of the way."

I jump in. "Thereby saving me."

Hunter throws me an amused glance. "And that was that."

KJ frowns. "That was that?"

"Yep."

He looks from Hunter to me and back again. "Where's the trap?"

"In the shed. It was a leg-hold trap. Nothing we haven't seen before."

That was covered in Hunter's blood.

Hunter stares at KJ, his gaze unblinking. It seems my man can convincingly lie.

KJ shrugs, looking away. "Cool. I just wanted to check. We figured the poachers were gone."

Hunter's shoulders relax imperceptibly. "Yeah, we did too."

Riley frowns. "So, what does that mean for us?"

"I'm thinking we put the cameras back up, see if we can keep an eye on them. We'll certainly have to make sure we keep up the patrols around Resolve."

KJ nods in agreement. "I'm also going to find a way to make the lines our cameras use as safe as possible. A lot of sensitive information could be picked up by them."

Like how many wolves are here. Like Hunter and I out on our runs.

Josh heads for the door. "I'm going to do a check of all the cameras, make sure everything's working as it should."

Riley shoots to her feet. "I'll join you."

Hunter plants a brief kiss on my head. "I'm going to go get all the equipment together." He glances at KJ. "Maybe check Sakari and the others while I'm there."

Hunter is just out the door when KJ wheels back to his desk. "One day he'll trust my surveillance system."

But Hunter ignores him. I smile as I slide on to the desk beside him. "You know he needs to see for himself."

KJ grunts, seeming to be focused on his screen. He seems busy, so I figure I might as well do a round myself and go to stand up.

But then KJ speaks up again "Personally, I've only shifted once."

Shock has me pausing half-way up. "Pardon?"

"I shifted the first time, like we all do," he throws me an apologetic glance, "like most of us do, at sixteen, and I haven't been a wolf since."

I frown. I haven't met a Were anywhere that doesn't wish they could shift more often since the drop in wolf numbers. KJ must have a pretty powerful reason to totally reject such a big part of himself. But this topic is a little close to home, so I decide to play it light. Settling back on the edge of the desk, I tilt my head. "Must've been pretty bad to not go there again."

KJ half-shrugs. "It's painful for all of us." His hazel gaze looks straight at me. "Was it painful for you?"

The words hit me like a freeze gun. What did he just say? Surely Hunter hasn't told him...especially without telling me first.

No. Hunter wouldn't keep something like that from me. Which means KJ's guessing. Probably testing me.

Except by the time I've remembered to move, KJ already has his answer. "My guess is it was something like your parents. Hunter was in danger?"

Man, this guy knows my family history.

My shoulders slump in defeat. Lying has never been my superpower. It's not even a skill. I move to the nearest chair. "When Hunter was shot."

KJ nods, no surprise apparent on his face. "He hurt himself in the trap too, didn't he?"

I pause again. How much has KJ figured out? "Yes. Nothing life-threatening though."

"Traps can do some damage though." He gazes at me thoughtfully. "So, you can heal now that you've shifted?"

"Basically."

KJ looks back at his screen, nodding ever so slowly. "Huh."

I push off the chair, rushing to stand on the other side of the desk. "We're going to tell everyone, I swear. We, I, just needed a bit of time to get my head around it."

To figure out what it's going to mean.

"I'd say it's going to mean something big."

I slump back. "I know."

He looks up at me, gaze steady. "Hunter's the key, isn't he?"

"You're one smart Were, KJ."

None of this could've happened without Hunter. And I know deep in my soul, that this Legacy is just as much his as it is mine.

KJ grins despite it all. "I keep trying to tell him."

"That I need him as much as he needs me?"

He angles his head, the grin growing. "That I'm one smart Were."

I roll my eyes, my own smile lightening my chest. "That bit he already knows."

KJ sobers, scratching beneath his beanie. "He carries every life he's lost on his watch." He wipes his hand down his face. "And possibly a few dozen others, knowing Hunter."

I sigh. That probably includes his father. "I know. They weren't his fault."

"Not according to him."

I sigh again. "He'll see what we see, KJ. Hunter protects those around him, the death toll would be so much higher if it weren't for him."

KJ smiles. "There's no one I'd trust with my life, or these wolves' lives, more."

I nod, feeling like there's some sort of double meaning in there. It feels like KJ is placing the wolves' lives above his own. It has me wondering again why KJ is so determined to save these wolves, particularly when he shuns the wolf within him.

But we've had enough deep and meaningfuls for one day. "Hey," I tip my head to the side, smiling at him. "What doe KJ stand for?"

Now it's KJ's turn to freeze. His brows are half-hiked up, his mouth partially open as he holds himself in suspended animation. Whoa, not the reaction I was expecting.

KJ opens his mouth, and I wonder if he's got some weird, wacky name, when my phone rings. Pulling it out of my pocket, I see Mom's name flashing on the screen. I point at him. "Saved by the bell."

KJ's grin is instant, probably a whole lot relieved. I head for the door, wondering if Hunter has told him how single-minded I can be if needed. There's no way I'm letting this go.

I'm about to shut the door behind me when I pop my head back through. "Oh. This stays between us, just for now. Okay?"

KJ throws out a jaunty salute. "Secrets are my specialty."

I smile a thanks and shut the door. I missed a call from my parents last night and they're probably wondering why I haven't called them back.

Keeping the smile in place, I take the call. "Hey, Mom."

My mother's face fills the screen. "Hi, honey." Oh, and Dad is with her. "Hey, gorgeous girl."

"Hey, Dad."

Mom leans forward. "You didn't ring last night. We just wanted to make sure everything's okay."

"Sorry, I went for a night walk with Hunter. Long story, but we found a trap, I tripped, and grazed my shoulder."

Dad's frown is instantaneous. "You went for a night walk?" I didn't think it was possible, but the frown deepens. "You were hurt?"

I roll my eyes. "Nothing major. Josh said it wasn't deep and will heal in no time."

Mom glances at Dad. "There was still a trap out?"

This is why I wasn't in a hurry to call them back. They'd realize the seriousness of what we've found pretty quickly. "Yeah. We're not sure if it's an old one, or if poachers are hoping there are more wolves out there."

"Ava." Dad's tone is low and serious. "We wanted to talk about this last night. We think it's time you came home."

Mom smiles, jumping in to back Dad up. "This was only meant to be for a week or two, just to drop off the vaccines. And your studies are falling behind."

I'm about to point out I'm home schooled, and I'm pretty sure I'm ahead of most teens my age, but Dad is already nodding.

"And this shows it's time. It doesn't sound safe out there."

I wait for the sales pitch to finish. I've been expecting this. "I'm perfectly safe with the Rendells. They take being protective very seriously."

Which is a pretty big understatement.

I put my hand up as they both go to speak again. "This is the quiet neck of the globe, remember? And Dawn is still here."

Mom's green eyes seem to reach out and grab me. "What's keeping you there, Ava?"

Now that stumps me. I knew when I met my white wolf I'd find my soulmate. Soulmates my parents can understand. After all, their love was destined by a prophecy as old as Weres themselves.

But to tell them about Hunter, about why I want to stay,

means I need to tell them I've shifted. And then there will be questions. And advice.

And a Legacy to live up to.

I just want a little more time with Hunter. For him to realize there's no way I can do this without him.

And maybe I want a little more time to just be the golden wolf who's visited him on the tundra for the past two years. I know it's selfish, and I know telling them is inevitable, heck, KJ has already figured it out. But I can't bring myself to tell them.

Not yet.

"There's something about this place, Mom. The wolves—they need me."

Dad crosses his arms, looking every part the Prime Alpha. What am I going to do if he insists? I've never defied my parents. But then again, I've never kept the truth from them either. "What are you saying, Ava?"

"That I love you guys and I'll come home. But I just need a little more time."

Essentially, I'm asking them to trust me.

Mom and Dad look at each other, and I wonder what they're thinking, what they're communicating to each other in that soul-deep way of theirs. I'm their only daughter. They've been waiting just like everyone else to see what I would mean for the world. Their love for me would be pitted against the knowledge that I was born with a responsibility.

Dad turns towards Mom more fully, as if they're going to have a private conversation. "I don't like this, Eden. We can't keep her safe."

Mom sighs. "I know, Noah. But..."

I hold my breath. Yes, but...

"She's been hurt, and there aren't the numbers to protect her over there."

All I need is Hunter.

Mom bites her lip. "Yes, but there're also less people over there. This is something she wants."

Dad doesn't respond, and I have no idea if that's a good thing.

"Ava has never asked anything of us."

My breath whooshes out. Mom's right. I've spent my whole life waiting for some sort of sign, from them, from my pack, from the universe, about what I'm supposed to be, do, choose. I still don't know, but I know that finding Hunter, then choosing Hunter, is right.

I know the moment they reach a decision because they imperceptibly nod.

Mom turns, her smile gentle and loving. "Okay."

Dad nods too, but there's no accompanying smile. "For now."

Relief has me sagging against the wall. "There's something really important happening here, guys. I just want to figure out what it is."

Dad is trying not to frown again. "Just be safe, okay?"

I smile, feeling the love right across the miles. "I love you too, Dad."

"And you need to contact us every day."

"Just like I have been?"

He arches a brow. "You didn't yesterday."

How can they be overprotective even with all this distance between us? Now that is an achievement. "I texted."

"Anyone could send a text."

I draw out the eye roll this time. "The joys of having an Alpha and a cop as your dad."

Dad's face relaxes. "You look after the most precious thing that's come out of all of this."

My chest warms. "I will Dad."

Not to mention Hunter will too.

We hang up and I stay there against the wall. I know I'll need to tell them soon.

I'm so absorbed in staring at my silent phone that I don't feel Hunter approaching until he's coming down the hall.

He looks down at the phone I'm holding. "Who was that?"

"My parents."

Hunter's brows go up. "And?"

"Amongst other things, they're worried I'll fall behind with my studies."

"My guess is, you're way ahead."

Nor have I ever wanted to go to college.

Hunter stills. "But you don't want to be like me, Ava. It's a steep price to pay."

He's talking about having to drop out of school so he could be Alpha. I let out a long breath. "They wanted me to come home." Hunter's face looks like someone just punched him. I quickly step forward, arms coming up to cup his face. "I told them I need to stay for a little longer. We have wolves to looks after."

Hunter relaxes, but not completely. "A little longer?"

I smile, fingers lacing with his hair. "My parents have always looked out for me, they know I inherited all the expectations of the Prime Prophecy. It's going to take some time for them to be okay with letting me go."

Hunter glances down, then back up. "Did you tell them about us?"

I still. "Not yet. I just—"

He leans down and kisses me. "I know why and I get it. You don't need to explain."

Does he? Does he understand I'm protecting him just as much as myself? When he goes to pull back I hold him in place, extending the kiss. Sometimes it's easier to show Hunter how I feel rather than tell.

When he pulls back, his copper eyes have darkened to the shade that has my heart swelling and my pulse rate spiking. "Point made, Ava Phelan."

I can't help but slip in another quick brushing of lips. "That's good, Hunter Rendell. Because I'm going to be around a whole lot longer than a little longer."

His smile is slow and beautiful. It starts in his gorgeous eyes and ends in the fingers that tighten around my waist. "Good. I wasn't looking forward to packing."

8

AVA

The following day back at Resolve, and Hunter's words are still on a merry-go-round in my head as I sit at my desk staring at my computer.

In part, because the fact that Hunter said he would come with me tells me exactly how much he loves me. The tundra, the wolves, his family, and pack, are Hunter's world, and their safety has been his life. The fact that he would leave them for me is... mind-blowing.

But mostly, it's because it shows how far Hunter will go to put me first. Leaving here would be another weight on his shoulders. If any of the wolves died after he left, they'd be another life he held himself responsible for. It touches me somewhere deep.

And it cements my commitment to be the one who puts Hunter first.

"Ava?"

My head shoots up to find Dawn looking at me. "Sorry, I was just thinking. What did you say?"

KJ, standing beside Dawn, nudges her with his elbow. "She was off with the fairies, was she?"

I straighten. "Worst joke ever, KJ."

Except Dawn bursts out laughing. It's the sort of laugh a proud mother indulges in when their child does something cute or smart. KJ beams and Dawn slips an arm around his shoulder. Despite the awful joke, I can't help but smile. The connection between these two is a strong one, forged of years spent together working toward the same goal.

Hunter enters the comms room, his brows hiking up in amusement. "Did I miss the joke?"

I shake my head. "You really didn't. Dawn was just saying the food reserves are getting low."

I throw a glare at KJ, proving to him that I was listening.

Hunter nods. "I was just checking, and Dawn's right. With Sakari needing more, we've almost run out."

KJ sits back in his computer chair, threading his hands behind his head. "Off to do a takeaway run then?"

"Looks like it. I'll head out once the sun is on its way down."

I shoot up from where I was sitting. "I'll come too."

But Hunter's already shaking his head. "I don't think you should come."

I narrow my eyes. If this is because of last night and my graze... "Ah, because?"

Hunter huffs out a breath. "Because if I can't find any road-kill, I'm going to have to get it myself."

Oh.

Dawn's Fae green eyes soften. "It might be best. He's usually not out long."

Great. Now I look like some lovesick teen who can't be away from her guy for a couple of hours.

KJ puts his arms out wide. "If you stay here, you hang with the cool peeps."

As much as I like hanging out with these guys who have become my new family, something niggles me. You know what? I'm okay with looking like a lovesick teen.

I come over to grasp Hunter's hand. "Well, we're going to look really hard for roadkill then."

HUNTER IS HOLDING the door to the truck open for me later that day when he grasps my arm. "You don't have anything to prove, Ava. It's okay to stay back."

In the twilight, Hunter is breathtaking. The shadows darken his almost black hair while the last rays of light caress his angles and planes. Even frowning he looks hot.

I sigh. "This is your fault, you know."

He blinks, pulling back a little. "It's what?"

My blink has a lot less surprise and a whole lot more fluttering. "Your fault. You have me thinking I can just about do anything as long as I'm with you."

Hunter's grin takes a second but when it comes, it's glorious. I grin right back and then climb into the cab. He shakes his head, still grinning as he climbs in beside me.

He puts the keys in the ignition, then stops. Turning to me, he sighs. "I'm serious. It's no biggy if you sit this one out."

Do I have something to prove? Yes. But it's not what Hunter thinks.

"First of all, I was being serious." I make sure I hold his gaze. "Anything is possible, but only with you, Hunter. And second, I'm not trying to prove anything to anyone. I refuse to be some squeamish princess who can't do what needs to be done."

"You're not some squeamish—"

I put my hand up, pressing my fingers on his lips. "And third, I'm a lovesick teen who doesn't want to be away from her guy."

I feel the lips pull up as I see the smile bloom. I drop my hand as Hunter starts the truck, shaking his head again. He glances at me again as he puts it into gear. "Next time, I'll just agree."

I laugh. "Smart move."

We head out down the highway, the almost-night air a swirl of cold in the headlights. Hunter drives slowly, keeping an eye on the rear-vision mirror to make sure no one zooms up our rear end out of nowhere.

"I basically just do a big loop." Hunter scans and talks. "That way I cover the main highway, where people aren't smart enough to slow down, as well as a couple of the smaller roads, where the wildlife are more likely to hang around."

"Makes sense. So, we're just looking for dead bodies?"

He glances at me. "Yeah, basically."

I nod. "I can do that."

Hunter returns to scanning, that Were sight of his searching the dark. I lean forward, remembering I have that ability now too. But the roadside is bare, the tundra stretching out beyond the reach of the headlights.

I remember what Hunter said about having to get it himself if he doesn't find something on the road verge. "Are there times you don't come across any?"

Hunter's glance is brief. "Sometimes, but it's not often. Usually, I'll come across an elk or even a hare or two. It's enough to tide the wolves over."

Except this is the most wolves Resolve has ever housed. And we don't know how long they'll be staying there.

I sigh. "Although now that we know Sakari is further along, we can't afford to not find something."

Hunter seems to tense. "Yeah, that's true."

Turning in my seat, I take in his profile. "You're worried about her, aren't you?"

Hunter remains staring out the windscreen. "A lot's riding on this litter."

I scoot over, placing my hand on his thigh. "You're right, there is. But she has us all looking out for her. I doubt that anything could happen that would mean we lose them."

This close, I can see that a muscle is ticking in Hunter's jaw. It's a level of tension that seems out of proportion. Sakari's had litters before, sure she's lost one, but Resolve successfully raised the last batch of pups. I'm about to ask why he's so worked up about this, when Hunter straightens.

"There!"

He's pointing at a lump just on the edge of the headlight beams. Oh. We've found one. I shuffle back, telling myself it's a good thing. This way we didn't have to go hunting.

Hunter pulls over beside it and my aching heart sees it's a moose. Big body lying on its side, its gangly legs stretched out in rigor mortis.

This time Hunter grasps my thigh. "You sure you're okay?"

I swallow. "Hey, circle of life and all that. If it's already been killed, then what's the value in it rotting beside the road, right?"

Hunter is watching me closely. "Basically."

Nodding, I grab the door handle. "I can do this, Hunter."

Hunter grasps my hand, covering it with his warm palm. "I know you can. Just by coming along you've shown you're the strongest person I know."

Before I have time to reply, Hunter has jumped out of the truck. I pull in a deep breath and hold it as I climb out too. I can do this.

But my steps slow as I approach the dead moose. It's a male, the scars on his head a testament to the antlers he would have shed after mating season. His eyes are staring straight ahead, shocked but lifeless at the same time.

I kneel beside him, hand hovering above his brown fur, but not touching. His thread is gone, violently severed when he was hit by a moving vehicle. There's no longer any sign of the spirit and life that it once had. I tell myself it's a carcass, a life that's no longer here. But I still feel the loss of its connection in this complicated fabric that is life.

I brush his shoulder; the body is cold and hard. I finally pull in the breath I was holding, and all of a sudden, I'm not feeling so strong. He smells musty and wet...and dead. In fact, I feel ill.

Dawn was right. I shouldn't have come.

I stand, not able to meet Hunter's eye as I confess in a whisper, "I'm not feeling well."

Hunter's by my side before I can ever register he's moved. His hands, so warm and so strong—so much stronger than mine —come up to cup my face. "Ava, the fact that this makes you sick doesn't make you weak." His hands tighten around my cheeks and I can't help but look up. "The fact that it makes you sick, and you still came, still got out of the truck, and still took the time to honor his life—that's what makes you the strongest person I know."

Oh.

I pull in a shuddering breath, but this time all I can smell is Hunter.

"None of this is nice—the sights, the smells. There's a reason Riley doesn't come on these trips."

Double oh.

I nod, a little speechless. "Okay."

He smiles as he steps back. "I've got it. I usually do this on my own, remember?"

Squatting, Hunter slips his arms beneath the carcass and then, like he's lifting a bag of flour, hoists it onto the back of the truck. He lays the moose down, almost gently, and the truck sinks with the weight.

Whoa, that show of strength is impressive.

Watching him, thinking of what he just said, means seeing the dead moose still hurts. But it's no longer overwhelming.

Grabbing the flask on the back seat, Hunter gives his hands and arms a quick wash. Only a Were could do that out on the autumn tundra. Getting wet isn't something a human would want to do out in this cold.

We climb back in the truck, and feeling like I've achieved something, I sit back, content to be here with my man. In the darkness of the cab, his face should be full of angles and planes. But his lips are curled up ever so gently, his face relaxed. I slide over so I can stroke back the hair that brushes his forehead, emotion filling up my chest. Hunter grasps my hand, taking his eyes off the road to kiss my palm. My whole body turns to goo as I sigh. This guy...

Hunter leans forward, squinting. "Now what are the chances of that?"

Straightening, I try to see what he's looking at. "Of what?"

My new Were sight sees it a second later. More roadkill. My stomach clenches—my guess is that the wolves of Resolve just got lucky.

Hunter pulls up alongside it and I brace myself again. If I thought seeing one dead animal was an achievement, then two are even more impressive. Hand on the door, Hunter glances at me, but all I do is raise a brow. It saves time if we don't go through this again. With a half-smile that is part exasperation, part impressed, he climbs out and I do the same, suppressing my own half-smile.

The smile dies quickly when I step around the truck, though. It's an elk this time, smaller, somehow more fragile looking. Just like the moose, the thread that gave it life is long gone. This one's eyes are closed, but there's no semblance of peace on its face. Violent deaths are the hardest ones to accept.

I drop to my knees, this time not hesitating to brush its soft fur. This one is a female. Seeing it again so soon after the last is somehow harder, but also getting easier. Her energy has returned to the cycle of life. All I can do is acknowledge that part she played while she was alive.

Hunter kneels beside me, reaching out to brush the elk's head. His hand pauses. "This one isn't roadkill."

"What?"

Hunter's frown is as dark as the night. "It's been shot. Possibly dumped here."

I yank my hand back when I see the red wound at the back of her head. "Then why would they leave it here?"

Hunter pushes upright slowly. "Damned good question."

Standing, he does a slow circle, sharp eyes scanning the dark. I look around, wondering what he's looking for. There's a low hill to our right, the road falls away into a ditch beside the elk on our left, but for the most part, we're surrounded by flat landscape.

Squaring his shoulders, Hunter turns back to the truck. "I've got a hunch." He opens the door to the passenger side and looks at me. "Let's go for a drive."

I climb in, feeling a frown wanting to be born. "A hunch?"

Except Hunter doesn't answer. He starts the truck and heads back down the road, leaving the dead elk behind. I look back at its motionless body. "Shouldn't we be picking it up?"

Hunter's lips are a thin line as he focuses on the road. "We will."

But it seems we're doing something else first. "Where are we going, Hunter?"

The glance he gives me is brief. "I just want to check something out first."

The frown finally scrunches my forehead. Is he being deliberately evasive? Surely, he knows we're in this together. I sit back, tense, but willing to wait this out.

Hunter will tell me.

9

HUNTER

D riving down the dirt road, I know I don't have much time. I don't glance at Ava, still hoping I'm wrong. Because if I'm right, then what I'm considering is risky.

But I've never been one to shy away from tough decisions.

We've only gone a mile down the road when I pull over. Ava is looking at me, confusion pulling down her brows. "Why are we stopping here?"

I unbuckle my seat belt, turning to her. "I need you to drive."

Those pretty brows arc up in surprise. "Sure."

I climb out, glad she's not asking any more questions. I can't tell her what I'm about to do. She scoots over to the driver's seat as I stand with the door open, tense and taught. When she realizes I haven't walked around, the confusion returns.

I lean in to kiss her before she can ask. "I want to check something out. Give me a couple of minutes, then follow. Headlights off."

This time the frown holds far more than confusion. Ava is getting frustrated. "Hunter, you need to tell me what's going on."

"It's probably nothing, but I need to find out."

"What's nothing?" She unclips her seatbelt, getting ready to hop back out. "You're not making any sense. Tell me, Hunter, we're in this tog—"

But I shut the door before she can finish. Her mouth is already open, her hand trying to wind down the window, when I shift. I would've liked one last look at her before I shoot off down the road, but I don't give myself the luxury. I don't need to find out how much she's honed her Were reflexes.

The road back to the elk is as empty as it was when we drove up. If my gut is right, then that's what the poacher who left the bait there is also banking on.

Well, he's about to get a wolf come and check out his trap.

But he'll get more than he bargained for.

Running fast, I slice through the cold air. Once Ava saw that I was heading back to the elk rather than continuing down the road, there's no way she's going to wait the two minutes like I asked her. She'll turn the truck around and follow me.

Another reason this was the right way to do this.

I smell the elk before I see it. The scent has me growling deep in my chest. If there were any wolves in the area, they'd be doing the same thing. The poachers haven't realized we've captured them all, but right now, that works to my advantage. When he sees me, I'm guessing from some little pocket on the rise, he'll think he's hit the jackpot.

Which is also when this gets dangerous.

I start zig-zagging, slowing down and speeding up, setting up an erratic rhythm. I'm not going to make myself an easy target for this bastard. As I see the lump of elk lying beside the road up ahead and nothing's happened, I'm not sure if I feel relief or disappointment. It looks like I was wrong, and this was just some schmuck out doing target practice.

The crack comes a split second before the soil explodes beside my foot. I veer left, heart hammering. That was a bullet meant for my chest. Dammit. I wasn't expecting it, which means I now have to wait for another shot.

Because I'm ready for it, I move the moment I hear the second crack. Throwing myself to the right, I crumple and tumble into the ditch. When I come to a stop, I do a quick check. There'll be bruises thanks to the rough nose-dive I just took, but no holes. Giving myself a second as relief courses through my battered body, I sag. Ava won't need to be healing me tonight.

Shifting, I try to calm my breathing. I need to hear what happens next. As long as the idiot believes he just shot the white wolf heading towards his bait, he'll be on his way. There's only a moment of silence before I hear the sound of an engine.

Ava.

At least she's keeping her headlights off like I asked. Not only does it mean the poacher won't know she's coming, but it also means she can't drive like a banshee because I just ran off on her. Half the reason I did this crazy plan was to make sure she didn't get hurt.

A second engine, this one louder and coming in faster, tumbles over the first. Coming out of the ditch, a wave of cold anger starts in my fists and spreads through me as I crouch behind the dead elk. Come on, you bastard. Come and see what's waiting for you.

Headlights sweep the area as the motorbike heads straight for me. He's expecting to find a dead wolf in the ditch beside me, probably already thinking of where to start skinning. He slows as he nears, smart enough to know that maybe his target isn't dead yet. Several yards away he kills the engine, angles the headlights at the elk, and climbs off. Grabbing a rifle, he raises it as he walks forward.

The moment his shadow brushes the edge of the elk, I jump. Spearing through the air, I get a jolt of satisfaction as I ram into him and yank out an "oomph." We crash to the ground and the jolt is quickly quashed by a wince as my bruises get bruises.

Another set of headlights wash us with light as I yank him up. Just in time, Ava.

"What the—"

The guy struggles, only to find the hands on his collar shaking him. I don't bother being gentle. Let him discover what he's up against. "Shut up, you bastard."

He goes quiet as he relaxes. I wouldn't say limp, which has me on guard.

The guy is dark haired and pale skinned. There's something about his smooth features, the shape of his eyes, that reminds me of a snake. Is this the guy who shot Sakari's pups? Is he the one who killed and skinned the last of the northern wolves?

Could this be the guy who killed my father?

My hands reflexively tighten, and I feel him tense. I shove my face close to his. "The smart thing to do would be to stay still."

The truck stops, its headlights bright and blinding. The car door opens. I can feel Ava watching and I almost relax my grip. Her gentle heart is probably feeling sorry for this guy.

"Let me go," he grinds out.

Teeth gritted, I keep my hands clenched. This guy needs to realize he's not in charge.

"He's more likely to talk if he can breathe."

Ava's voice is gentle, but dry, and is probably the only thing I'd listen to right now. She's right. We need some information.

I release Snake with a shove and he stumbles back. I straighten as he rights himself, feeling the barely banked anger pulsing through my veins. Ava steps up beside me, managing to look calm and confident, even though I can sense her unease.

Snake squares his shoulders, thinking I wouldn't notice as he surreptitiously glances around.

"The wolf's long gone. I made sure he was."

He looks around as he wipes a streak of dust from his chin. "You were waiting?"

I shrug. "Figured a wolf would come along at some stage." Then glare at him. "Giving us a chance to chat."

Snake must be getting cocky, but his pale gaze glares back. "You know I can walk away. No crime's been committed here."

I cross my arms. "How many have you killed?"

"I haven't killed anything." He glances at the dead elk. "Well, apart from that one."

My arms unwind, too much energy pounding through them. He knows I'm talking about wolves. "How. Many?"

Snake straightens, seeming to relax. "Enough."

Before I can decide what to do with that, Ava steps forward. "How do you do it?"

He narrows his eyes. "It's pretty straight forward."

"No, I mean, how do you kill them but not feel their pain?"

The guy tenses. "They don't feel any pain," he growls.

But Ava is already shaking her head. "You know that's a lie." She waits, but he doesn't answer. "So how do you do it?"

I'm not surprised when he tries to run. He didn't strike me as smart. As Snake sprints for his bike, I entertain the idea of letting him climb on and think he's home free before I take him out. But I'm too pissed. Loving the existence of Were speed, I tackle him a second time. This time, I don't care how hard the ground comes at us. He deserves it, and it's possible that I do too.

As I crash on top of him, he starts pushing, hands wildly shoving, legs flailing. I grunt when his boot connects with my shin. Reigning in the anger is hard, but I manage it. Gaining the upper hand, I pin him to the ground, but Snake doesn't seem to realize he's lost.

He pushes up, straining against the arms holding him down. "I enjoy it."

I know the words are meant to incite me. I push forward to tell him he can shove it, but as I breathe in, his scent hits me. For some reason, it bypasses my lungs and spears straight through my brain. Rage, hot and red, explodes like lava through my bloodstream.

This ends now.

"Hunter!"

The panic laced through my name doesn't have the power to reach me. It was inevitable that Ava would see who I really am. I push back a little, and the guy probably thinks he just got an escape window. But it's all the space I need to draw back my arm. Wondering why I'm holding in the fury, my fist connects with his face.

His head snaps back with a grunt and he goes limp. Satisfaction thrums through my veins and I punch him again. My arm is just winding back to go one more time when I feel a palm on my shoulder.

"Hunter—"

But the fury is a force to be reckoned with. It flashes and flows, an animal that wants out. Snake's eyes are wide with fear above his bloody nose.

Ava needs to see how far I'll go.

"You're just as connected to him as he is to the wolves."

My anger deflates like a punctured lung. I can't see the threads that Ava is talking about, but she can. And whether I like it or not, there's one extending between me and him. Somehow connecting us. Possibly making us equal. And even though I'm not sure who I am, I do know I'm nothing like him.

My arm drops, coming down to grab his collar again. Pulling him up, I growl in his face. "Why would you go to such lengths to catch a wolf?"

Snake pauses, and I hold him there, the promise of violence

coursing through my body. He doesn't need to know I no longer intend on acting on it.

Proving he's not a total idiot, he nods. "There aren't many left."

"And?"

"It's good money for their skins."

This time when that anger flashes again isn't for me. Ava's heart would be aching knowing she's seen what she's seen for nothing but money. "Who's paying you?"

For the first time, Snake is silent.

Ava leans over my shoulder. "Hunter is his own man. If he decides to ignore me, there's nothing I can do."

Snake swallows and a little smile seeds in my chest. She knows. And she's playing him.

"I don't know."

I draw him up, figuring he needs to see what's in my eyes a bit closer up.

His own pale eyes widen. "I'm telling the truth! We don't know who it is."

We...

"All we know is he goes by Helix."

There's a peace at Resolve that I've never experienced anywhere else, and it's during evenings like this that I really appreciate it. Hunter and Ava are out getting wolf food, probably kissing more than looking for road kill. Riley and Josh have gone home to watch The Bachelor with Ruth...probably trying to get a kiss in whenever they pretend to fill up the chip bowl in the kitchen. Dawn has gone back to her place to take a much-needed break.

Which leaves me here, alone and loving it.

I've come to accept that not finding a mate is going to be a by-product of being a pseudo-Were. Dating one of my kind isn't happening. The last thing I'm doing is opening up the possibility for my line to continue. Plus, what Were wants to be with someone who has rejected what we are? And humans are out of the question. I can't reconcile what some of them are doing to wolves, no matter who started it.

You have that many variables limiting your data set, and well, you have a sample size of zero. Even if there was some unique outlier out there, how the hell am I supposed to meet her? She'd have to find me out in the arctic boondocks, or I'd have to leave the place where, if I really concentrate, I can forget who I am.

Not. Happening.

Flicking through the screens, I double check the wolves are all asleep. Even Achak has taken a break from pacing the perimeter of his cage and is curled up, possibly snoring. Considering he was born in captivity, his restlessness was unusual to start with. But the fact that days later, he's still going, is even weirder. Unusual enough for me to wonder how Furious can't still be in his bloodstream.

But we checked again, then did another run just to make sure. His tests came back clean. No sign of the virus nor any immune response to it.

Dawn and I agreed we're going to have to tell the others. We just have to decide what our next step is going to be.

Moving over to the adjacent screen, I click through the tabs. Things have been quiet on the digital front, which could be a good thing.

Except I've generally found that these quiet moments lull you into a false sense of security.

Opening Alistair's Facebook page, I scan the contents. He's still updating it regularly with whatever snippet of lame information he can find. It must be killing him that he's not finding any fodder for his lies.

The page starts buffering and I sigh. Great. He's going live again. Is he interviewing someone who saw a wolf in the distance and got worried? Is he showing documentary footage of wolves hunting in the wild? It's the closest he can find to blood and gore when it comes to wolves.

I shudder as I think of what would've happened if he'd got footage of Zephyr attacking the woman he brought to Resolve. The last thing humans need is more evidence that wolves are dangerous. Anger bubbles in my belly. It's because of Alistair that Hunter had to shoot the wolf he'd been protecting his whole life.

I unclench my fingers around the mouse, wondering if Alistair would've still become a journalist if his father had never been attacked. To be honest, it's what Weres are capable of that keeps me here, even though it's late and I'm tired and I don't have Hunter's deep love of coffee—his blood type may be caffeine, there's only so much of the stuff I can drink. Weres don't need numbers to be a threat. They have the strength and the power.

I feel it course through my blood every time I stare too long at a horizon that calls to me.

When the video starts, I maximize the screen. Information is the best defense we have right now. Alistair has his face close to the camera, eyes wide as he puffs a bit. He's always been prone to drama.

"I have breaking news, good people of Jacksonville."

The chair creaks as I shoot upright. Jacksonville? What's he doing back there?

"Not long ago, what I've been warning you about almost came true, right here, in the heart of wolf territory."

Dread is a heavy, black pool in my gut. I don't like where this is going.

He steps back, and the camera pans out. I hate that he's got enough kudos to have some intern with a camera following him around.

Yep, it's definitely Jacksonville. He's in a clearing somewhere in the reserve, pine trees a wall of green behind them.

And he's not alone.

A burly dude is a bit further back, an unmoving pile of fur at his feet. The guy curls his lip as he nudges it with his boot. The animal wobbles as the waves of motion flow through its inert body.

It's a dead wolf. One who was recently killed.

Alistair has stepped forward, pointing out his microphone. "Chuck, can you tell me what happened here?"

Chuck jerks the gun hanging on his shoulder further up. "Was out doing my allocated cull."

"And thank you for that community service. You're keeping us all safe."

Chuck grunts and I don't know who I want to taser first. Wolves aren't the problem with this planet...

"Well, I had to go further than usual, there just ain't as many of them."

"So your efforts are working. Wonderful."

This time Chuck slides a glance at Alistair. He doesn't appreciate being interrupted. "And this thing," he nudges the dead wolf with his toe again, "Came at me like a fuc—"

"Remember," Alistair glances at the camera with a nervous smile, "We want families, those who are most vulnerable, to be able to see this, Chuck."

Chuck's brows shoot down, but he must figure he can't pummel Alistair while a camera is zoomed in on them. "Like a freight train. It was crazy mad. Running at me like it was possessed."

"This is a familiar story, Chuck. My father lived this."

"Well, it's a good thing I had Happy Ending with me." He pats the rifle over his shoulder.

You've got to be kidding me, that's what he named his gun? Happy Ending?

"Took a good few shots, too."

The dread is no longer a pool in my gut. It's a cold, dark weight defying gravity as it climbs up my spine. Alistair's father didn't see what Chuck did. Alistair's father saw a violent Were trying to scare humans with what we are capable of.

Chuck has seen something almost as dangerous...

"That sounds like a very dangerous situation. Your life could have been at stake."

Having Alistair repeat my thoughts isn't helping.

Chuck grunts, his brows almost touching his nose. "Closest I've ever come to meeting me maker, that's for sure."

Alistair has started spewing his twisted statistics, but I zone them out. The camera is moving, and I need to see something. I need to know this is just a hyped-up poacher looking for his five-minutes of fame.

The camera pans down to the wolf, zooming in on its pale grey form. It conveniently skims over any sign of gunshot wounds or blood. Alistair is saying something about this is the only way you should see a violent animal such as this one. Dead.

I clench my hand and slam it down on the desk.

The wolf has an unmistakable line of foam along its mouth.

11

HUNTER

Watching Ava on the screen as she sits with Achak, I flex my knuckles. The bruising is almost gone thanks to Were healing. Unfortunately, I'm not sure Ava has recovered yet.

Sighing, I look up from my desk. I've hidden behind all the things that we've had to do since we returned last night, but I know we need to talk about what happened. "I've asked Gareth to come in."

Riley raises her brows. "As in Dad's-brother-from-another-mother Gareth?"

I sigh as I rub my forehead. "Yeah. He's the best person to deal with this guy."

Unfortunately.

After realizing we had no reason to bring the guy in, we'd got his name. Kyle White. I still prefer to think of him as Snake. Letting him go went against everything my mind had been screaming at me, but he was right. No wolf had been killed.

Josh glances at the two of us. "Who's Gareth?"

The fact that Josh's been here for a month and doesn't know is something that doesn't sit well with me. Gareth, for all his angry nay-saying, is still part of my pack. "He's a Rendell."

"He was also our Dad's best friend." Riley flips her fringe. "They grew up together with Mom, a bit like Huey, Dewey, and Louie."

Josh nods like that sounds familiar. "They would have been close then."

"Those two were peas in a freaking pod." My sister looks at me, gaze heavy with implications. "They held the same strong views on a lot of things."

Like captive breeding.

I rub my brow. "He's also a park ranger. He knows the law when it comes to this stuff."

We all straighten a little as our Were ears hear his footsteps down the hall. He's early. Ava is still with Achak. She wanted to be here for this chat.

The door opens, and Gareth's tall form stops there, like he's not sure whether he wants to take the next step.

Despite it all, I smile. This guy was like an uncle to us. "Gareth, thanks for coming. I'd like to you meet Josh Phelan-Channon."

Gareth nods a greeting as Josh smiles back. "Nice to meet you, Gareth."

Gareth grunts before turning back to me. "You called, Alpha?"

So that's how we're doing it, huh? I come to stand beside the map we have spread out on one of the desks. "We caught a poacher last night."

His defenses relax enough for his eyebrows to twitch. "Where?"

I point to the road Ava and I were on. "Closer than I would have liked."

Having no choice but to enter, Gareth comes over to look. His eyebrows finally release from their cranky formation as he sees where I'm pointing. "That is close."

"Yeah, and he was using a dead elk as bait."

He rubs his jaw. "So he didn't use a trap?"

"Nope."

Gareth finally looks up at me, those Rendell eyes of his are heavy and serious. "So, he was waiting. He really wanted to catch a wolf."

The sound of footsteps trickles through the open door and even if I hadn't heard it, I would have known it was Ava. Something happens to my body whenever she draws near. A lightness, a warmth...a rightness. It's the most addictive thing I've ever experienced.

When Ava enters, Dawn is with her. Ava's eyes instantly connect with mine and I glory in our connection. Everything aligns when I acknowledge she's mine and I'm hers.

Ava turns to Gareth. "Kyle tried to shoot Hunter."

Riley gasps as Gareth's brows head back to a frown. I shoot Ava a disgruntled look. I wasn't going to share that bit.

"But he missed. We caught him, got his name and a confession." I sigh. "And then I had to let him go."

Ava steps beside me. "Because if there's one thing Hunter always does, it's the right thing. No matter how hard it is."

"Damn straight," my sister mutters.

I'm not sure, but I think I see Gareth's lips twitch. Josh certainly grins. I almost feel like blushing. The support is touching, but undeserved.

I pretend that didn't just happen. "The authorities need to deal with him. He's killed wolves and is still trying to."

Gareth seems to pull in a breath, glancing around at us all. "There's nothing they'll do."

"What?" Riley storms over to stand on my other side. "He's a killer!"

Gareth holds up his hands in a don't-shoot-the-messenger

gesture. "We all know it's been legal to shoot wolves for a long time."

I shake my head. "Not when numbers are this low."

Ava moves in, her hand slipping into mine. The movement isn't missed by Gareth as he rubs his chin again. "I've caught a poacher before."

Josh wheels his chair forward. "You have?"

"Yeah. About eighteen months ago. He'd just shot a wolf." Gareth's shoulders seem to sag. "Took him into the cops and they looked at me like I was a tree-hugging hippie."

Dawn has sat at her desk. "I thought it was just me they looked at like that."

Ava frowns. "You've tried talking to them too?"

I remember when Dawn tried to see if we could get the wolves some sort of added protection. I'm not sure who had been more disillusioned when she returned with her answer.

Dawn looks away. "Just like most humans, they see the wolves as a threat, and poachers are a way of keeping their numbers under control."

Riley's hands clench. "Well, they've been very efficient."

I glance at Gareth, a question forming in my mind. "Did he skin it? The poacher you caught. Had he skinned the wolf?"

Gareth looks at me strangely. "He was too busy trying to intimidate me."

I suppose that's a good thing.

Gareth slowly straightens. "With a skinning knife."

Ava's intake of breath gives voice to all our shock. The poachers have been skinning wolves for longer than we realized.

Gareth steps forward. "Someone's been skinning them?" He asks quietly, but I've known Gareth long enough to know what that means. The Rendells have protected the wolves of this region for a long time. Hurting them hurts us.

"Yeah. They get paid for it."

Ava's hand squeezes mine. "By a guy called Helix."

Dawn gasps and she seems to pale. It wasn't far off the expression I saw on Ava's face when Snake landed that piece of news on us.

Josh has shot upright. "There's a guy paying for wolf skins?"

KJ enters, a sheaf of papers in his hands. "We thought the poaching seemed too coordinated. It looks like someone is turning them into mercenaries."

I glance at the paperwork. "Did you find anything?"

But KJ shakes his head. "Not yet." He half-grins. "Googling Helix gives you a whole lot of info on DNA. But he doesn't know what he's up against."

Gareth takes another step forward, coming to stand before me. "You knew all this?"

I raise my brows. "It hasn't been a secret...for anyone who was willing to listen."

Gareth's chest expands on a breath, his eyes flaring. "We're up against some serious stuff, Hunter."

No shit. Wolf numbers nudging the edge of extinction. A virus we hope is gone. And now a prick called Helix paying people to exterminate them.

Every muscle tightens as I feel my own barely banked anger flash. "And you still think captive breeding is a bad idea?"

He leans forward, his face looking like a bunch of thunderclouds. "You have to draw a line somewhere, Hunter."

I ignore the sting that barb just dealt. "And watch them go extinct?"

All of a sudden, Ava is standing beside me, almost in between us. "None of us want that."

Gareth instantly deflates, which doesn't surprise me. Ava is like a balm to soothe any negative feelings.

She's also spoken the truth which Gareth hasn't been willing to acknowledge. We all want the same thing.

He steps back, now studying her. When Ava doesn't back down, he looks away, frowning.

"Right." Josh claps his hands. "Looks like we've got some planning to do. I'll grab the coffee."

I smile, glad for the change of tone. "Good to see someone else understands the importance of caffeine."

The room seems to take a breath, and everyone shifts a little. Gareth heads for the map, and to my surprise, doesn't go any further than that. I expected him to leave the first opportunity he could. Josh and Riley are leaning over their phones as they stand beside the coffee machine. Dawn has walked over to KJ as they pour over the paperwork he brought in. Hopefully, they can glean something from the little information he found.

Ava releases my hand and heads for the door. I don't think much of it until she walks straight through, not once looking back. Ava always touches or glances before we say goodbye, even when we're in the same building. It's like a promise that it won't be long. I only noticed now that it's so glaringly missing.

I follow her out the door. She was quiet as we returned home last night, and I tried to tell myself that was normal. We had a lot to digest. But there's been a sadness to her I didn't want to acknowledge. This stuff must've affected her more than I'd realized.

I find her at the end of the hall, like she wasn't sure where to go next. There's something about her that says she's hurting.

I step closer, but don't touch. "Don't let Gareth get to you. He's holding onto the old ways like a lifeline."

"I haven't. I respect his commitment, if not his convictions. My guess is he's deeply connected to his pack."

Right. If it isn't him, then...

Ava's hands explode out with such force that I step back. "I don't like what you did last night."

I freeze. "I wanted to do more than punch him, Ava."

She narrows her eyes at me. "I'm not talking about that."

I blink. Ava saw that I'm no compassionate soul like she is last night. That I'm capable of more than she realizes.

She pushes away from the wall. "You could have been killed, Hunter!"

I relax, knowing a guilty conscience isn't good for my stress levels. "I'm sorry. It was a risk, but I knew he would be far enough away for me to hear the shot before it reached me."

Ava shakes her head, her eyes looking like they're aching green pools. "That's not the point." She looks away. "You took the risk alone."

I take a step back. "I...Alone?"

"Yes, Hunter. Alone. I've been thinking this whole time we're in this together. But last night you worked like the solo wolf you've always been."

"Ava—"

"Seeing that you don't trust me hurts. It really hurts."

It feels like I've been gutted by a train. I've hurt Ava. How do I tell her I was trying to protect her? Dammit. Just like her parents always have.

Double dammit. Who was I really protecting?

And who am I protecting by not telling her the truth about Sakari's pregnancy?

I close my eyes for a long moment, knowing I'm about to do this. We can't do this if I'm not honest, no matter how much it scares the hell out of me. "You're right."

"I know."

That almost draws a smile. What I'd do for her confidence about what the right thing to do is.

I'm trying to figure out where to start when the silence is fractured by a ringtone. Ava grabs it from her pocket but I hold out my hand for her to stop. "Whoever it is, call them back. I have something I need to tell you."

Ava pauses, then drops her hand. The phone rings a few more times, then stops. She stands there, waiting.

I swallow, knowing I could be killing the most beautiful thing I've ever experienced. But maybe, just maybe, Ava's infinite compassion will understand why I did this.

"When I killed Zephyr—"

"Because you had no choice."

I swallow again, recognizing the warmth that just bloomed in my chest for what it is—hope. "Yeah, well, things were looking pretty hopeless. I felt like I was letting everyone—"

My stilted speech is interrupted again as Ava's phone rings a second time. She frowns, pulling it out of her pocket. "I'll put in on silent." But as she glances at her screen, the frown intensifies. "It's my parents. They never call twice in a row."

I nod, wondering if this is the universe punishing me by drawing out this awful moment. "You'd better grab it then."

She hesitates. "I'll see what they want, then we'll finish our talk."

"Sure." Unfortunately for me, the truth ain't going nowhere.

She hits the green button, lifting the phone to her ear. "Hey, Mom."

"Ava, are you okay?" You wouldn't need Were hearing to overhear this conversation. The woman's voice on the other end of the line sounds high and strident.

Ava glances at me, confused. "Sure, Mom. Why wouldn't I be?"

"Ava." This time it's Noah's voice. "We've got you on speaker phone. We heard about last night."

Ava mouths "Josh" as she rolls her eyes. "We came across a poacher. But we're all fine."

"Poachers are dangerous people, Ava." Eden's voice is low and serious. It's like she's talking from personal experience. "And there were shots fired."

I gesture, asking whether I should leave but Ava shakes her head, grabbing my hand for good measure. She sighs. "Yeah, there was, but no one was hurt." She glares at me as she says the last words.

This time, her father speaks. "We want you to come home."

Everything stops for several heartbeats. Noah's voice rings with the authority of an Alpha. What's more, it's underscored by the love of a father. And to top it all off, I'm about to give Ava a pretty good reason to go home. But I don't back down from the decision I've made. What we've done can't stay a secret.

"Dad—"

"No, Ava. You're too important. I won't have you unprotected."

She frowns hard. "I can't leave yet." She glances at me. "And Hunter is keeping me more than safe."

I can imagine Noah is shaking his head right about now. "Things are getting too serious too fast. Jacksonville is the safest place for you right now. These wolves need you just as much."

I don't think anyone needs Ava more than I do.

"Mom. You guys raised me. You know I'm strong enough to do this. I'll be home as soon as I can."

My guess is Eden is the easier of Ava's parents to convince. I'm hoping she'll be the voice of reason.

"Ava." Eden's voice is quiet but sure and it already has my heart sinking. "We're both asking you. We can fight this fight together. Here."

Ava flops back against the wall, her eyes closing as she grimaces. "You don't understand..."

Standing there, helpless, I wish I knew what to do. Short of telling them she's shifted, how are they going to believe that she can hold her own?

Ava's wintergreen eyes open and grab mine. She pulls in a breath and seems to calm.

"Honey—"

But Ava cuts Noah off. "Dad, Mom, can you hang on a sec?"

"Sure. But whatever argument you come up with isn't going to change our minds."

Ava rolls her eyes as she grabs my hand. I give her a what's-going-on look, but she just tugs me back to the control room.

Inside she heads to KJ. "KJ, can you put this call up on the screen?"

"Sure."

Ava goes to hand him the phone but then pauses. "Is the line secure?"

KJ snorts. "Is Hunter's birthstone a coffee bean? I've encrypted this sucker until I barely recognize it myself."

"Good."

With the phone in his hand, it's only a few seconds before Noah and Eden are up on the screen. They look a little surprised to see us all in the room, but Noah quickly finds his frown again. "Having an audience isn't going to change the decision."

"I thought it was a request."

Noah arches a brow and I wonder if they've seen this side of Ava. Ava underscored by conviction is the only Ava I've known. It's the Ava I fell in love with.

Ava glances at me, and I can tell she's decided something. My chest is tight, my muscles locked, as I wait to know what it is. If it didn't feel so serious, I'd consider smiling. Is my girl giving me a taste of my own medicine?

Ava draws in a breath and grasps my hand. "Mom. Dad. I don't want to leave because this is where my heart is. With Hunter."

I stall, standing there, as Noah and Eden's gazes fall on me. Against the odds, pride fills me. Ava is publicly choosing me.

Eden smiles. "We figured something like that had happened. You've been spending a lot of time with Hunter."

"Including when you were injured and when you came across a poacher with a gun," Noah growls.

Ava hasn't lost her steady gaze and unflinching stance. "What happened when you found your soulmate, Dad?"

Soulmate. The words spear through my chest with their truth. Ava has my heart because she's my soulmate.

Noah is down and out speechless. Eden's eyes, the ones so like Ava's, have grown wide. She moves forward, her face coming in closer. "You've..."

Ava nods. "I shifted. After Hunter was shot."

And we kissed for the first time.

Whoa. It's all out there.

Everyone is silent. Noah, Eden, Dawn, Gareth, Riley, and Josh. Even KJ knows this is a big moment, and he already knew Ava had shifted.

Ava watches her parents, waiting. Noah's mouth has slammed down into a thin line. Eden is a little slack jawed as she blinks over and over. They look at each other, and I don't need to see Ava's threads to know these two are deeply connected. Simultaneously, they reach out their hands and clasp each other. Their eyes seem to be having a whole conversation.

Meanwhile, I'm not sure if I have the capacity to breathe. We're at a tipping point, and it's hard to tell which way it'll go. Elation surges through me that everyone will know Ava is mine. That I'm hers.

But what will it mean? My golden wolf is about to become a part of this fight, and I'm not sure where I fit in that impressive picture.

And how will Ava's parents feel about me being in it?

Together, Noah and Eden turn back toward us. Eden smiles, but it's Noah who speaks. "Welcome to the family, Hunter."

I nod, finally allowing myself a breath. "It's an honor. Ava is my heart."

As I say it, I realize something. Noah's words of welcome just became the final nail of the coffin that housed my secret. Ava's news is going to spread faster than the speed of light. She'll finally be seen for what she really is: someone with so much compassion and strength and conviction you'd think it's about as real as the possibility of a glorious, golden wolf. She'll be our beacon of hope.

And the mate of the great golden wolf would never do what I've done.

Ava deserves someone better than that. Weres deserve better than that.

Which means I'm going to pretend for as long as I can.

12

SAYEN

W ho would've thought that working with Eden would have a whole lot of parallels to working with Dawn.

I suppose the lab here is pretty similar to the one at the Tate ranch. Growing up with one of the richest packs in this part of the country had certainly had its perks. Fifteen years ago, John and Marie had jumped at the opportunity to clear the Tate name, seeing as it was several of their pack members who had joined Kurt Channon and his quest for Were domination.

So, when Dawn offered to establish the lab at their ranch, it had been up and running in record time. A lot of the early blood work on understanding wolf health and genetics had been done at the Tate ranch. Most of my teens had been spent in those white walled rooms, communing with microscopes.

For most of my childhood and adolescence, Dawn had mentored me. When she'd left for Jacksonville, I felt like I'd lost the closest thing I had to a mother. Dawn had trusted me, taught me, and saw my potential. With her, I finally had the opportunity to prove that I could follow in my father's footsteps.

And just like Dawn, Eden trusts me. John and Marie, the ones who had raised me once my mother died too, had talked up my skills and dedication. I wonder how they can be so naive considering what happened within the Tate pack almost two decades ago.

"How are John and Marie going?"

I startle, straightening up from the Petri dish I was leaning over, dropper suspended midair. Eden can do that. It's almost like she's reading your mind, and holy hell, that makes me nervous.

"I just spoke to them yesterday. Marie sends her love." I can't help the smile. "She asked if you needed any more biscuits."

Eden chuckles as she wheels away from her bench and grabs a pipette. "Tell her Beth only singes them nowadays." Her Fae smile reaches me across the room. "They're almost edible."

Noah's mother, Beth, is infamous for her ability to burn anything within six feet of a stove. I haven't tried it myself, but legend has it, you won't ever forget the taste of Beth's cooking once you've had the privilege.

Resuming like nothing's amiss, I let a clear bubble of fluid drop onto the Petri dish. It spreads, sitting like a colorless eyeball looking up at me. How can such a minuscule bead carry so much? I wrap a sense of purpose around me. Now isn't the time to get cold feet.

Without looking up, I put out the feeler. "I know they already did, but they wanted me to pass on their congratulations again."

Eden's pause is much subtler than mine. If I wasn't straining to listen, I would've missed the creak of her chair. She resumes adding the stabilizer to the next doses of therapeutic vaccines like nothing is amiss. "What did they think of the news?"

Ah, the news—the bombshell news of their daughter.

Ava has shifted.

In fact, Ava met a guy and then shifted.

It's been the talk of the Were community. My pack. Her pack. Any Were that has a vested interest in the fate of the wolves.

I've soaked up all the talk. Those who say they weren't surprised. Those who keep asking what it's supposed to mean. I've paid particular attention to those closest to me—they're the ones who know the truth. But it's how Eden and Noah feel about the news that I need to find out.

I slide the lid on the Petri dish, shutting in the contents. "They're so happy for you and Noah. They think the world of Ava."

Eden finally looks up, her face soft. "She loved spending time at your ranch. I would have liked you to meet her."

I shrug. "I spent most summers on the Reservation with Mom. Seems it wasn't meant to be."

"You'll meet her when she comes home."

Placing the Petri dish in the incubator with the others, I slide it slightly to the side. I need to remember which one this is. "Sounds nice. Will that be soon?"

Eden looks away. "I'm not sure. She seems determined to help the arctic wolves."

I suspect Hunter has a lot to do with that. Some Were that no one knew existed who just became a household name overnight. I begin to wonder what makes him so special, but tell myself I don't care. It works for me that Ava isn't coming home anytime soon. Having another pair of eyes in this lab isn't something I need. "Well, their numbers are much lower than ours."

"Only a handful left." Eden sighs. "It's just hard, having her so far away when things are so unsettled."

"Why don't you tell her to come home?" Our elders are the ones who know what the best thing to do is.

Eden looks surprised. "I trust her. Ava has always had a sense of what's right. I know that's the direction she has to move in."

Huh. It seems I have more in common with Ava than I realized—I also know what's right.

Shutting the door of the incubator, I check the temp and humidity. Forty-eight hours and they'll be ready. "Next batch of therapeutic vaccines are cooking."

Eden smiles that smile of hers. "Wonderful. You really are a gem, Sayen. I couldn't have produced as many as we have without your help."

The door opens before I have to formulate a response and Noah enters. I tense. Spending time with Eden is a whole lot easier than being around him. Like there's some invisible thread between the two of them, his gaze seeks out Eden's like he knew exactly where she was.

"How you two going in here?"

"Well, Sayen has the next batch stewing." Her shoulders slump. "I'm pretending I'm making progress."

Noah's blond brows crinkle. "We knew it would be a long shot."

Eden drops her pen on the bench. "We could try to make an actual antivirus if we had a sample of Furious."

Noah rubs her back. I doubt he's even conscious he's doing it. "There hasn't been a confirmed case of Furious for a while. We're all hoping we won't need one."

"We need it to. If it rears its ugly head again, we'll be back to fighting an unknown enemy." She looks up. "It worries me, Noah."

His gaze holds hers and it's like I'm not in the room. "We didn't know what we were up against when the whole Prophecy started. Now that she's shifted, it's doing it all over again."

They're talking about Ava. My mother never got to worry about my future. With my father dead she'd returned to the reservation to be with family as she'd drowned in grief and shame. Only to find that the poverty and crime promptly short-ened her lifespan.

"This is bigger, Noah. I can feel it."

"I know. It's not just Furious. But she's your daughter. She's my daughter. We've always believed in her."

He bends down and their foreheads touch as they briefly brush lips.

I look away, working hard not to grimace. Instead of their love softening anything in my chest, it just reinforces everything I was told as a child. They're lost. They're holding onto nothing but hope.

They're doing it all wrong.

"It's not the same out here, is it?"

Hunter turns back from surveying the landscape around us. The quad is to our left. The outcropping that I'll forever call ours is to our right. In front and behind is the vast expanse that is the arctic tundra. There's so much raw power, but you can feel it's all balanced on a knife's edge.

He nods, knowing exactly what I'm talking about. "It's quieter."

Considering the tundra is built of nothing but the wind pushing silence around, those words break my heart. Without the wolves, an essential element of the fabric around us is missing.

I slip my arms around his waist. "We'll fix this."

Hunter's smile is crooked, and I haven't decided if it's my favorite yet. "Well, now everyone is kind of expecting us to."

I rest my forehead on his chest. "No pressure, huh?"

"Not really. I believe in you."

I let myself frown since Hunter can't see my face. Until Hunter starts seeing the truth, I can't tell him the secret that proves what I've known all along. "Well, I believe in us."

Hunter sighs as his arms come around me. "I'm not surprised this is where we met. I used to come here a lot."

I look up, willing to go with the change of subject to see where it will take us. "Because of the wolves?"

Those copper of eyes is burning deep. "Mostly."

"But there was another reason?"

"This is where Dad would bring me for Alpha training. He knew how important our role was."

My chest aches. Catching the poacher has stirred up so much for Hunter. His father died protecting the wolves. Not only that. His father was killed by everything we're up against. "He'd be proud of you, Hunter."

Something shifts in Hunter's eyes but he looks away before I can grasp it. "I think the wolves knew it was special. They seemed to love this spot as much as I did. But then I saw you, and my heart became forever connected to this place."

I watch his handsome face, taut with strain. But he's still deflecting, staring out at the horizon like it has all the answers. "There's a lot of history here."

"There sure is."

"I'm looking forward to making a whole lot of future."

Hunter's gaze snaps back to mine. Shades of amber move through his copper eyes. The embers of past pain flare and I hold my breath. Slowly, they lighten, moving through brilliant shades of dawn, finding the light of hope. His lips relax, his eyes soften. "Me too."

And that's all I needed to hear.

Pushing up on my toes, I touch my lips to his. This sensation, this is the promise of our future.

This is the touch of our love.

Hunter half-sighs, half-groans as his hands dive into my hair. Cupping my face, he angles his head and deepens the kiss.

Expanding the sensations, delving into our passion.

Whoa. That went somewhere I love a whole lot faster than I expected.

But this, Hunter, is what recharges me. My faith. My hope.

So I push up a little more, wanting to do some delving myself.

Within the space of a gasp, we're wrapped around each other, hands clutching, tongues roaming. What started out as a promise has just become a pledge. There's too much emotion for it to be anything else.

When hands become restless and start searching, we pull apart. There's some unspoken agreement that we can't let this get away from us. I know why I don't want Hunter committing before he's ready, but for the first time, I begin to wonder why he's doing the same.

Hands clasping my head, Hunter smiles down at me. "Not sure we'll be able to do much of this once we've finished today's job."

Laughter bubbles up at the truth in his words, but then I push up for another quick peck. "I'm pretty sure they're getting kinda used to it."

Hunter's chuckle is music for my soul. "You've got a point."

He releases me and heads to the quad, opening the compartment on the back. Pulling out the equipment we'll need, he heads over to the outcropping. I join him, disappointed this is our last one. Spending time out here with Hunter is going to be a treat that's probably going to become less and less frequent.

Hunter was right. Now that Weres know I've shifted, a collective breath has been sucked in. And everyone is holding it, waiting to see what's going to happen next.

The only problem is, I don't know what that is.

"Hold this?"

Hunter passes me a mallet, finding I already have my hand out. We've established a rhythm as we've reinstalled the cameras out on the tundra. We'd brought them all in once the last of the wolves had been captured, but now that the poachers are still hanging around, we decided they could still be useful.

It doesn't take long for the stake to be hammered in and the camera to be positioned. We work together to connect the small solar panel, and with the press of a button it begins streaming.

Standing, we stare at it. These cameras acknowledge that the fight against the poachers isn't over. I ask what I already know the answer to. "You want to catch him, don't you?"

Now that this mysterious Helix exists, this all just amped up to a whole new level. Everyone knows the poachers won't stop until we know who that is. Money is just too great an incentive.

Hunter's lips flatline. "Damn straight I do. I want to catch every last one of them."

I ignore the uneasiness sliding down my spine. Hunter's words were hard, full of icy anger and even colder determination. "You think that one of them is your father's killer."

"One of them has got to be." He pauses, but I can feel there's something else. "Does that worry you?"

I don't even need to think about that one. I shake my head. "No. I know you're angry. What happened wasn't fair." I slip my hand into his. "You want justice. I get that."

Hunter's hand grasps mine like a lifeline. He doesn't look at me as he speaks. "You don't know what I'm capable of, Ava."

I don't let those words have any more air-time than they deserve. I know what Hunter has had to do to save the wolves. "Yes, I do, Hunter. You're capable of great determination, loyalty, and sacrifice." I nudge him with my hip, not letting this go any further. "Not to mention you're not a bad kisser."

Hunter's lips twitch as he fights the smile. He turns to me, his eyes sparkling with humor. "It's all the practice."

I bite my lip. "I mean, it's practically gold standard kissing."

The smile slips through and I feel my chest warm. Hunter

steps closer. "Although I'm definitely going to need more practice before you can make that judgment call."

I mold my features into a frown, no matter how much I want to smile, too. "That's true. I wouldn't want to make a preemptive call."

He arches a brow as his eyes heat up and I feel my pulse do the same. Sexy Hunter is one I wish I could see more often.

"Well, maybe I could show you a selection?"

My breath hitches. "A selection?"

He steps in, head leaning down as he whispers, "Yeah. A selection."

"Ah, well, that sounds...nice..."

It only takes a small movement for our bodies to be flush. "There's the 'you take my breath away.'"

Hunter leans down, the air between us still and silent as he pauses, studying me. The emotion—the depth and breadth of it —has any air in my lungs evaporating even before our lips touch. A heartbeat passes and he claims the last millimeters between us. His lips are soft, full of love, but so much more. Only Hunter could communicate a forever sort of commitment in just one touch.

He pulls back and I blink. "I see what you mean..."

Something flares in Hunter's eyes and I'm not sure if it's satisfaction or pride. His breath fans my face. "And the 'I don't think I can ever get enough.'"

This kiss is one of possession and passion. His hands frame my face, controlling the pressure and angle. His lips are all hot and soft, fast and firm. I sink into them, letting him know that I never doubted I was his. I know I got my message across when his groan rumbles through his chest.

He pulls back, swallowing. I look up at him, waiting, possibly challenging, him to see what will come next. Somewhere in the land of reality, I feel his phone vibrate in his pocket.

The hint of a smile isn't what I expected. "And I call this the 'we need to get back kiss.'"

This brush of the lips is brief. Although there's the 'this ain't over' promise in the caress, Hunter steps back.

I pout. "I'm going to be honest. That one is my least favorite."

Hunter's laugh is such a beautiful sound that before I know it, I'm smiling right along with him. Clasping hands, we head back to the quad.

The drive back whips up the good feeling our time together has given me, despite all the challenges we're facing. Now that I'm finally Were, the cold air is nothing but invigorating. There's too much hope sparked by everything's that happened. I settle down behind Hunter, knowing that even though we don't have any answers, together, we have the power to find them.

We park the quad in the shed, and like we always do, hold hands as we enter Resolve.

Hunter pulls his phone out of his pocket, brow tense. "If that's KJ again..."

I glance over. "He's been messaging you?"

"About a million times. I told him what time we'd be back this afternoon."

I stop, thinking of Sakari and Achak. "Is there something wrong?"

"No. If it was anything urgent, he would've rung. This is because we're running late."

I can't help the grin. "Well, I think that could be my fault."

Hunter shifts closer. "I could show you my 'let's teach him patience' kiss..."

There's the click of the speaker above our heads. "Don't even think about it!"

KJ knows he doesn't have to shout into the speaker, but he's obviously decided to do it anyway. Hunter and I grin at each other, and I'm hoping he's getting the same idea I am. We continue our inward trajectory.

"And no, that was not meant to be a challenge, you two!"

Hunter sighs as I giggle. Holding hands, we head down the hallway. It seems KJ has something he'd like to discuss.

In the control room, we find everyone is already there.

KJ looks up, then pointedly turns to Josh. "I'm glad you asked, my friend. Yes, I have been looking into the technology we'll need to install remote-controlled tasers on the cameras."

Hunter rolls his eyes as we come to stand by his desk. He leans back, crossing his arms. "You're going to fry your beanie one day with all your crazy ideas."

Riley giggles. "Have you seen how many he has in his drawers?"

KJ shrugs. "Sometimes crazy is just what we need."

Dawn stands, her face calm, but not smiling. I glance at Josh, sensing something is up. Josh does his 'I have no idea' look.

Hunter's copper gaze assesses them both. "So, what's up?"

KJ wheels his chair forward, grabbing a piece of paper. "Achak's blood is clear."

Josh frowns. "How is that possible?"

I look at the faces around me. Josh is right. How is that possible?

"We're not sure. We've run multiple tests, and they keep showing the same thing."

Dawn nods. "His blood is that of any other wolf."

I sag back, butt hitting the edge of the desk. I'm not sure how I feel about this. Surely it's a good thing if Achak never had Furious? It means all the worries we've had about whether he can return to the wild are no longer an issue. Except...

I walk over to the screens. We opened the door to Achak's external enclosure yesterday. I was hoping it would ease his restlessness. Except now he just paces the fence line, a feral energy seeming to be permanently powering him. Why else would he have attacked me? Why is he acting like he is now? "It doesn't make sense..."

KJ looks down at the paper, his frown full of confusion. "I know." He sighs as he looks up at us. "It also means we don't have any more leads."

I hear Hunter's breath whoosh out. "Achak was our one link to Furious. Are you sure?"

"According to what we have here."

Dawn steps forward, and I have a feeling this was all leading to something. "I'm going back to the mainland, for a week or two. We just don't have the facilities here to do what we need to do."

Hunter nods. "Makes sense. When are you thinking of leaving?"

Dawn glances at KJ. "Tomorrow. The sooner we get started, the better."

I look at KJ, wondering why Dawn seems to be so focused on him. Hunter must be wondering the same thing, because he opens his mouth to speak but KJ cuts him off.

"I'm going with her."

KJ stares at Hunter as his words hang in the room.

Hunter uncrosses his arms, disbelief seeming to undo him as he points at KJ. "You're going to the mainland?"

KJ throws him an unimpressed look. "Is there fur stuck in your ears? That's what I just said."

Riley is looking confused. "But you hate the mainland."

Josh holds up his hands. "Although, I'd like to point out that fresh fruit and vegetables are far more affordable there."

KJ can't seem to hold Hunter's gaze. "Dawn suggested it, and I think she's right. Two people can achieve far more than just one."

Hunter is rubbing his forehead. "I don't get it. You've always been so adamant that you won't go back there."

Go back there? I know KJ had a history before he arrived at Evelyn Island, and whatever it is has molded the choices he makes now.

"Sure, it's not something I'm looking forward to. But—"

Hunter straightens. "You can't go."

KJ frowns. "Well, I kinda can."

Hunter is staring at his cousin with such intensity, I don't know how it doesn't singe his beanie. "We have Sakari here." He pauses, like that's important. "And the other wolves. You're the one who's tracking their data."

Josh raises his hand. "I could do that. I used to help out back at home with that stuff."

Which is true. Medical data and all its jargon is Josh's first language.

KJ looks like he's clenching his teeth. His jaw is tense as he grinds out his next words. "It's the only way I can find out more about Furious."

Hunter pulls in a slow, controlled breath. His hands clench and unclench. Although I'm standing right next to him, for some reason he feels like he's just found himself all alone. "Fine."

With that, Hunter stalks out of the room.

KJ scratches his chin. "I'm not gonna lie. He took it better than I expected."

Dawn walks over and places her hand on his shoulder. "You two have worked closely for a long time. He'll see that this is what you need to do."

Riley is frowning as she looks at the door her brother just went through. I'm not sure what this change means. Surely Dawn and KJ going back to the lab at Jacksonville's captive breeding program is a good thing? I get that Hunter would miss his cousin. But something about his reaction felt...dispropor-tionate.

Turning, I follow him out the door and find him only a few feet down the hall. He's leaning back against the wall, one leg propped up, arms crossed.

As I approach, Hunter unfurls his arms, pulling up a small smile. "Sorry. Kinda overreacted in there. I just didn't see that coming."

I wave away the apology. There's something else going on here. "Why is it so significant that KJ is going to Jacksonville?"

Hunter's eyes close as he leans his head back against the wall. "I can't tell you."

He can't tell me? It never occurred to me that there would be something between us that we hadn't shared. I draw out my response as I digest the realization. "Okay."

"I would if I could, Ava. But this is KJ's story to tell, not mine."

"This has got to do with why he hates being a Were, doesn't it?"

"Yeah. Pretty much."

Hunter watches me as I mull that over. He seems to be holding his breath and my chest tightens. I slip my arms around him, even though I'm not sure how I feel about him keeping information from me. Logically, I know this is KJ's secret, and not his. But something is prickling along my skin. It's a sense of unease I can't place.

As strong arms wrap around me and the feeling that I'll never tire of swells through me, I acknowledge I trust Hunter. He'd tell me this if he could.

But as his head comes down to rest on mine, I realize some-thing else.

I asked the wrong question.

I pause and bury my head into the hot muscles of his chest. Minutes pass and I'm not sure if I'm waiting or wondering.

All I do know is, that I didn't ask why KJ leaving is something that would rattle Hunter so bad.

And as we head back to the control room, I realize I'm avoiding.

Because I don't ask.

14

AVA

Visiting Achak is a daily routine now. Back in Jacksonville, his need for independence had meant I didn't need to be around much. We didn't need to see each other often to know our connection was a strong one.

But since we've captured him and brought him to Resolve, it's been different. Very different.

It's been raining, meaning the soil is sodden as I head out to his enclosure. We put him in the biggest one, the one closest to the wilderness, but even that wasn't enough. I can feel his tension before I see him, and I know he's pacing again.

The soil is a mud track along the boundary fence, a no-man's-land worn down by agitated energy, and Achak is battering it again. He's half-way down when he sees me. For the first time today he stops, letting out a small bark.

I enter the enclosure, glad for the double gate because Achak rushes me the minute I open the second one. Finding the first tightly shut, I feel the burst of frustration as he turns away. He lopes over to the fence again and I follow, a heaviness in my gut.

Kneeling down beside the fence, I ignore the cold squelch of mud. I wait to see whether he wants to spend time with me.

Achak trots over and stands before me, his red-grey coat spiky from the rain. He paces no matter what the weather. His canine gaze is steady as he takes me in. Our thread comes into my consciousness, a glowing, golden fiber stretching from him to me.

I lean my head against the wire fence that's keeping him prisoner. "I'm so sorry, Achak."

Coming around, he sits beside me, his furred body leaning into mine. My eyes pricking, I wrap my arms around his damp body. This is the wolf who I'm so deeply connected to that he followed me across land and water. And not long after he found me, I caged him again.

And yet, he's offering me comfort.

"I'm trying to keep you safe, my friend."

Achak doesn't move. It's possibly the stillest he's sat since we brought him in. I wonder if he's thinking how lame that excuse is. This is probably the least safe he's ever been.

What will happen if they decide Achak doesn't have Furious? Does that mean he'll be considered aggressive after what happened back in Jacksonville? Or do the tests get more frequent now? Have I turned him into a lab rat who everyone wants to wring answers from?

I sigh, leaning back to look at him, not liking what I'm about to suggest. "Maybe you should go back with Dawn and KJ."

Achak leaps to his feet and moves away. He wouldn't have understood the words, but I channeled my intent through our connection. His reaction makes the suggestion feel like even more of a betrayal than what I've already done.

He stands a few feet away, staring at the horizon. I follow his gaze, wondering what's calling to him so strongly.

"You want to stay."

Although he doesn't come back, Achak seems to relax. Despite how much he hates it at Resolve, Achak doesn't want to leave the tundra.

My shoulders slump. That wasn't the answer I was expecting. I know our connection is strong, but there's something else going on here. Standing tall and strong, his red-grey coat a thick mane around his head, Achak stares at me. His steady gaze is trying to tell me something.

You can fix this.

I sigh. That's what everyone thinks.

I hold my hand out, letting him know what everyone seems to be forgetting.

I can't do this on my own.

Without hesitation, Achak comes back. He powers straight past my hand until his forehead comes to rest against mine. I smile as my chest aches. It's not often I ask Achak for anything. It's deeply touching to know that when I do need something, that's the sort of answer I'll get.

As we stay there for long moments, I breathe in his soggy scent. The words seem to be stuck in my brain. It's like I'm missing something.

You can fix this.

I pull back as it hits me. Achak knows something I don't.

He doesn't blink as I continue to stare.

And now that I can see this, why does it feel like a familiar feeling?

The click of the speaker has Achak's ears twitching. KJ's voice projects through a second later. "Five minutes, peoples."

Achak steps back, as if realizing that's his cue. I sigh. "This sure would be easier if I had a clue."

I push up, glancing down at my knees. Two brown lines of mud extend down the front of my jeans. "Good thing the cameras only show from the shoulders up, huh?"

Achak turns away and I know he's going to go back to looking for the non-existent weak points in the fence. I brush his tail with my hand as it sweeps past me. Looks like we're both going back to where we started—a plan based on hope.

Heading down the hall, I stride like I know what I'm doing. Following my gut has got me where I am now. With Hunter. Fulfilling my potential.

But as I get to the door, I pause. They'll all be waiting in that room. Dawn may even be getting a little edgy as the moment the teleconference for the Assembly starts. But Hunter would know I'm on my way. Even if he couldn't feel it, he'd be able to see it on the screens.

Although I still hesitate. There are moments I'm so sure this is all heading in the right direction. But then there are the moments I see Achak hating his confinement, the moments I count exactly how many arctic wolves are left, moments when I'm scared my worst fears will come true—that I'll have to do this alone...and I realize exactly how many pieces make up this puzzle.

And all those fragments keep moving on me.

I startle when I hear footsteps coming down the hall to my left. I thought everyone would be in there.

I'm glad when I see Josh walking towards me, his familiar grin lighting up his face. He slips an arm around my shoulder, staring at the door just like I was. "You excited?"

I throw him a wry glance. "Were you excited when you had that interview for med school?"

"The only reason I didn't vomit on their shoes is because you texted me just as I was about to go in."

I smile. I'd forgotten about that.

"I think those words are probably quite relevant right now."

I elbow him. "I told you to look on the bright side, if you break a leg, you'll be learning how to fix it."

"Admittedly, it doesn't seem immediately applicable. But those words were just what I needed to hear."

I look at him, wondering what he's trying to tell me.

Josh squeezes my shoulder. "You basically told me I had it in the bag. It never occurred to you that I wouldn't get in."

I roll my eyes. "You've been preparing for that your whole life."

He grins. "Ditto."

Oh.

Wrapping my arm around his waist, I squeeze him back. "You're my favorite cousin, you know that?"

Josh snorts as he steps to the side. "Considering two sets of twins who even our grandmother has named The Terrors are my competition, I'm not sure that's an achievement."

I giggle. The eldest twins, Breanna and Belinda, think it's a challenge to lock everyone out of the house. The younger, Layla and Luna, think their noses are where marbles should be kept. Josh places his hand on the doorknob and looks at me, eyebrows raised in question.

I straighten as I nod. "Let's do this."

Josh winks and pushes the door open. "Did I mention you're also my favorite cousin?"

I shake my head. His dad only has one sibling—my father who only ever had one child. And his mother's siblings all scattered once their father, Kurt Channon, wreaked his havoc. As far as we know, I'm not only his only cousin, but also his closest known relative.

Inside, KJ steps back from the microphone that's connected to the speakers. "About time. You don't know what I was about to threaten."

Josh throws him a grin. "That you'd watch our every move?"

KJ shakes his head, but doesn't manage to hide the spark of a smile before he heads back to his desk.

Hunter's eyes warm as he takes me in. "I told you she wasn't far away."

KJ is rapidly clicking his mouse as he stares at his screen. "Yeah, well you also told me that coffee would maintain your sunny personality."

Riley's the one who giggles at that one. I walk over, slotting in next to him like I belong there. I smile up at Hunter, telling them all that there is indeed a sun glowing within him. If it were just the two of us, I'd ask him to show me what his greeting kisses involved.

But we're here for an Assembly. Probably the biggest one yet.

Because now I've shifted.

No one's asked what color wolf I am. They probably assume I'm a white wolf like Dad, maybe even some shade of grey like his mother. Hunter and I have spoken, and we've decided we see how this Assembly goes before we share that little nugget. We need to get a sense of what Weres and Fae are expecting from us before we raise the stakes even more. Shifting late, as impossible as it is, has happened in my family before. But being a wolf that glows and shimmers? That's going to set some pretty high expectations.

And we're still not sure what we're fighting.

KJ looks up at the screens. "Everybody take their places. We're about to go live."

Riley grabs Josh by the hand. "And that's our cue to leave." They head out the door, probably planning on eavesdropping on the other side.

I feel Hunter pull in a breath at the same time I do. It's actually comforting knowing he's just as nervous as I am. We decided last night we'd stand together. Hunter was foolish enough to suggest that he remain to the side, maintaining his role as the Rendell Alpha, but I'd quickly shut that one down. Golden wolf exists because of Hunter.

Which means hope exists because of Hunter.

Dawn takes her place standing beside her desk. Hunter and I stand in the center of the room.

One by one, the screens come alive. They fill up with Alphas, Fae Elders, and lastly my parents; the Prime Alpha and his mate, the Queen of the Fae. It looks like everyone has made an effort to turn up for this Assembly.

Hunter's fingers reach out and link through mine. I feel his edgy energy and let it meet mine. This is definitely intimidating.

Dad speaks first. "Welcome everyone. Thank you for your attendance. As you know, we're here to discuss the latest developments."

The images on the screens all nod. That's exactly why we're here.

"I assume everyone has had an increase in poaching?"

Once again, there's a wave of nods, but this time they're accompanied by frowns.

Mom's face is frowning like all the others. "We know this Helix is paying for wolf pelts. Poachers now have an even bigger incentive outside of just trophy kills."

"Humans." The word is growled quietly from the Lyall Alpha.

River, one of the Fae Elders, looks pained. "They don't understand what they're doing yet."

"I doubt they will." This time it's the Bardolph Alpha rumbling his dissatisfaction.

Hunter and I inhale simultaneously. There's far more frustration than we'd expected.

Dad holds his hand up, asking for silence. "Let's not forget we're human too."

There's quiet, and the two Alphas frown, their eyes sliding to the side.

Dawn seems to have waited for a pause, because she speaks up. "And from what we can tell, Furious isn't finished yet."

Everyone has seen what Alistair broadcast on his page. Unfortunately, it's received the most traffic of any of his posts. People are starting to take note.

Dawn's face is somber as she continues. "And Achak's blood, the wolf we believed survived Furious, has come back clear."

More rumbles echo through the speakers.

River asks what I'm sure everyone is wondering. "What does that mean, Dawn?"

KJ is watching Dawn closely, and I wonder what he's thinking. He doesn't seem so sure that it's all that clear cut with Achak.

"I'm returning to the Tate lab to do further testing. We're hoping to have a concrete answer within the week."

John Tate nods. "We have everything ready."

"But if he's clear, then we have nothing?" Lyall Tate has pushed upright again, looking like he wants to jump through the screen and get some answers himself.

I look at Mom. She's the one who's been working so hard on this. Her face is resolute. "We'll find something else."

"So, we've got some guy called Helix determined to line his house with wolf fur, and a disease we're hoping to hell doesn't take off?"

Mom nods, unruffled. "Those are the challenges we face, yes. But we also have strength and determination."

Hunter finally speaks. "And we have Ava."

That silences everything. I resist the urge to swallow as every eye turns to me. They all know I've shifted. I take in their expressions, a mix of curious, hopeful, some of guarded distrust.

How do I give them hope when I don't have the answers?

Dad nods. "Ava is the child of the Prime Prophecy, and she's now Were."

Mom smiles at me, pride glowing from her eyes. "She's human and she's the daughter of the Fae Queen. She knows the power we all carry."

And I am the mate of Hunter Rendell. I straighten as my hand tightens around his. That's where all my power comes from. Yes, it was born of the Prophecy, but its Legacy is that of love. And that's all thanks to the honorable, amazing, wonderful Were beside me.

But that part I can't share.

Not yet.

"So, what's the plan?"

And there's the question this meeting has been dovetailing to. What's next? More specifically—what am I going to do?

For some reason, the threads take that moment to flare into view. It's amazing how they can show that despite the distance between us all—we aren't as separate as we think. Mom and Dad, the Fae and the Were. If they were all here, the web connecting us all would be a rich one indeed.

What the people taking part in this Assembly don't see is that humans are just as much a part of this as we are.

They need to see what I see.

What about Helix? He's part of this fabric too. Except Helix is fast-tracking the wolves' extinction. Which shows something very wrong is happening here. The tear is bigger than any of us realized.

I straighten, lifting the hand that's clasped in Hunter's. "We stop Helix. We find a cure for Furious."

I look around, willing to meet disbelief and distrust, latching onto the faith that's trying to grow.

"We save the wolves."

15

KJ

T here sure are more pine trees than I thought there would be on the way to the Tate ranch. It strikes me as odd enough that I sit up straighter in the car. Yep, definitely more pine trees, and they seem to be increasing in density.

I turn to Dawn. "How much longer till we get there?"

Dawn remains focused as she navigates a bend in the road. "Not long."

Hmm, Dawn is usually more precise in her responses. "Will John be there?"

The flicker of a glance she slides my way has me tensing. "Possibly not."

"But he's the Tate Alpha. Why wouldn't he be there?"

"KJ." She draws my name out.

"I'm not loving that tone, Dawn. When anyone has ever used my name in that tone, I've always ended up disappointed."

She opens her mouth, but I'm not finished.

"And when I say disappointed, I mean 'someone just crushed the way I saw the world' disappointed."

Dawn sighs. "We're not going to the Tate ranch."

I spin in my seat, alarm ringing through my nerves. "You told me that's where we were going."

"I know, KJ." Her look is full of compassion, but for some reason, it feels like pity. "But then the wolf with Furious turned up in the reserve. It was logical that we go to Jacksonville."

Jacksonville.

The pine trees seem to be crowding in as the car slices through their shadows. "You didn't tell me on purpose."

Dawn's hand moves like she's about to reach out, but it settles back on the steering wheel. "You wouldn't have come."

"Of course, I wouldn't have."

There are two people on this planet who know why I don't want to go to Jacksonville. Hunter, I trusted with my secret within days of meeting him. You don't need to spend long with Hunter to know he's someone you can trust with your dirty past.

But Dawn, I debated long and hard. As we worked closely together, I'd watched and weighed. Would she realize that no-one can know this? Would she look at me differently?

And I've never regretted telling her.

Until now.

"I'm so sorry, KJ. I don't like lying to you."

I look out the window. "But you did."

She sighs again, and I hate that I notice it. One, thanks to my Were hearing. Two, because it means I still care about how she's feeling.

"We need your brain to help solve this. I couldn't let this get in the way."

The anger is hot and fast. It always is. I clench my hands and teeth as it sweeps through me like a freaking tsunami. It calls for me to react. To show her that I'm not some pawn, that this isn't something that can be overruled like that.

I breathe in. It's a struggle to get the air down my constricted throat and into my cramped chest, but I do it. And when it's done, I do it again. Anger isn't something I can afford to feel.

Dawn's right. I wouldn't have come, which means one less person facing Furious.

And we can't let that happen.

I consciously untangle each muscle. It's like trying to mold steel, they're that rigid, but I've done it plenty of times before.

My shrug is stilted and kinda jagged, but it's a shrug nonetheless. "Well, if it's what the fans want…"

She smiles, the strain around her eyes relaxing a little. "I knew you'd step up." This time she does reach over and squeeze my knee. "You've always been willing to do what needs to be done."

Which is the common ground that first drew me to Dawn.

I squeeze her hand right back. "We're going to win this, just you wait and see."

Her smile grows as she turns back to the windscreen. "That's the plan, KJ."

My false bravado gets a reality slap as we pass the Jacksonville sign. When I promised myself I would change this Legacy, I knew there would be challenges. Big challenges.

And I was okay with that. Like Dawn said, I'm willing to do what it takes.

But being here?

If you were to draw a circle that outlined my comfort zone, then you'd find Jacksonville somewhere in the next galaxy.

I shake my head as we skirt around town. It doesn't surprise me that the universe is punishing me.

As we pull into the carpark of the captive breeding program, I have a mantra going through my head.

It could be worse.

It could be worse.

Beanies could never have been invented.

Climbing out of the car, I pause. The building looks innocuous enough. I notice the plaque—United We Conquer. Could that be any vaguer? That fuzziness is exactly why this all started. Some Weres decided to twist it to justify their own agenda.

Dawn takes a few steps, then registers I'm not with her. Her face softens as she stops too. "I wish I could tell you that you don't have to do this."

I shrug. "Me too, but that train of inevitability was put into motion long ago. It's not your fault."

I head to the building, striding like someone who knows what they're doing. I grab the door and hold it open for Dawn. "Welcome home."

She smiles as she shakes her head. "Home has never been this place."

As we pass through, I wonder what she meant by that.

I know it's rude, but I barely acknowledge the guy at the front door. All I know is he's Were, and that's enough for me. The hallway we walk down is lined with photos of wolves. There's not fifty, but there's definitely a quite a few shades of grey. They're largely at the center, but there's also several of wolves in the reserve.

Dawn stops when she notices me looking. "From our founding members, through to all the success we've seen born."

"That's quite an achievement."

"The work they've done here has made a significant difference to wolf numbers in the reserve."

Unless poachers reduce their numbers so much that they can't bounce back.

Or a virus wipes them out.

We keep heading through, Dawn using a card to enter a back area. We stand there for a moment, but the place echoes with emptiness.

Dawn glances around. "There doesn't seem to be anyone here."

Drawing in a breath, I register other recent scents. Relief is a welcome feeling. "Nope." I tap the black bag hanging on my shoulder. "So, where's this mecca of all laboratories?"

Dawn's green eyes twinkle. "You wearing socks?"

I grin back. "Looking forward to getting them knocked off."

Dawn uses her pass again at the next door and we enter a room. The lab isn't big, but it's decked out. Microscopes, sleek and modern, sit on a bench along one wall. Shelves, their glass doors showing more glass containers, line the other side. The back has the incubator and a—

"You have a biosafety cabinet?"

"Yes, it means we can keep samples as sterile as possible."

I nod slowly. "Impressive."

The other side of the room is lined with benches too, but this time, instruments sit proudly on it. I take two steps and stop. "A vaccine bath?" Holy moly! "Don't tell me you have a Craigie Tube?"

"I just ordered that. It'll help us to learn about Furious."

If we get a sample.

I shake my head as I correct myself. When we get a sample.

I glance down at my shoes. "Yep, socks are gone."

Dawn claps her hands. "I knew you'd love it." She steps further in and turns back to me. "We'll be able to do so much here, KJ."

"Do you know what I'm seeing?"

"Your version of heaven?"

I grin. "Answers."

The sound of a cell ringing has Dawn pulling her phone out of her pocket. "That's Eden. I'll let her know we're here."

Answering, she heads back out. I hear her warm greeting as she heads further down the hall.

I turn on the spot. What we could learn here! It's obvious they've set it up for making the vaccine. Unfortunately, from what we've seen, it doesn't work. But all we need is one lead…

Plus, if I hang here, I can probably avoid running into too many of the locals.

I'm heading over to the incubator to see what they've got cooking in there when the door behind me opens.

I turn, smiling. "I think I may need to move i—"

Except it's not Dawn who's frozen in the doorway.

Definitely not Dawn.

This girl is young, probably my age, and is as caramel-skinned as Dawn is white. Despite being on the small side, I straight away register she's Were, but I won't hold that against her. There's a lot of those around here. She pauses, then pulls up a smile, but for some reason, I don't feel the welcome. "Hi."

Whoa. Now that I'm past the 'she's a Were' stage, I suddenly realize how gorgeous this girl is. She's all strong angles and striking features, somehow serious and intense. It floors me for a second. "Hi."

"Ah, I'm Sayen."

Sayen. It's not a name I recognize so she must be from one of the packs further afield. Glad my brain is working again, I smile back. "I'm KJ. Nice to meet you."

She pushes her fingers through her long dark hair. It flips back, but then waterfalls back around her face and she leaves it there. Interesting. I can recognize a defense mechanism when I see one. I wonder if I should lend her a beanie. "So," she glances around. "Where's Dawn?"

Ah, so she knew we were coming. It rankles that Sayen did when I didn't, but I can't blame her for that. "She just took a call. She'll be back shortly, I'd say."

She looks back at me, her waterfall hair framing her features. For some reason, it focuses my attention on her lips, which my brain oddly registers as quite lush. Another smile pulls up her striking features. "I hear you'll be helping around the lab."

Yep. She definitely knew I was coming. "Apparently so." I angle my head, curious. "What do you know about Furious?"

The smile seems to freeze for a second. "Probably as much as you."

"If it's more than you can write on a candy wrapper, you're doing better than me."

The smile fades and she arches a brow. For some reason, it feels like the most genuine look I've had from her. This girl is certainly intriguing...

The door opens, and this time it's actually Dawn. She sees there's now two in the room and her smile beams. "Oh great, you two have met!"

Sayen's smile is back. "We were just talking about Furious."

The smile grows some more. "Wonderful." Dawn's gaze ping-pongs between us. "Because you two are going to be spending a lot of time together."

Then it hits me. This is probably why Sayen was all sorts of awkward. Dawn's decided to play matchmaker! Like hell, she will. She can take that mother hen idea and shove it in the biosafety cabinet.

I head to the nearest microscope. This is the only friend I plan on making on this little trip. "Well, I'm gonna get started. Let me know if you find anything."

I know it's a bit rude, but Dawn needs to remember a few key points about me. Sayen's a Were, and there ain't no way I'm going there.

16

HUNTER

A s Sakari slowly sinks to the ground, the sedative stealing her consciousness, it feels like all her energy hasn't disappeared—it's been transferred to me. It zips through my veins like a hyped-up triple-shot, getting harder and harder to hide.

"You okay?" Ava has stepped in closer, her wintergreen eyes looking up at me with concern.

I channel the feeling she evokes so I can draw up a smile. "Sure. I always worry for her."

Ava's face softens as she rests her head against my shoulder. "I know. You have a strong bond with her."

Man, I'm glad she can't see my face. I'm saved from trying to find an answer as Josh and Riley come in.

Josh flexes his shoulders. "Ready to go, cousin-of-mine?"

Ava scrunches her nose at him. "You sure you know what you're doing?"

He lifts up the bag of medical paraphernalia. "You do stuff with this stuff."

Ava shakes her head as she walks towards the gate. "If you screw up, I'll let her bite you."

Josh chuckles—probably knowing Ava could never let anyone get hurt—as they head toward the gate.

The tension manages to grow and condense at the same time. It bursts through my body as it simultaneously forms a lump in my gut.

You can already see that Ava is doing whatever magic she does. An expression seems to swallow her whole body; serene, sure, and ethereal. I feel it draw me in. I've noticed recently that I can almost feel it myself. It's a low hum, like an electrical current or a fast-moving stream that starts somewhere in your chest. If I thought it was more than my imagination, I'd say it seems to raise my awareness. It almost feels like there's something just outside of my consciousness.

I shake my head. The stress of Sakari's secret is getting to me. Once the pups are born, we'll know what we're dealing with. Then, I'll either tell Ava...or I'll lose her.

Sakari is lying still, breathing slowly and rhythmically. Ava kneels beside her head, gently stroking her as Josh sets himself up. He pulls out the portable ultrasound machine, frowning in concentration as he unwinds wires and presses buttons.

Riley slips her hand through mine. "I hope she's going okay."

The tension thrumming through my body feels like it's made up of shards of metal. "Me too."

"I'm sure she'll be fine. She seems really strong."

"She's certainly a survivor."

One of the last few...

As Josh places the ultrasound on Sakari's growing stomach Ava leans down to touch her forehead to hers.

Josh's face splits into such a big grin that it triggers one in Riley. He looks up at us. "Three strong heartbeats."

Riley clasps her hands beneath her chin. "That's awesome!"

I don't move. Ava's focus on Sakari is intense, and I'm not sure what that means.

Josh looks back on the screen in front of him, moving the little wand around. It's Ava who has my attention, though. Her breathing slows, matching that of Sakari's. Ava talks of the threads, and although I can't see what she's described, it's practically a throbbing river around her.

"What's up, Josh?" Riley's voice holds a frown.

Snapping my attention back, I see Josh leaning closer to the screen, eyes narrowed and tight. My step forward as I come up flush against the wire is almost reflexive. What's he seeing?

Josh's head flicks in our direction as he stays focused on the screen. "I'm not sure. I think my measurements must be wrong."

Riley frowns. "But you spent the last three days reading up on this."

"That's why I'm double checking."

Whatever is in Josh's tone, it has Ava looking up. It takes a couple of seconds for her gaze to refocus as she returns to the reality the rest of us live in. She glances at me and I wish I could ease her concern.

I look away before she can get a sense of how much this is rattling me.

Josh picks up the clipboard sitting on the ground beside him. He scribbles something down then flips back a page. He drops it, reads what he's written, then goes back to the previous page. I grip the wire, glad for the sharp pain.

Josh looks up at Ava, his face saying he's not sure what to feel. "The pups have almost doubled in size."

Riley's brows shoot up. "Whoa."

Ava nods like she isn't surprised. "They're strong."

Josh looks back at Sakari. "And big."

Riley steps up to stand beside me. "What does that mean, guys?"

Josh shrugs. "I'm not sure. We probably need to ask Dawn and KJ."

Where the hell is KJ when you need him?

Riley glances at me. "I suppose at least it means they're healthy."

I nod, not trusting myself to speak.

Ava straightens up. "They're definitely healthy."

She looks at me and her eyes are swirling pools of green. My heart thunders in my chest. What has Ava seen?

"Maybe…" But I can't do it. I can't lie that maybe we got the due dates mixed up again. "We'll just have to keep monitoring. If they're healthy and strong, then that's a good thing."

But Josh's frown is back. "It means her weight gain probably wasn't hers again."

Dammit. Guilt is growing like a cancer in my gut.

Ava stretches her hands down Sakari's body. "She's still thin. It's like the pups are sucking her dry."

"I'm going to give her a shot of iron, just in case."

As he pulls out the syringes and bottles, Ava goes back to calming Sakari. Josh is as efficient and confident as Dawn would be as he administers the dose. I wouldn't be surprised if Sakari is partially conscious for this, but her leg never twitches. With Ava here, we can give her the lowest dose of sedative each time we need to do this. I hate the relief I feel that this isn't something we can do too often, because I know I'm not thinking of Sakari.

"All done." Josh starts packing up, and Ava starts a little as she looks up.

With one last stroke of Sakari's head, Ava leans down. I wish my Were hearing didn't pick up what she says next. "Your babies are going to be beautiful, Sakari."

Once they've joined us on the other side of the fence, I realize I need to get myself under control. I already know what sort of person I am thanks to what I've done, but Ava is determined to believe otherwise. The fact that I'm selfish enough to keep this farce going shows exactly how wrong she is.

We watch as Sakari slowly comes to full consciousness. Ava is still, but I can feel how unsettled she is. Like I've taught myself to do, I shove down the blackness that's my core, focusing on the girl who needs me.

Ava fits into my side as we watch Sakari stand up and shake herself off. With a last look at us for the indignity she's just been put through, she trots back to her den. My arm is wrapped around Ava's waist before I realize it's there. I've planted a kiss on her soft hair as my chest tries to contain it all. How can so much love live beside so much disgrace?

Riley's cell rings and she pulls it out of her pocket. "It's Mom." She heads to the door. "I'll see what she wants."

Josh follows her. "I'll go clean up, then send these results to Dawn."

Ava barely notices them leaving. She's still focused on the dark entry to the den. She can't see Sakari anymore, but I know she can feel her.

"You okay?"

She finally looks up at me, her lips tipped up in a sad smile. "Yeah. Just thinking."

As much as I don't want to know, I follow her train of thought. "You were really focused on Sakari."

"I tapped into our connection." Her eyes seem to blaze with excitement as they swirl with confusion. "I can feel the pups, Hunter. Each one of them."

That doesn't surprise me. To be totally honest, it scares the crap out of me.

"I felt their heartbeats. They're strong, Hunter. Really strong."

"That's good." Except I can tell there's more.

"I felt…" She shakes her head. "It doesn't make sense."

I wait, throat so constricted I can barely breathe.

She casts a confused glance at Sakari. "I'm not sure. It must be because you have such a strong connection with her."

"What, Ava? What did you see?"

Her wintergreen eyes snare me and I couldn't move if I tried. "I felt your thread in there, Hunter."

I rear back like she just slapped me, only to catch myself. "But—"

Ava shakes her head. "I know. I told you it didn't make sense."

My heartbeat is like thunder on my eardrums. That can't be possible. Unless...

Ava's hand caresses my cheek. "I still don't know what these threads and powers mean. It's probably nothing."

She's reassuring me? I grasp her hand, kissing the palm. "It was just a surprise." Which isn't a lie. "I don't want anything to happen to Sakari."

Which is also the truth. I'd go back and make a different decision if I could.

Ava's eyes flare at the caress. "And what am I going to say to that?"

The fact that this girl can get a smile tripping at the edges of my lips is a testament to how amazing she is. "That she has a team around her determined for her to be more than okay."

Ava doesn't hold her smile back. "Damn straight she does."

Wrapping my arms around her, I let her goodness warm me. Actually, that was just what I needed to hear. It gives me hope that Sakari, maybe even her pups, are going to be okay...despite the traitor in our midst.

We both hear Riley just before she opens the door. She comes in with her hands over her eyes. "Are you guys dressed?"

If I had something to throw at her, I would.

Ava grins. "Just give me a sec."

Riley's mouth pops open beneath her hand, and I've got to

say, I'm a little shocked myself. My girl winks at me. "Figured you wanted some time to find something to throw at her."

My laughter surprises me, like a wave you didn't see coming. Ava winks again like this happens all the time, but the glow in her eyes tells me how much she's enjoying the moment.

"Ava." Riley has her hands on her hips. "If you didn't just make the rarest thing in the world happen and make my brother laugh, I'd be throwing something at you!" She flicks her fringe. "I almost had a heart attack."

Josh pops up behind her. "Who needs CPR?"

Riley elbows him. "Hunter if Ava keeps making him do the impossible."

"Sorry," Josh's hands come up in a not-happening gesture. "Not qualified yet."

I'm shaking my head even though the smile on my face doesn't seem to be going anywhere. "What did Mom want?"

That sobers my sister up. "She said Gareth is on his way over."

Well, that killed the smile. "How does she know that?"

"She said he was over at ours and they were talking."

Huh. "What were they talking about?"

"She wouldn't say, only that she told him she believes you're doing the right thing."

Josh lets out a low whistle. "Way to poke the Were, Mrs. Rendell."

So that's why Mom decided to send out the signal flare. Gareth's coming and he probably has a prickle up his butt.

With a sigh, I head to the door, Ava by my side thanks to our joined hands. "I'm always happy to talk to our pack."

Back in the control room, it feels like the quiet before the storm. The screens flicker through their silent images, and with Dawn and KJ gone, there's no paper printing or theories flying around. I head to the screens—the only movement is on Achak's screen as he continues with his pacing. I've never seen a wolf object to captivity with the same level of determination as this guy.

I'm tempted to turn it off whilst Gareth is here—the last thing he needs to see is a wolf hating his cage—but I never saw myself as someone who shied away from the truth...until Sakari. That secret is eating away at me enough, I refuse to add any more.

Ava squeezes my hand, reminding me I need to keep this in check. She can feel I'm uneasy and unsettled, because she's the compassionate soul that she is, but also because our connection is so strong. The guilt and shame are the parts that wouldn't make sense to her. The irony that trying to suppress the bastards only inflates them is part of my punishment.

I study her beautiful face. "You okay?"

She nods. "Are you?"

How does she always know how to get to the heart of things? "I'm good." I lean down. "I have you."

Lightning fast, she pushes up and brushes her lips against mine. "Yes, you do."

There's no time to respond, because we all straighten as we hear footsteps down the hall. Gareth is here.

The door opens, and he takes several steps in as he looks around. He smiles at Riley, pretty much dismisses Josh, and pauses on Ava. Although his gaze is far from friendly, she smiles. But even Ava's sweet welcome isn't enough to melt Gareth's defenses. He looks away, his gaze settling on me.

"Hello, Gareth."

He nods. "Alpha."

I wonder how he can call me that considering how much he's hated the decisions I've made. "It's good to see you. How can we help?"

"I heard KJ's gone to the mainland."

I nod. "With Dawn, the Fae Elder."

Gareth crosses his arms, his frown a deep fold across his forehead. "Doesn't that leave this place even more unprotected?"

My hands want to clench but I don't let them. "We're dealing with this virus just as much as the poachers."

"You've captured all of the wolves, contained them in here, and then left them defenseless?"

Riley steps up to Gareth. "It's not like they have a pack to protect them, is it?" She flicks her fringe. "Gareth, you're like an uncle to me, but it's time you stop blaming Hunter for what he's had no control over."

"Hunter has done what no-one else had the courage to do." Ava has stepped forward too.

"I'd expect you to say that." He points to where Achak is pacing. "You're the one willing to do that to a wolf."

Ava flinches and this time my hands do clench. They become fists of protectiveness, ready to make sure Gareth knows how little he's talking about.

But Ava places a hand on my arm as she holds Gareth's gaze. "And I suspect the pain I live with every time I see that, is the same pain Hunter lives with, too."

Gareth's mouth slams shut. I almost feel sorry for him.

When a shrill beeping pierces the silence, it takes me a second to register what it is. But when I do, I instantly turn to the screens, scanning.

Gareth is by my side a second later. "What's that?"

The cameras I expect to be flashing are all clear. "A movement sensor attached to the cameras we have out on the tundra."

"To keep an eye out for the poachers?" Gareth sounds almost...impressed.

"Yeah. Although it's usually nothing but an elk—"

The bottom row of screens was the last to be checked

because they're the closest to the village. But it's there that I see what triggered the alarm. I lean forward, trying to get a sense of what we're dealing with.

"What is it?" Josh is on my left, peering over my shoulder.

Gareth does the same on my other side. "There's nothing there."

He's right. There's nothing on the screen. "That's the problem."

Josh straightens, his face somber. "Something's knocked over the camera."

Gareth tilts his head to the side, aligning himself with the horizon at the top of the image. The rest of the space is taken up by blurred, wet dirt.

"Could've been a hare." Riley's joined us, her face showing how likely she thinks that theory is.

I look at Ava. "We'll need to check it out."

"I'm coming with you."

I turn to Gareth, not expecting those words to have come out of his mouth. "No need. Ava and I have got it."

Except Gareth is already heading to the door. "I may not like what you're doing here, but I'm a Rendell just like you are, Hunter. I'm coming."

Now he decides to play pack? But he knows I won't say no. Working as a pack is one of the strengths of being Were.

I sigh. The Rendells haven't worked as a pack since I became Alpha. "We'll take the quads."

Gareth is already out the door. "I'm getting off that thing the minute I can."

I'm about to follow him when I sense something. Ava hasn't moved.

Standing by KJ's desk, she smiles at me. "You two go."

I spin around. "What? Of course, you're coming."

She's already shaking her head. "I'm going to stay here and

keep an eye on the wolves. Achak is really agitated, and Sakari is still recovering."

"But..."

I glance around the room. Riley shrugs, having no idea what's going on. Josh has already moved to stand beside his cousin. He drops his arm around her shoulders. "She's probably right. Without KJ and Dawn here, we need to keep a Fae at Resolve."

I respect Josh for that—he's supporting Ava, even though he doesn't know why Ava's decided this, especially after how hard she fought for me to take her when we were vaccinating the wolves. He doesn't even know she's a wolf so golden she takes your breath away.

Then it hits me.

Gareth is coming, and if Ava comes, she can't shift if she's going to keep her golden wolf status a secret for a while longer. And if she doesn't shift, she could slow us down.

But I know there's a question hanging between us. What if it's a poacher? What will happen if I come across another one?

Ava got a taste of what I'm capable of when we came across Kyle. He stands for everything we're up against. Would I be able to stop myself if she wasn't there?

I don't know the answer to that question, but when I look back at her, I'm floored. Trust is shining from Ava's eyes. Her wintergreen gaze is steady and sure. She smiles, and that simple, beautiful gesture is full of faith. "It's fine. You've got this."

I turn away before I discover what I'd do next. Tell her I love her? Show her how misplaced her belief is by revealing the truth about Sakari?

As I head to the bikes, I rub my head with punishing force.

Even if we come across a poacher today and I don't annihilate him, eventually I'm going to prove her wrong.

17

HUNTER

T elling Gareth I need to call Mom, I veer down the hall and out the back door. Gareth nods, figuring I'm probably updating her that we're heading out, and strides away.

I press the speed dial button, tension knotted in my gut. There's a big part of me that doesn't want to make this call.

When KJ picks up his phone, I get straight to the point. "You alone?"

"Are you going to ask me what I'm wearing next?"

My hand clenches around my cell. If it's not a yes, then KJ will make sure he is when I ask my next question. "Good. I need you to talk me through what you did to the pups."

There's a pause. "Ah, why?"

"I realized I don't actually know what's involved with all this genetic engineering. I think it's important that I get my head around it."

"Okay." KJ draws the word out, telling me he hasn't fallen for the decoy. "Well, first thing is to find and isolate the DNA we want."

"From the Were DNA."

"Exactly. Then I duplicated it and inserted it into some

carrier bacteria. Once it stabilized, I injected that into Sakari's fertilized eggs."

"And the genes are integrated from there. Got it."

"Awesome." KJ sounds relieved. "How did the checkup go today?"

"Hang on. I just realized I have one last question."

"Sure." KJ's tone is open and cheery, but I know him well enough to detect that the note of caution is back.

"Whose Were DNA did you use, KJ?"

Silence slams down the line. I'd speak, but I'm pretty sure it would crack my jaw.

"I didn't have a lot of time..."

I wait out KJ's stalling, dreading what's coming next.

"I couldn't use mine. You know that." KJ's voice is low, laced with the shame he carries.

I'm shaking my head before I remember he can't see me. "You've shown not everything is inherited, KJ."

"And that answer is why I used yours, Hunter."

The words hit me so hard that my legs buckle, and I find myself crouching beside the building. My eyes are screwed shut as my fingers dig into them.

KJ used my DNA...

"Hunter? You still conscious?"

I squeeze two words out past my clenched jaw. "I'm here."

"I know I should have asked you—"

"Damn straight you should have."

"But they needed the best—it was a no-brainer that it would be your DNA in there."

Suck in. Push out. Suck in. Push out. Breathing is all I focus on right now.

No wonder Ava can sense me in the pups.

I push myself up even though I feel like I weigh the equivalent of a semi-truck. When I find my legs aren't as stable as I expected, I lean back against the wall.

"They're growing faster than they should, KJ."

There's the slightest intake of breath. "Right."

"Just like Weres do."

"I know that."

KJ's voice is getting testy, but he needs to realize what we're up against. "They have human in them, KJ."

"We can't jump to conclusions. I get that it seems wolf and human genes have some overlap in Weres. But they may just be fast growing wolves."

My head falls back and I welcome the thumping pain as it hits the bricks. "What have we done?"

KJ's sigh carries through the cell. "This doesn't have to be a bad thing, Hunter. We're trying to give them a fighting chance."

By turning them into something they're not. KJ may not be willing to admit it, but we've done the wrong thing.

I just don't know how to fix it.

My eyes fly open. "When are they due?"

"Well, if they've grown again..."

I'm going to assume KJ is doing some calculations rather than leaving it at a non-answer.

Except the silence draws out. "KJ," I growl. "When will they be born?"

He sighs. "It's hard to tell. All we can bank on is sooner than we expected."

Damn. Damn. Damn. The air feels like it's shrinking around me, like someone just upped the pressure. I'm running out of time.

The sound of a quad bike starting has me pushing away from the wall. "I've gotta go. How's the lab looking?"

"It's pretty decked out. If there's anything in Achak's blood, we'll find it."

Good news is a nice change. "Great."

"I know carrying the responsibility of the world is your superpower, Hunter, but you're stronger than you give yourself credit for."

I don't want to hear the false ego boosts. "I've got to go out on patrol."

But KJ manages to get one last line in before I hang up.

"Which means those pups are going to be stronger, too."

IT'S BEEN over two years ago since I've been out on the tundra with Gareth.

Back then, the three of us—Dad, Gareth, and I—would share the patrols. It was the odd weekend that was the real treat though—we'd do them together. They are some of the best memories I have of Dad.

Gareth and Dad were close. It's like they were cut of the same Were cloth. KJ says they've got to be related, no matter what their DNA profile would say. They drank the same favorite beer from the glasses they 'borrowed' from a bar during their college days. They thought each other's jokes were hilarious, even the ones they'd heard before. I'm pretty sure it was only when Mom came on the scene that they finally spent time apart.

But even then, as Dad started a family and Gareth committed himself to bachelorhood, they never stopped fighting for the same things.

Accelerating, I welcome the cold wind on my face, almost wishing I could feel more of its sting. After several nighttime snowfalls, the landscape around us is more snow than dirt. The white blanket isn't thick, but it's letting you know it's here to stay.

Gareth follows closely behind me, another stark contrast to the way things used to be. Back then, Dad led, and we followed. But Gareth doesn't know where the cameras are because it was made very clear I'd be making this decision on my own.

I accelerate some more, telling myself I want this over and done with so I can get back to Ava. When Gareth keeps up despite the breakneck speed, I start wondering if he's trying to escape something too. I don't look back though. We no longer have that sort of relationship.

I only slow when we near where the camera is set up. The area is relatively open, the camera not far from a track created by the animals of the tundra. Evelyn Island's only town is a mile or so away, and in tundra terms, that's not that far, which is why I didn't expect anything to be messing with it.

But as I slow, I see I'm coming to an intersection. Our trajectory is about to cross the tracks of something else that's been here. I stop, taking in the heavy marks that have crushed the snow enough to show the mud beneath. Gareth pulls up beside me, his brows hiking too.

I climb off, knowing exactly what I'm looking at, but still not quite believing it. "They're polar bear tracks."

Gareth nods, confirming that the massive, wide prints are exactly that. "A male from my guess. Recent too. After last night's snow."

I look up. You can't see the town from here, but still... "They never come this close to civilization."

Gareth squats, fingers outlining the depression. "Not that I've seen."

I scrabble for theories. "Unless he's really hungry."

Gareth stands, his forehead hunkering down low. "Or there aren't any wolves keeping him away."

I open my mouth only to find I don't have a comeback. Wolves and polar bears avoid each other, knowing they're competing on the same rung of the food chain. With the wolves gone, it's possible that polar bears would be sniffing around this close to the town. It's possible Gareth is right.

I turn away, heading back to the quad. Of all the days for Gareth to come out…

But Gareth isn't finished. "You guys have messed with the order of things, Hunter. What did you expect would happen?"

I spin on my heel, the wet snow making the movement slick and fast. "That there would be no perfect solutions, Gareth. That maybe their numbers would go down instead of up."

Thunder moves across Gareth's face. "That's exactly what your father and I were working towards fixing."

Two more steps and I'm in his face. Practically eye to eye, I stab my finger in his chest as I grind the words out past my clenched jaw. "And it wasn't working."

Gareth's indrawn breath is short and sharp. They would plot and plan long into the night as Mom brought them coffee after coffee. They charted the wolves' territories. They tracked their movements. All the information I had when I was out on patrol was thanks to Dad and Gareth.

But their numbers kept falling.

"And you think your idea is better?" Gareth growls. "And what if this doesn't work, Hunter? What then?"

I deflate, feeling like a lead balloon. "Then no one wins, do they?"

I feel heavier as I walk back to the quad, maybe a bit bruised. What's the point of going over this again? Gareth will never see how hard the decision to establish Resolve was. Or how little I wanted to make it.

Climbing on, I don't look at him as I speak. "The camera isn't far away."

The polar bear tracks head straight over the camera. I doubt it was barely a blip on his radar as his massive body moved through here. At least the tracks now head away from the town.

I straighten it up and jam the stake back into its hole. Pressing some buttons, I'm impressed to find it still works. If the big guy comes by this way again, then at least we'll know about it.

"How many cameras are there?"

Gareth hasn't left his quad, either not wanting to be near me or realizing there's not much he can do to help. Or both.

Wiping my wet hands down my jeans I look around. "About ten. We put them back out when we learned the poachers hadn't given up."

I'm on the quad and have its engine revving before Gareth can respond. I don't want to hear whatever his response is going to be. The care factor seems to be dropping with the temperatures.

I drive back slower, even though I'm keen to get back to my girl. It's like all my energy has fizzled out. Did Dad ever feel like this? Like the boulder he'd been pushing uphill kept growing like a snowball?

We're only a mile from Resolve when a scent strikes me.

My whole body freezes and the quad comes to a halt. "Can you smell that?"

Gareth frowns as he pulls up beside me, angling his head. "Petrol." Then his nostrils flare. "Humans."

I scan, finding the direction it's coming from. What would humans be doing out here in the middle of the tundra? Too far from town, but too close to Resolve for my liking.

I turn the quad to the east. "I'm going to check it out."

"Yes. We are."

If I had a sense of humor right now, I'd point out how much Gareth sounds like Ava. Instead, I make like an arrow for whatever unwanted surprise we've just stumbled across.

It's over the next rise that we find it—a small camp made up of three tents. As we approach, three men stand up from their camp chairs. Heat flashes through my veins as I recognize one of them.

Pulling up, I don't glance at Gareth as I mutter one word. "Poachers."

Gareth seems to grow as he pulls in a breath. "Bastards."

Exactly what I was thinking.

We approach, and Kyle steps forward, apparently their self-appointed leader. One man, a square slab of beefy frown, crosses his arms. The other, tall and thin and lacking a chin, blinks at us rapidly. He reminds me of a turkey.

Kyle smiles his bloodless smile. "Nice day for a ride, gentlemen."

My blood is beginning to hit lava level. Why does this guy get to me so much?

"What are you doing out here, Kyle?"

I feel Gareth's surprise that I know this guy's name, but he's smart enough to keep his eye on the scumbag.

Kyle rolls his eyes. "What do you think I'm doing? A family camping trip?" He glances back at his comrades, showing exactly how he would feel if he discovered he was related to them.

"You're wasting your time. You're better off trying somewhere else."

Kyle shrugs. "Prices have gone up. I'm willing to play the waiting game."

Prices have gone up? That's the last thing we need.

I step forward and Brick and Turkey contract around Kyle, their eyes full of warning. "Who's Helix, Kyle?"

Kyle's smile is slow and satisfied. "He could be anyone, for all we know."

Brick elbows Turkey. "Could be you, Mike."

Mike grins. "Helix could be the last person you expect them to be."

Gareth snorts. "You don't know."

Kyle arches a black brow. "I could be Helix."

Fury is pumping through my body, a beast that wants to be unleashed. Only someone with a whole lot of hatred in their heart could do what Helix is doing.

And that's exactly what Kyle is made of. Hatred.

Except right now he has two bodyguards. And I have a pack member here. I can't have Gareth implicated in whatever is going to be inevitable. I stare at Kyle, and I stare hard, making sure he reads the promise in my eyes.

I will find you alone.

Kyle imperceptibly nods. His almost-smile says he'll be looking forward to it.

The only saving grace right now is that he doesn't realize that all the wolves are at Resolve. If he wants to camp out in the cold waiting for a wolf to shoot, then this is probably the safest place for them.

As we head back to the quads, I throw out one last remark, wondering why I'm even bothering. "By the way, there's a polar bear out here."

But Kyle doesn't look surprised or worried. "That's what I thought, too."

I pause beside my bike. Why is this guy talking in the past tense?

Gareth scoffs. "What else would it be?"

Kyle turns his head towards him like he has all the time in the world. "Some pelts are worth more than others."

Gareth shakes his head in disdain. "That wasn't arctic wolf tracks."

"Not a standard one, no." My world freezes as Kyle's eyes light up. "There are bigger ones out here, we've seen them."

Horror freezes my lungs. Kyle's seen a Were in wolf form?

Brick nods slowly, his lip pulling up in a sneer. "We got a score to settle with one o' them."

Turkey bobs his head beside him. "It's been a long time coming, but when we do, it's going to be the ultimate trophy."

Kyle's fisted hand in the air is a short, sharp movement. Brick and Turkey's lips instantly clamp shut.

They're hunting Weres? And have been for a long time?

I shake my head in disgust. "I figured you guys were crazy, but that's some next level crap."

Kyle's snake features never change. "I'd imagine Helix will pay big money for that pelt."

Neither Gareth nor I respond, instead we're climbing on the quads. The spray of snow and mud is deliberate as we drive away. I hope they choke on it.

We're side by side as we head back to Resolve. No matter how hard I accelerate, Gareth is right there with me. I'm not sure what that means, but I'm not slowing down to ask. There's stuff that needs to be discussed. No one will be able to shift while Kyle and his buddies are around.

In the shed, I'm already climbing off when Gareth cuts his engine beside me. I throw my goodbye over my shoulder as I head to the main building.

"Hunter."

I stop, one foot already out the door as I turn back. "Yeah?"

Gareth scratches his elbow and I immediately recognize the gesture. Gareth is uncomfortable and I'm guessing I know why. "I'll take care of Kyle and his idiots. They won't find what they're looking for."

"That's not what I was about to say."

I blink. "Right."

Gareth straightens, like he's made a decision. "You were right."

"Pardon?"

"About the captive breeding." I turn to completely face him. Did he just say what I thought he said?

Gareth's eyes are heavy with truth. "If we'd left the wolves out on the tundra, they'd be gone by now."

I try to find a response to that, but my mind is blank. My chest aches and I realize I haven't taken a breath. It's like I didn't want to break the moment...just in case I was dreaming.

Gareth glances at the horizon behind me. "Those guys aren't going to stop."

Especially since they get a nice little bounty for their efforts.

And now it seems there's a personal vendetta against giant wolves.

"Ah, thanks." I hover in the doorway. Those are words I never thought I'd hear, but now that I have them, they've stumped me.

Gareth straightens as he moves to stand before me. "We need to protect the ones we have here."

Struggling to keep the emotions in check I nod, acknowledging the promise in his words. Gareth just made a commitment for us to work together.

As a pack.

Supporting my decisions.

As an Alpha.

18

SAYEN

M eeting KJ for the first time knocked me off kilter. I hadn't expected him to be quite so...smart. No, that's not it. I've met smart guys before, and that didn't have me forgetting what I'm here to do. I hadn't expected him to be so... positive. Confident. Optimistic.

Afterward, I realized it's probably because he's delusional, which will make my job easier.

My uncle had made sure to remind me, along with the others of my pack who have never forgotten—I may be one of the youngest, but I've also been given the greatest role to play.

Especially now that KJ is here.

Heading to the incubator, I grab the bottles we filled yesterday. KJ doesn't look up from the seat he claimed the first night he arrived.

Fighting a sigh, I slide one into my pocket. I never thought I'd meet someone as focused as I am.

Then I met KJ.

I'm glad I got everything I needed to get done before he arrived, because he spends all of his time at the center. And I mean, all of his time. When I arrive, pale light just peeking over the trees, so does KJ. When I leave long after closing, gritty-eyed and exhausted, KJ is just starting to pack up.

And he's certainly not making my mission any easier.

It's been several days and all he's done is focus on anything smaller than a pinhead. He's probably going to become a permanent hunchback spending all that time leaning over a microscope.

But today it was agreed I take it to the next level.

I let the sigh gain life, puffing out with emphasis. "Are you sure you don't want to come, KJ?"

KJ doesn't look up from the microscope. "Nope. Thanks anyway."

I've checked three times over the past three days, and the answer has always been the same. If he wasn't so dedicated, I'd be thinking he's avoiding going outside.

As I carefully place the small glass bottles in the vet pack, I think about the pointers I've been given. Smile more. Be friendly.

I go to push my hair back, but I stop myself. If I had a heart, this would be a whole lot easier. But before I can come up with something, the door opens.

It's Dawn, but she's not wearing her usual smile. She looks around but quickly centers on me. "Sayen."

The zipper I was pulling pauses. "Yeah?"

"I'm really sorry, but something's come up. I can't go out with you today."

I frown. "Oh. It can't wait?"

Dawn coming was going to be one of my draw cards.

Dawn is already shaking her head. "The Fae Elders decided to meet. I need to be there."

I pull the zip all the way around, frowning in thought. "Eden will be there too, then. And I think Noah is working today." Two missions are now in jeopardy.

Dawn glances at KJ before looking back at me. "There's no one else?"

I echo her head shake. "There're only the two keepers here today, and we've been ordered to have someone at the center at all times, remember?"

That order came straight from the Prime Alpha after it was discovered exactly how determined the poachers are. My hands tighten around the bag. And that they're being paid even more for wolf pelts.

Dawn glances at KJ again and I hear his chair shift.

"No."

Her eyebrows shoot up in surprise. "What?"

"I'm not going, end of story. The next lot of samples will be ready in twenty minutes. I want to run some more tests on them."

The same tests he's been running since he arrived. It's like each time they come back negative it raises his determination to prove the results wrong. Knowing what's in those test tubes, I almost feel sorry for him...

Dawn's hands come up in surrender. "I never suggested it. I know you don't want to go out there."

He stares at her. "I can't."

Dawn's smile is gentle. "I know." She turns back to me. "I think we're going to have to postpone."

Bloody KJ and his weird-ass attachment to the lab.

"I could go—"

"No." Dawn is shaking her head, knowing I was going to suggest going out anyway. "We'll have to do this tomorrow." She glances at her watch. "I'd better go. Don't break anything, you two."

Dawn shuts the door, cutting off the possibility of any further conversation.

KJ's chair creaks as he sits back down. In about three seconds he'll be leaning back over his microscope.

I pick up the vet pack and head to the door.

"What are you doing?"

I stop, hand on the doorknob. "Going anyway."

KJ stands up. "What? Dawn just said it will wait till tomorrow."

I roll my eyes at him. "Furious waits for no-one, KJ."

I yank the door open, glad my urgency isn't fake. I need to get this stuff out there today.

"Wait!"

I turn around, brow arched. Is KJ going to try and talk me out of it only to discover I personify determination? The sucky part is going to be doing it with a smile.

KJ turns off his microscope. "Those samples will be here when I come back."

My smile is reflexive. Looks like I'll be getting two missions done in one day!

What's even more rewarding, is the spontaneous smile I get back. KJ's hazel eyes light to a glowing kaleidoscope of shades of earth and hues of green. It's so dazzling that I look away. At least getting KJ to fall for me is going to be a pleasant mission.

Unlike my others.

"So, you're a Tate?"

Of all things for KJ to make conversation about, it had to be that? I keep my eyes on the dirt road slicing through the plain we're crossing. "Yeah. My mom was from the Maiyun pack in the west though."

"The Tates were almost as problematic as the Channons."

It takes some focus to stop my hands from clenching on the

steering wheel. "Yes, there were some supporters amongst them."

"There sure was. One guy was Kurt's right-hand man."

And he died trying to show what Weres could be.

"What about you? Where's your pack?" As I ask the question, I realize I don't know and how unusual that is. Every Were is defined by their pack.

KJ looks back out the windscreen, his face tightening. "My parents are dead. I left my pack."

That silences me for a second. He left his pack? Why would someone do that? And how?

KJ yanks his beanie down another inch until half his ears are covered. "So, what's this testing we're about to do for?"

Change of topic, huh? Despite my curiosity, I go with it. I'm trying to get KJ to like me, after all. "We're just checking whether the vaccine has conferred any immunity. We're sampling the wolves that've been released because they're the easiest to track."

I tap the device next to me. Its screen shows a dot directly north of us.

"And has it?"

I repeat what I've told everyone who's asked this question. "Yes, which is good news. It gives them a fighting chance."

"Except it's not working. We've had infected wolves who'd been vaccinated."

I keep my gaze straight ahead. "True. But there are so many variables at the moment. We don't know if that'll be the case if Furious shows up again."

When I glance over, KJ is studying me. I've pushed my hair back before I can stop myself.

His hazel gaze is thoughtful as he turns away. "There's something about Furious..."

This stuff is what I'm here to find out. What questions are forming in KJ's smart mind?

"There sure is. It's not like the standard strain of rabies."

"It's not!" KJ sits up a little straighter. "It travels through the bloodstream rather than the nerves," He ticks off one finger. That's right, KJ was the one to discover that nugget of information.

"There doesn't seem to be the paralysis phase," he ticks off another finger.

And it seems KJ knows his rabies stages.

But he pauses on the next finger. "And we haven't figured out how it's spread."

Crap. He's getting closer than we expected. "What do you mean? Rabies is spread by saliva."

"In two locations though? Places that are nowhere near each other? And, so far, each incident has been isolated. It just doesn't make sense."

I shake my head, clearing away the nervousness KJ's words are causing. "That's why we're here. To make it make sense."

KJ looks back at me, something warming in his eyes. "Yes, we are, Sayen."

His gaze, his use of 'we', have me looking longer than I should. I focus back on the road, frowning. I hadn't banked on this, and I'm not sure what to do with it.

KJ clears his throat and picks up the tracking device. "The wolf isn't far away."

I nod, thankful for the neutral territory. "She. Suki is a gorgeous black wolf, released a couple of years ago."

KJ pulls the device a little closer to his face. "It's odd that she's not moving, isn't it?"

Uneasiness slides over my skin. I'd noticed that too. "Yeah." I look at KJ. "She's likely to be pregnant, so she's napping or something."

He arches a brow. "Probably."

Which shows KJ knows how unlikely that is for a wolf in the middle of the day. Even one carrying pups.

I pull over half a mile from the dot on the screen. "We'll need to walk from here."

KJ is already unbuckling his seatbelt. "Lead the way."

When KJ goes to grab the vet pack, I snatch it before I can stop myself. His eyebrows shoot up high enough they almost touch his beanie.

I flush, knowing I just slipped up. "All good. I'm used to doing this bit."

KJ shrugs as he retracts his hand. "Seems I'm destined to be surrounded by independent women."

Why do I like that KJ doesn't seem bothered by that?

We head out, the dot taking us into a heavily wooded area. The scent of pine is strong as I draw it into my lungs. Suki has always tended to hang in the safety of the trees.

"I hadn't realized I missed the woods."

KJ had slipped behind me, and he looks startled when I turn around. He shrugs, seeming to pull himself together. "I was just thinking out loud. I grew up in New Hampshire."

As someone who's woven a web of lies around herself, I instantly recognize KJ's words for what they are—fiction. But someone trying to catch a guy wouldn't ask any questions that could rock the boat, so I just smile and look away.

We've only covered a few more feet when I stop, uneasy at what's on the receiver. KJ looks over my shoulder, seeing what I'm seeing.

I look back at him, my heart rate hiking at having him so near. "Maybe the receiver is faulty."

KJ glances ahead, probably calculating that Suki isn't far away. "As unhelpful as that would be, I hope so."

Noticing the wind direction, I indicate we head east. Right

now, we're downwind, meaning Suki will smell us coming. KJ nods and we set off again, now side by side as we monitor the screen I'm holding.

Another fifteen minutes of hiking and Suki stays where she is. Silently, we take a left so we can start closing in on her. When the dot isn't far away, I stop to pull out the tranquilizer gun.

I bring my fingers to my lips, a gesture that seems to focus KJ's gaze on my mouth. "We'll need to be quiet from here on in," I whisper.

His eyes widen as he nods, and I'm not sure why that expression fills my cheeks with heat, but it does. Getting angry with myself for such strange reactions, I turn around. This was never part of the plan.

We creep through the trees, silent and alert. From memory, there's a small clearing here, not far from a river. It's just the sort of place deer might venture into, seeking fresh grass. It's just the sort of place a wolf would check out to see if a prey animal was risking being open and vulnerable.

The gloom gives way to light as we approach the edge of the trees. KJ fans out to my left. We're going to need to see her before she sees us.

I hold my breath as I scan the clearing, then the edge of the clearing, then the monitor, just to check. Yep, this is where she's supposed to be.

But the clearing is empty, the trees unobstructed. Suki isn't here.

I go to move forward but KJ raises his hand as he leaves the edge of the trees. Surprise stalls me for a second. KJ is making sure he goes first? I've always been expected to be on the frontline, be the one who takes the risks. Why do his actions annoy me and somehow warm me at the same time?

I stride out, not willing to look at that too closely.

KJ starts slowly, but quickly picks up the pace until he's in the center of the clearing. He looks around, listening. There's no startled movements, no shifting of shadows. A part of me wishes a round of growls would erupt, telling us we've intruded.

The screen in my hand hasn't changed. Frowning, I hold it up. "It doesn't make sense."

KJ angles his head, scenting the air. He freezes a second before I smell it—faint but undeniable—too.

Blood.

I spin on the spot, frantic to find its source. KJ's movements are slower, more concentrated. He takes a step to the right and stops. He pauses and looks down.

Following his line of sight, I gasp.

Nestled in the grass is a black strip attached to a small black box. It's Suki's collar and transmitter.

KJ picks up the collar, face twisted with disappointment. Slowly, shaking ever so slightly, his hand closes around it, muscles and sinews tightening. I want to look away when the pressure has blood seeping out between his fingers.

Another wolf lost to a poacher.

I hold myself, unsure how to feel...wishing for the pain to subside. I know more than anyone that these deaths are going to happen. I can't do what I do if I let the pain get in the way.

I send up a silent goodbye to Suki. The pain doesn't go, but I take what flashes through me instead. Anger.

Just like I've always been told, human greed is so easy to manipulate. Offer some money and they're happy to kill. It shows me what we're doing is right. That soon enough, others will see this too.

My hands clench. "It's not fair."

"It's really not."

I look at KJ, wondering how far I can push this. "And it's not okay."

I'm surprised when he flinches, but he nods. "No. It's not okay."

How did I know he'd agree? It sends a shaft of something through my hot chest. "There's going to come a time when what we're doing isn't enough."

KJ holds my gaze. "That time has already come, Sayen."

My chest expands, trying to make room for the unexpected sensations. Could they be right? Could KJ be someone who'd understand what needs to be done?

I look away before I say any more. Every goal is made up of small steps. Each building on the other.

Just like what I have to do next.

"We'd better get back and tell the others what's happened."

Still holding the bloody collar, KJ starts walking towards the trees. "You do the people stuff. I only do the wolf stuff."

Tucking my hair behind my ear, I let him go first. One, because KJ's comment intrigues me and I know I'm not meant to ask. Two, because of the second task I have for today.

As we hit the edge of the trees, I unzip the bag on my shoulder. As I place the unused tranquilizer gun back in I grasp something else. Tightening my hand around it, I'm almost glad we found Suki gone today.

I've been dreading this, hating it even as I made it happen. But now I can direct that hate where it belongs. As KJ walks ahead, I slip my hand out, watching him. Thankfully, he seems focused on his own thoughts.

Slowing a little, I reach out to brush a tree as I let the small glass bottle drop. It falls to the pine-littered ground soundlessly, slipping amongst two gnarled roots.

Collecting my hatred and wrapping it around me, I send my location followed by a text. *Package has been dropped. Use a target in the northern quadrant.*

"Texting your boyfriend?"

Startled, I find KJ looking over his shoulder. For a moment my heart hiccups painfully, but his teasing face stays focused on mine.

As relief allows me to breathe again, his words have a small spurt of joy zinging straight to my chest. KJ is checking whether I have a boyfriend. Smiling before I realize, I angle my head. "The closest I could come to a boyfriend is if I grew him in a Petri dish."

KJ smiles back, his hazel eyes catching the light. "Yeah, I think you know your way around a lab better than I do."

I grew up knowing a lab was my future. "Magic can happen in a lab."

KJ slows, then stops. Like I'm his shadow, I stop too. His brows crinkle, a sign of confusion. His eyes darken, something that has my heart hitching. "The most impossible of things can start in a lab."

I know there are layers to what KJ just said, but I'm too over-whelmed to process what they are. The hot hatred is gone. Instead, there's tingling, there's a sense of lightness.

There's a complication.

I start walking before those feelings can grow into something else. Something dangerous. Something...weak.

KJ doesn't say a word as he falls in step beside me. The walk back to the truck is wordless, and I don't even peek to get a sense of what KJ's mulling over.

Navigating this mission is going to be trickier than I expected. KJ showing an interest is good. That's what's supposed to be happening.

But what would certain members of my pack say if they discovered I was developing something as naive and foolish as feelings for KJ?

19

AVA

Gareth isn't sure where I fit into this puzzle that's been built around us. Since he started spending more time at Resolve, even becoming part of the patrol roster, he's obviously reconnected with Riley and Hunter, even come to like Josh, the only other outsider. But with me, he's more cautious. It's like he's waiting to see what's going to happen next before he commits to liking me.

Which I kinda get. I'm not really sure how I fit into this puzzle either...

I smile when Hunter brings me a cup of tea as I sit at my desk. You can see Gareth and Hunter used to be close, and you don't need their thread to be visible for that. It's the ribbing about embarrassing moments that happened years ago or their identical eye rolls when Riley says something particularly outrageous. All I can do is hope that I'll slot in somehow...

The sound of a cell vibrating cuts Hunter's responding smile short. Pulling his phone from his pocket, he glances at the screen, his brow tightening quizzically. "It's Mom."

Spinning around, he perches on my desk as he answers. "Hey, Mom. All packed?"

Packed? Did I miss something?

Hunter's brows bunch up. "What? And she's okay?"

Instantly on high alert, I throw privacy to the wind and focus on Lauren's voice carrying over the line.

"Yeah. Fell over in the bathroom. Something about almost dropping her curler."

Hunter pushes himself upright. "You're still going to go, aren't you?"

Lauren tuts. "I didn't feel this was a good time to go, anyway. I'm thinking I'll cook a veggie pie."

"Mom, you know we can cook. You should go. You always go."

"Hunter, I don't want to argue about this. Margie breaking her arm is a sign I'm meant to stay."

Hunter's lips flatline. Lauren has been the matriarch of her family for two years, he knows there's no point arguing.

Riley is already by his side as he says goodbye with a huff. Concerned, she looks from the cell to him. "What's up?"

"Margie broke her arm so Mom's not going."

Confused, I reach out to tap his side. "Not going where?"

Riley throws a quizzical look at her bother. "A wedding on the mainland. A friend from her college days that she hasn't seen in years."

Gareth's brows shoot up. "And she's going to cancel?"

Hunter frowns. "Yeah. Says she needs a plus one. She was really looking forward to it, too."

Memories of Hunter, eyes sexy and sultry, pointing out that sometimes his Mom isn't home for the night float through my mind. But the image doesn't warm me like it should. For some reason, I didn't know...

Hunter glances at me, for the first time in a long time, eyes unreadable. "I had to convince her long and hard as it was. She kept trying to back out and only agreed to go this morning."

Which I suppose explains things. But, still...

He turns back to Riley, looking at her with eyebrows raised.

Riley steps back, alarm like a siren on her face. "Oh no. No. No. No." She shakes her head. "I'm not going."

"You know how much this means to her. And things have been so intense."

The shaking intensifies. "I'd be the youngest person there. You know they'll talk about the good old days! They'll probably go way back to baby stories." Riley's voice is rising with each statement. "Maybe even birthing stories!" All of a sudden, victory flashes across her features. "Plus, I'm pretty sure I'm on shift tonight."

Hunter's shoulders sag and I wonder if he's considering going himself. I'm about to throw myself on the sword, reminding myself it's only one night, when Josh clicks his fingers. "Gareth should go!"

We all turn to the only adult in the room. Gareth's eyes widen with alarm as his mouth pops open. "I can't. Things are too unsettled."

Hunter arches a brow. "The wolves are the quietest they've ever been."

Which is true. Even Achak only paces about half the time now.

Josh shrugs. "It's only one night."

Riley pushes her fringe back, eyes pleading. "She deserves this, Gareth."

Gareth's mouth snaps shut. He scans us all and even before he says it, I know what his answer is. Gareth's connection to Lauren is a strong one.

"Okay."

Riley whoops as she throws herself at him with a hug. Gareth grins as he hugs her back.

Josh is smiling too. "Weddings are a great place to meet potentials. I think you might be a very smart man, Gareth."

Gareth scoffs. "You want to go then?"

Josh's response is the same as Riley's. His face fills with horror as he pushes back on his desk chair. Riley giggles and Hunter grins, but I wonder if they notice the slight tinge of pink to Gareth's cheeks. Is it possible that Gareth wants to go? My eyes widen. Gareth was best friends with Hunter's dad. He would have spent just as much time with Lauren when they first met...

Gareth heads to the door, his phone in his hand as he dials. "I'll let her know. And I won't take no for an answer."

Hunter grins at his retreating back. "Man, I hope his suit still fits."

Gareth throws him a glare from shutting the door.

Josh puts his hand up. "Is this when I mention I'm on shift tonight?"

Riley elbows him, obviously worried Gareth might still hear him. But the door remains closed.

With Gareth gone and Riley and Josh rejoicing over the near miss, Hunter goes back to scanning the tablet in his hand. With the excitement done, I pause. Lauren was going away tonight—how did I not know about that? More to the point, why did I not know about that?

The uneasy feeling that I've been trying to ignore for some time wells up and I hate it. Hunter's love for me is undeniable. It's in his words, his touch, his very essence. But there's a part of me that feels like something is out of alignment. Like I'm missing something. I shove the thought away. Trusting Hunter means looking beyond the uncertainties. With so much hanging in the balance at the moment, everyone is uneasy.

I focus on my tea. Once I finish this, I'll go visit Achak again. I'll feel better after that.

I'm BACK, realizing that Achak's restlessness is the last thing I need right now, when Hunter's phone buzzes again, this time a text. He rolls his eyes. "Probably Mom sending a disgruntled message. They'd be on the plane by now."

But when Hunter pulls out his phone, he stares at it for long seconds. He looks up at Josh. "Can you get the news up on the central screen?"

Josh's dark brows hike up in surprise. "Sure. Anything we're looking for?"

"Who knows? KJ just said 'turn on the news.'" Hunter's fingers tap as he thinks aloud. "What, Alistair making trouble again?"

The reply is almost instantaneous, and so is Hunter's frown. He looks up at me, eyes dark and muted. "He said no."

Everyone is tense as we wait for Josh to connect to a national news station.

With a click of the mouse, the screen comes to life. Josh walks around to join us. "He didn't say which one, so we'll have to see if this gives us anything."

A female reporter, brunette and somber takes center stage beneath an umbrella. Some distance behind her is a white screen, blurred by rain. Police tape flaps across it and blue and white lights flash and glare around her.

My stomach clenches tight and doesn't let go. It looks like a crime scene of some sort.

I gasp. "Josh. That's the Elkhorn Flat picnic area!"

Josh's face lights with recognition. "It is, too."

The Channons and Phelans had several wonderful after-noons there. The picnic area is little known because it's a bit of a hike. But for those who find it, they quickly discover the wide expanses of green grass framed by old growth pine forest means you'll be coming back.

Why is KJ getting us to check out some awful murder scene or something? Is it because it's our home turf?

"Welcome back to this heartbreaking news." The woman stares straight into the camera, her eyes grave. "The good people of Jacksonville have been shocked to hear of today's terrible tragedy."

I'm standing and walking toward the screens, my eyes never leaving the one in the center. Oh no. Is it someone we know? Hunter's hand slips around mine and I cling to it. Dread is spearing cold fingers through my chest.

"A violent attack has left a family of four dead. Details are still coming in, but it seems a hiker discovered the grisly murder scene while out enjoying this usually peaceful setting. The victims are yet to be identified but are believed to be the bodies of two adults and two children. The bloodshed was so significant that the hiker has been taken to the hospital and treated for shock."

Her hand comes to the earpiece as she focuses on the voice updating her. Her indrawn breath is barely audible, but it has me freezing. Her mouth drops open before she quickly recovers.

"I'm sorry. We've just had an update. Police have confirmed what we already knew—this was no standard attack." She pauses, her gaze steady as she lets the tension build. "I've just been informed that evidence suggests a wolf has killed this poor family." She listens into the earpiece again, "Evidence that includes wolf tracks approaching and leaving the crime scene, and," she swallows, clearly looking ill, "and the nature of the injuries. Forensic teams are suggesting that despite the significant carnage, it was a lone animal."

She shakes her head. "What an awful tragedy. One that's

going to rock the nation, possibly anywhere these animals roam freely. Are our reserves no longer safe? How will authorities respond?" She nods sagely. "Keep watching this channel for all the latest updates."

The camera flicks over to scan the area. The beauty of the reserve is nothing but a backdrop to the metal barriers keeping the reporters back, flashing lights like some garish disco, and that awful white screen. Behind it are four lives; four threads forever severed.

By a wolf.

The room has been shocked into silence. Everyone knows that no wolf would do what just happened in that peaceful picnic area. No wolf who was sane.

Which means Furious is back.

And Furious has killed.

The silence is beginning to hurt. Or is that my heart struggling to beat in my too-tight chest?

The dead air is finally ruptured by a noise. A sob bursts from Riley as she brings her hands to cover her face. Josh engulfs her in a hug, sharing her pain.

Turning, I seek Hunter like the wounded seek healing. Without words, he's there, arms surrounding me. I fold into them, reaching out to comfort in the same way I'm receiving it. We hold each other tight, breathing shallow like we're in pain.

My fingers tighten around his arms. Hunter is hurting just as much as I am, but rather than compounding my pain, feeling it somehow divides it. I'm glad, I'm not sure I could hold this all on my own.

Pulling apart, we look at each other. This virus is not only still alive, but it's now hurt humans.

Humans who will want justice.

Probably revenge.

I'm not sure where to next, but I do know what our next move will be. I clasp Hunter's face. "We need to talk."

Hunter nods, his gaze dark and heavy.

Josh and Riley have moved to the nearest desk and have perched on it. They stare at the floor, eyes showing how hard this is to process, their hands clasped between them.

Hunter clears his throat. "We need to get home, Riley. We can follow the news there."

Riley's eyes flash the same copper fire I've seen in Hunter— the sunset glow that speaks of unmoving determination. "I'm staying here. With Josh."

Hunter's chest fills with a breath but deflates just as fast. "Okay."

Surprise sparks across Riley's face. "Okay?"

"Yeah, tonight isn't a night to spend alone." He glances at Josh. "And I don't want one person here on their own. Especially at night."

I suppress a shudder. Hunter thinks that Resolve is going to be a target?

Josh nods. "We'll stay on alert."

The drive back to Hunter's house is quiet, the air heavy with implications. I curl up tight into Hunter's side as my thoughts spin on an axis of grief. There are people out there now trying to navigate a world with four less souls woven through the fabric of their lives.

Because of a wolf. An animal full of pride and peace. A wolf who's still out there somewhere. I curl in tighter as I wonder whether there'll be more deaths and I hate the feeling of inevitability that comes with that thought. Hunter reaches down to run his fingers through my hair. I focus on the gentle stroke, my one link to something positive right now.

Inside the house, Lauren has left a note saying there's a

vegetable pie in the fridge. Hunter holds up the note in question, but I shake my head. "I'm not hungry."

"Me neither."

We head to the lounge room to find Lauren has already unfolded Hunter's sofa bed. Hunter turns on the TV and making myself comfortable, I curl my legs in. For the first time since I shifted, I'm cold.

"Come here." Hunter sits next to me and when I go to move in closer, he lifts me up and shifts me to his lap. I snuggle down, wishing the strength of the feeling between us is enough to keep out the pain.

We watch as the reporter keeps the nation updated. It's been confirmed the attack was committed by a wolf. Authorities are conducting an intensive search for the animal before any more lives are lost, but it will likely be hampered by the rain. The family of the victims has been notified. They've asked for privacy as they come to terms with their loss.

Flipping through the channels, we discover that every network is now covering it. The picnic area is alive with lights and reporters. Police and state troopers mill in the background, several dogs on leads leaping and barking with excitement. Furious has well and truly made the news.

I tuck my head in, unable to stomach any more. "Another wolf lost." There's no doubt the animal will be shot. With Furious, so far, that's the only thing that's saved lives.

Apart from Achak.

"It could be dead already."

I look up, wondering what he means.

"Rabies burns itself out. No animal survives it."

Apart from Achak. Now I'm hoping that maybe he never did have Furious...

I settle back into the hard chest, knowing it's time we face what this is going to mean. "Hunter. Humans were already scared of wolves."

"Thanks to people like Alistair."

"Well, he's now got the ammunition he's been searching for."

Hunter doesn't respond, but the tension radiating from his hot muscles tells me he's already thought of this.

We're going to have to stop this. Somehow.

I lean back and look up. "I'm going to have to announce that I've more than just shifted. Show them who I am."

Hunter is still and silent. His eyes, so beautiful and so grave, say it all.

We have no choice.

It's time.

Slowly, he leans down, his gaze grabbing mine and not letting go. We seal the promise with a kiss. A gentle kiss. A kiss heavy with the weight of tomorrow.

We fold into each other, reconnecting with what this legacy has also created. Despite the recent deaths and looming threats, there's love here. Pure and strong. My hands move up into his hair, glorying in the texture of silk and strength. Hunter's warm palm cups my cheek, anchoring me, angling me so we can have it all.

We pull away, breaths heavy in the quiet room.

Hunter rests his forehead on mine. "I'm here for you, Ava. Never doubt that."

I blink away the moisture his words elicit. Why are those words so bittersweet? But before I can even wonder, Hunter brushes my cheek again. "You need to try and get some sleep. Tomorrow is going to be big."

He's right.

Tomorrow, everything changes.

Hunter turns off the TV and the lounge is overtaken by darkness. My Were sight adjusts and I watch him rub his eyes with the palms of his hands. I go to move off his lap, almost missing how things were even yesterday, when I pause. The thought of going to my bed alone isn't appealing right now.

The quiet reminds me that there's no one else in the house. "I'm glad Gareth went with your mom."

Hunter nods, maintaining the pressure on his eyes. "It's good to know she has someone with her."

Every Were would know of what's happened by now. Tomorrow will be the time when we have to step up and respond.

I pause, not sure why I'm hesitating to ask this question. "Why didn't you tell me your mom wouldn't be here tonight?"

The tension I feel in Hunter is subtle. Someone else probably would've missed it. But I'm so deeply connected to him that I can't help but feel it. I'm just not sure what it means.

"I've been so caught up with all this stuff, I didn't realize till a couple of days ago."

I wait.

Hunter's hands seem to flutter at my side before stilling again. "And she only decided yesterday."

I wait again.

Hunter sighs. "I didn't want to pressure you."

Frowning, I do what I've never done before with Hunter. I pull back. In fact, I climb off his lap, sitting beside him. "Pressure me?"

It doesn't make sense. Does this mean Hunter's been holding back?

I shake my head, trying to understand it. "Why would you think I was feeling pressured?"

How could he not see that I'm ready for whatever he wants to commit to?

"Ava." Hunter's voice is strained. "You need to be sure before we were to do…anything like this." His arms wave to the bed, probably encompassing the empty house.

"I've been nothing but totally certain, Hunter."

He looks away. "I wish it were that simple."

Is this about the poachers again? "It's understandable that you'd be angry with Kyle. The poachers have taken so much from you. From us." I go to touch him, but I pull back, and I wish I knew why. "You stopped yourself from hurting him."

"You stopped me from hurting him. A part of me wants him dead, Ava."

Hunter's trying to shock me, but it hasn't worked. He's not telling me anything I don't know. It's the fact that Hunter would never act on those feelings that has my love growing, not because he thinks them in the first place.

I shrug. "You haven't frightened me off yet, Hunter. Is there anything else?"

There's silence.

"Because tomorrow whatever has been brewing starts. Humans, Weres, even Fae are going to be impacted by what's happened."

This time I wait. I can't think of anything that Hunter could tell me that would have me turning away from him.

"Ava." My name sounds like a prayer. "All I want is to be what you need."

I cup his face. "I had that two years ago, Hunter."

Hunter's groan is one of surrender. My sigh is one of sweet, sweet triumph.

I take Hunter with me as I lay back on the bed. Like I've tripped a switch, his passion soars, taking mine with it. His body covers mine, his weight hot and heavy. As each inch of me ignites, so does my anticipation.

Could we be finally cementing what is already so sure in my heart?

Holding his face close, I gaze into his desire-heavy eyes. "We have now, Hunter."

Those copper pools blaze with so many emotions, each so much more powerful than the last. As his head comes down, as his lips draw nearer, I know Hunter is thinking the same thing.

Tomorrow, everything will change.

20

AVA

The sound of snow wakes me the next morning. I lie still, marveling at what my Were senses can pick up. The details and the depths that I hadn't known existed. And today, on this morning, there's nothing else I want to do more.

Today, I draw in a lungful of the most amazing scent I'll ever experience. Hunter's sheets stopped smelling of him a few weeks ago, and I missed being able to draw his scent into my lungs as I fell asleep. Having him here with me, sleeping in his bed, is a gazillion times better.

I catalog all the places that are touching him. I'm lying on my side, my legs tangled with his. One hand is tucked under my chin, the other nestled against his chest. It's an effort to hold still so I don't wake him.

I open my eyes to find him watching me, meaning all that self-control was wasted. Sleepy Hunter is a sight to behold. Relaxed, his tense edges a little fuzzy, he looks younger. More carefree.

As we lie there looking at each other, I can feel when reality starts to intrude. Hunter's breathing becomes a little more regulated, his awareness expanding beyond our little bubble.

Today isn't a day we can stay in bed and revel in the glow our love has created. It was our first night together. It holds the promise of many more.

Hunter studies my face, his gaze intense. "Are you okay?"

He's talking about last night. I nod, wishing I could capture in words what I couldn't in the early hours of this morning. Stroking the fine stubble on his chin, I smile. "I'm glad we had last night."

I feel as well as watch the corresponding arch of his lips. "Me too."

I sigh. "Because I think life is about to get complicated."

His smile broadens as his eyes become serious. "I'm hoping that's not an understatement."

Despite knowing we need to get to Resolve, neither of us moves. In fact, I shuffle a little closer, hoping to hold reality at bay.

Today feels complicated.

Last night was wonderful. Magical. Unforgettable... Then why do I feel unsettled?

Hunter leans forward, his good morning kiss a gentle one. "Let's bring the veggie pie to the center. Today's going to be a long day."

Mentally, I shake myself. I knew today would be big. Of course, I'm going to be unsettled.

With a last brush of our lips, Hunter climbs out of bed. My body heats as his smooth skin loses the protection of the sheet. His broad back is all golden skin over shifting muscles and it stretches down to his boxers.

Hunter without a shirt. My hands free to roam. My heart feeling the fullest it ever has.

When he glances over his shoulder, I don't bother to hide how the sight of him has me feeling. Hunter blinks, then blushes, then shakes his head. "I'm going to have a quick shower."

The tinge of pink hasn't passed before he's out the door. I smile to myself. It's nice to know that maybe the same images are still fresh in his mind.

Except four people died yesterday. When my cell rings, it has me jumping. The ache at the thought of the deaths grows to foreboding. Surely the phone call isn't to do with that.

The screen tells me it's Josh and the foreboding morphs to dread.

I press the little green phone. "Hey."

"Hey. We need you at Resolve."

I scrabble out of the sheets. "We're just heading over now. Have they," I swallow, sensing something is about to be set in motion. "Have they found the wolf?"

"Huh? No, no news yet. I'm ringing about—"

His voice becomes muffled and muted and I hear Riley in the background, her words unrecognizable but her tone urgent. Josh curses. "Already? Yes, she's on the phone now."

Hunter is in the doorway, dressed and obviously concerned. It's comforting to know he responds so quickly when he senses something is up.

"Ava. You need to hurry. It's Sakari."

THE WHITE WOLF lying outside her den is barely recognizable. Sakari looks like an anemic sack of bones. She's curled up, her fur the color of chalk, her eyes looking too heavy to hold open. The contrast to the wolf she was has me clutching the wire. "How?" I whisper.

Riley hasn't stopped shaking her head since we stepped out

here. "She was restless yesterday morning, but she disappeared into her den. We didn't see her again till this morning."

Josh comes to stand beside me. "We called you the minute we saw how fast she's lost condition."

Except you can't look at Sakari and not know it's more than that. Sakari is sick. Really sick.

I look to Hunter who's rooted to the spot behind me. His face is stamped with one emotion—sorrow.

I swallow. Hunter would know I can feel Sakari's thread. He can probably read that it's thinned, possibly as gaunt as she is.

And there's no Dawn to diagnose. There's no KJ to hypothesize what this could be.

Like he's just read my mind, Hunter turns to Josh. "Can you get KJ on the speakers?"

Josh is already on his way to the door. "I'll make it happen."

Hunter's words spur me into action. I turn to Riley. "Get me some blankets. And some of that milk Dawn gives the sick wolves."

Riley nods and rushes off.

I look up at Hunter. "Will you come in with me?"

He swallows and nods. Hunter's always been so careful with Sakari. So cautious. It's almost like he never expected this litter to make it.

But he's about to learn that threads are stronger than that.

Sakari doesn't move when I open the gate, doesn't flinch when Hunter closes it behind us. She doesn't even acknowledge when Josh comes back in, holding up his cell. "I've got KJ."

KJ's voice carries through the speakers. "I'm here, guys." There's a pause. "Aw man…"

Hunter's lips flatline. "You can see her?"

"You know I can access the cameras." KJ's voice drops. "Yes, I can see her."

I stroke her head and feel Sakari sigh. "What could it be, KJ?"

"Josh has talked me through her symptoms, but Dawn isn't around." There's a shuffling of papers. "This is definitely not usual."

Tension is an explosion in Hunter. "You need to figure it out, KJ."

There's silence on the line.

Riley enters with the blankets and I carefully tuck them around Sakari.

Riley stands back, crossing her arms. "Could it be...Furious?"

I jolt at the suggestion that hadn't occurred to me. "But she's not violent or angry."

Josh shrugs. "But she was restless. And she's also pregnant. Who knows what that could mean?"

"Guys." KJ's voice is calm. "It's true that Furious isn't the usual strain of rabies. I'm thinking someone's messed with it somehow. Either way, I don't think that's what's happening here."

Someone's messed with it? I look up at Hunter, needing a gauge of what to think of it. But Hunter isn't looking at me. He's staring at Sakari, hands fisted, face hard.

More paper rustles. "I'm thinking it's a nutritional imbalance or an infection."

Riley frowns. "She's been eating more than two wolves put together."

Josh nods. "And we've had her in isolation, where would she have caught an infection?"

Hunter is staring at the speaker like KJ is in the next room. For some reason, he's waiting for him to solve this.

I brush his arm. "I'll heal her."

Hunter's mouth opens like he's going to object, but then he slams it shut. Whatever his protest was going to be has been shut down by the knowledge that this is all we've got. He nods, his face becoming resolute.

Hunter looks at Josh. "Turn the cameras off."

But I hold up my hand. "No. Others need to see this."

We knew that my golden wolf status would be revealed today, that others would learn I can heal. Well, they're about to see it in action.

Sakari's breath seems to be coming shallower. I scoot around, bringing my face close to hers. "We're going to make this okay." I brush her forehead, but her eyes remain closed. "We're going to look after you and your pups."

With a deep breath, I dive into our connection. Each time I do this, it gets easier and easier. Within a heartbeat, I'm there with Sakari, the essence of what makes her the amazing animal she is. Another breath and I'm diving deeper, blending my energy with hers, finding our universal bond, the junction of our spirits.

When I find it, the golden motes are glorious. My mother told me she saw these once, the day she was crowned Queen of the Fae. What would it be like if others could see this? Not just a chosen few?

I focus on why I'm here before I get lost in the beauty that we all carry within us. Sakari is sick, and we don't know why.

Straight away, I feel myself drawn in deeper. It's like a vortex sucking at Sakari's energy. I let the pull take me down, sensing I'm coming closer to the pups. When I find them, it's like I just tumbled into a burst of light. Three heart beats, three threads, all their own life force, all entwined together.

I gasp. "They're so strong. So healthy."

I stay focused on where I am, so I have no idea what the others think of this. It's a relief to know the three little lives inside of Sakari are going well. Which means there's something else making her sick.

Calming myself with another slow breath, I try to find what I'm missing. The pups are healthy, which means it's Sakari's thread that's waning. As I explore this world of golden rivers, I start to see that it's Sakari all around us. I feel her love, her maternal commitment to protect these pups no matter what. I see everywhere they overlap and interlace. Although I've never seen this before, I instinctively know this is how a mother and babies are threaded together.

But it's Sakari's thread that's the palest. Although it's everywhere, it feels thinly spread. And it's somehow different.

There's a mismatch.

But how could that be?

I concentrate harder, whatever it is, it's elusive.

"Is she glowing?" It's Josh's voice, laced with surprise, sounding like it's coming from far away.

"Ava?" This time it's Hunter, concern knitted through my name.

I grasp his hand, the sensation wrenching a gasp from my lips. The feelings that are always there flow through me. But now there's something more.

It starts in my chest, warm and wild. It spreads out rapidly, showing me how much bigger this is than just me.

Suddenly, Hunter's thread is there with us. No, with the pups. Details become sharper, feelings become so much more substantial. It's like Hunter was already here before me.

There's no time to wonder as I draw in a sharp breath and hold it. Channeling this extra energy, I gift it to Sakari. The threads that were so anorexic a moment ago start to swell. The motes, a slightly different shade of gossamer, seem to welcome it, drawing it in like oxygen.

Riley gasps. "She's looking better already! It's like someone just gave her a boost of go-go juice."

I can feel Hunter's wonder. I can sense Sakari's healing. I can't help but experience the pup's thirst to grow. All so similar.

But somehow different...

I frown. I couldn't see it before, but with Hunter here, with the energy amplified, it jars me.

It doesn't make sense—

I open my eyes with a start, finding the return to reality harder than I thought. As I look up into concerned copper eyes, no, copper eyes full of fear, my muscles crumple.

The darkness rushing at me after the golden glow is a sharp contrast, but as exhaustion floods my limbs, I welcome it. Unconsciousness is about to become my friend.

I WAKE up to the sensation of fingers on my wrist as Josh's voice filters in. "Her pulse is getting stronger. I think we're out of the woods."

"Thank goodness," says a voice I wasn't expecting.

KJ? I thought KJ was away.

Then I scent him. My mate, I turn my head, needing, wanting Hunter, like he's the one who can figure this out for me.

"She's waking up." Josh's voice rushes out with relief.

But only one face fills my vision. Hunter is holding my other hand and I feel his grip relax. The worry seems to melt from his face as he brushes my hair back from my face. "Hey."

"Is Sakari okay?"

His hard lines dissolve into a smile. "She's the healthiest she's ever been."

I close my eyes for a second. "That's good."

They shoot open when KJ's voice intrudes again. "Knew you'd pull one out of the bag, Ava."

I smile, glad Hunter's holding my hand. "She's a strong girl, our Sakari."

My smile dims. Something is tickling the edge of my consciousness. Hunter was there too...

"Well, I'm not sure how it looked in the room, but you lit up like a Tesla coil. Sure makes for some interesting footage."

I push myself upright as Hunter watches me closely. He's barely said a word since I woke up. He looks wound tight, and I know I need to reassure him. "Send it to the others, KJ. They need to know this is what we can do."

Silence stretches through the speakers. "Are you sure?"

I wonder how much that question is aimed for me. Hunter swallows, the wild glint in his eye not quite gone. I wait for him. This is a two person decision.

Hunter's fingers tighten around mine. "I'm here for you, Ava."

I blink. Pieces seem to be falling into place around me. Before they can amass into whatever it's going to be, I turn to stare at the speaker in the corner of the room. "They need to know, KJ."

"Aye aye, captain."

There's a click and he's gone.

Josh pushes into my field of vision. "Whatever just happened isn't going to be in any medical texts, but I'm going to recommend you take it easy for a bit."

I arch a brow at him. "I don't need to take it easy. It was just a little more intense than the other times I've done it."

"The other times?"

It takes an effort to smile, but I manage it. "You should see what color wolf I am."

Josh's dark brows spike up. "You always were an overachiever."

I sigh. "That's going to be a story for later. Right now, I need to talk to Hunter."

Josh glances past me, before looking back. "Sure." Before he walks off, he squeezes my shoulder. "Any big plans can wait till tomorrow though, okay?"

I nod, even though the knowledge that it won't is heavy in my chest.

With Josh gone, Hunter pulls his chair in closer. "You sure you're okay? You haven't fainted afterward before."

I nod. I feel weak, but strangely clear headed. "It became more...intense once you were there."

Hunter nods, his eyes a swirling cauldron of copper. "You saved Sakari, but it took its toll."

I rub my forehead, feelings and thoughts starting to crystallize. "I need you to help me, Hunter."

"Anything."

I push up and Hunter leans back. I swing my legs down from the cot, glad to see that they look like they'll hold me. "I have some questions."

I don't know why, but it feels like Hunter pulls back a little farther. "Sure. I didn't see much when you were healing Sakari, just a lot of flowing color."

I shake my head, allowing myself the patience I need. Something is coming, and I know I need to be prepared.

"I never doubted your love for me, Hunter. You've always been there for me." I know without a doubt that Hunter would die for me. "But why does it feel like you're never there *with* me?"

Hunter doesn't say anything. To be fair, I'm not sure there's an answer. But the questions keep coming. Like a tumbling deck of cards, each one uncovers another.

"Why did you stop last night?"

Last night. The more the passion flared the more Hunter pulled back. He said he loved me. He pointed out that it wasn't the right time. I was happy and naïve enough to think that was enough.

Hunter blinks the slowest blink I've seen. His jaw works, the muscles a concrete mixer beneath his skin. He stands, taking a step away.

I don't wait for an answer. In truth, there's only one I need. "It's always been the pups, hasn't it? You were so worried about them." I swallow, knowing the words have finally arrived. "Why do the pups feel different, Hunter? What's been done to them?"

It's out. The question that's been waiting to be asked. That Hunter hasn't wanted me to. That I couldn't have conceived.

Hunter looks away. He swallows. He stares at the cot as he speaks. "We were desperate. We knew this could be the last litter of arctic wolves."

I brace myself, knowing this is going to hurt. Knowing there's no way I can prepare myself.

When Hunter finally looks at me, the agony in his eyes assaults me. I wrap my arms around me, knowing I don't want to hear this.

"They've been genetically altered. They have Were genes added to increase their genetic diversity."

I lick my lips, but it feels like my whole body just got hit by a tsunami of ice. It leaves me dried out and frozen.

Genetic engineering. Altering the most essential part of who we are. No wonder Sakari's been sick, she's carrying something that isn't supposed to exist.

"You never told me." The words come out as an agonized whisper.

Hunter steps forward but suddenly jerks himself back. "I almost did. So many times," He growls. "But my role is to protect you. Including from myself."

A tear escapes, a cold trickle down my numb cheek. "You'd give me your life before you gave me the truth."

Hunter looks away. "The truth is worth more."

His words feel like they slap, no, slam straight through me.

As I walk past Hunter, out the door, and into the hallway, I hold myself together. It takes more grit than I realized I had, but it's not a sobbing, mourning girl that walks out of Resolve. The cameras would see nothing but a girl walking steadily, her arms tight around her, maybe her gait a little stiff.

Out of the building, I keep walking. Past the car park. Into the tundra.

I'm glad it's the barren landscape that it is, stretched from one horizon to the other.

Because when I collapse, when I let all this agony out, I don't think anywhere else could hold it.

Once I'm out of reach of the cameras, my knees hit the snow. I grab my stomach as I double over. As my grief pours out into the white carpet, slick with my tears, I can feel it tearing at my heart. I know there's going to be enough to drench this cold soil, merge with the white snow, to ride the hills, to fill the valleys.

Hunter was supposed to realize. He was supposed to believe.

But I failed.

21

KJ

"I thought you didn't go out."

I don't stop jamming the backpack with the contents of the vet pack. "Bet you regret starting that then, don't you?"

Sayen frowns. "The packs are deciding what we do next."

Swinging the backpack over my shoulder, I throw her an unimpressed glance. Here I thought she was smart. "Great. I look forward to hearing what that is."

After whatever happened in the reserve, I've made sure we've barely spoken. Despite her past attempts at talking, Sayen seems to have focused on her Petri dishes. Maybe the wolf attack has made her more determined to discover a vaccine. Me on the other hand, I've been hitting dead ends every freaking time I think I've found a lead.

But now there's a wolf out there with Furious. With four dead humans in its wake. And I need to find it before they do.

I'm surprised to find Sayen at the door the same second I go to grab the handle. She presses her palm to the white surface. "They have people out there looking for them."

The one thing she has to remind me of.

Phelans. Channons. Probably some of her own pack—the Tates.

I shove away the surge of emotion that knowledge elicits. I won't be heading the same way they are.

"And then they'll kill it."

Sayen gasps. "You want to keep it alive?"

I glare at her. "Furious burns so hot that the virus decomposes before we can learn anything. We need to find a live one. It's the only way we'll beat this virus."

I pull on the doorknob but Sayen pushes back. The door remains closed.

You've got to be kidding me.

Sayen pushes in a little closer and I have to hold my breath. This close and I can see the worry in her eyes. "It's too dangerous, KJ. I've seen what Furious looks like."

If my senses weren't going haywire right now, I'd be able to process that interesting statement. Sayen's seen Furious? But I know my limitations, so I focus on the issue at hand—the door that someone's holding shut.

My hand tenses around the doorknob. "No need to worry." Hope sparks in her eyes. "I doubled dosed the tranquilizer gun."

Just as I hoped, my words have Sayen's hand slackening along with her jaw. With a grin, I yank open the door. Jogging down the hall, I don't bother to turn back. A quick recon isn't going to hurt anyone.

I allow myself a glance over my shoulder as I near the truck in the parking lot. I'm honest enough to admit I'm a little disappointed Sayen didn't try a little harder. I can't even see her peeking through any of the windows. Well, if she thought I wasn't serious, she's about to—

I leap back in surprise when she comes around the side of the truck. She angles her chin. "I'm driving."

Frowning, I heft the backpack, ready to turn away. "You're welcome to. But it won't be in this truck."

Sayen pats her pocket. "I wasn't sure which one we were going in, so I grabbed the keys to all the others."

Dammit. Now is not the time to prove my hypothesis that she's smarter than those lush lips suggest.

I plant my feet into the asphalt. This isn't a battle I'm going to lose. "I'm not good company."

Sayen shrugs. "Dawn seems to think so." She climbs into the driver's seat. "And you don't have any other way of getting to the reserve until I return."

She starts the engine and begins reversing. You've got to be kidding me. I leap to the side, and when she stops to put the truck into first, I open the passenger side door and climb in. The truck's already powering forward when I slam my door shut.

I look at Sayen, to be honest, a little gobsmacked. "What if you'd turned me into a pancake?"

Sayen looks away before I can see the grin that stretches her lips light up her eyes. She quickly quashes it. "It's good to be a Were, huh?"

Staring out the window, I dredge up the deepest frown I can find. Why is this girl so determined for me to embrace my shifter side?

I stay quiet on the highway, and so does Sayen. Suits me. I don't always like where it goes when we talk.

When she goes to turn off the highway, though, I have no choice but speak up. "We're not going to Elkhorn Flat."

She glances at me. "But that's where the attack happened."

"And forensics have been all over it. Not to mention the rain would've washed away any tracks. There's nothing else for us to learn there."

Plus, everyone would've assumed the wolf has headed back out to the reserve.

"So, where are we going?"

I point to the approaching handmade sign. "Lovers Lookout."

I ignore the sideways glare I get, and the warm flush in my chest—I'm not the person who named the place. I just need the highest point so I can get a good look at the lay of the land.

Silence is our chaperone as we wind up the mountain. Sayen isn't from around here, but the name of where we're heading pretty much says it all. A naturally cleared peak at the top was quickly commandeered by the lovebirds of the area as an adult free zone. If it didn't have me thinking of her lips, then I'd make a joke. I glance at Sayen's profile—dark hair, mocha skin, full lips.

Nope. Not making a joke.

At the top, Sayen pulls up. Just looking out the windscreen you get a sense of what the view is going to be. It has me undoing my seat belt before the engine's cut. Jumping out, I can't help the grin. It's probably the pine-scented air, it practically punches you in the lungs.

We walk to the edge of the clearing. There's no handrail at the edge of the rock, meaning you almost feel like you're floating above the amazing scenery. The view feels like it's pulling you in; some breathtaking vertigo you totally want to be part of. There's patchworks of pine and grassland, houses in valleys, trees hugging hills. The wonders of science and the joy of nature right beside each other.

"It's something, huh?"

Sayen stands there, taking it all in. Her hands bunch by her sides. "Worth fighting for."

I nod. "Which is why we're here."

The gravel crunches under my boots as I turn one way then the other, getting my bearings.

"Did you pack binoculars?"

I look back at Sayen. "What?"

She rolls her eyes. "If you're looking for the wolf."

I shake my head with a smile. She thinks we're going to scan for the wolf from up here? "I didn't pack three days' worth of food to do that." I glance out at the vista. "Plus, if we did find that needle in the haystack in half of Wyoming, how would we reach it?"

She frowns. "Then why are we here?"

Squaring myself off from the horizon, I narrow my eyes. "That's Elkhorn Flat over there." I point to the base of the mountain range on our right.

"Shouldn't you check that on a map?"

I roll my eyes. "It's Elkhorn Flat. If you squint, you'll probably see some of the emergency vehicles still there."

Sayen leans forward, scrunching up her eyes.

While she does that, I keep scanning. "It would've headed to an island."

"Ah, we're on a continent, KJ."

"We're landscape tracking. Animals need protection and water. Islands are pockets where those resources are found in abundance."

Behind Elkhorn Flat are the foothills of a mountain. Even from here, you can see the terrain is rough. There's also lots of vegetation, and foothills tend to have rivers.

Sayen looks at me. "That's where a lot of our captive wolves seem to head."

"That's cause they're smart. Good place for herbivores to hang out. And if there're herbivores, there're carnivores."

"So that's where we're going?"

I don't move. "That's where everyone else has gone."

Humans and Weres have all assumed that's where this wolf retreated to. It's definitely where any wolf we know would head. To protection. To food.

Straightening, I scan the surrounding area. "Wolves follow their prey. It's survival."

Sayen frowns. "So, it makes sense that's where the search focus is, then."

I keep scanning, not knowing why it doesn't feel like it fits. It never has with Furious. Deer and rabbits are plentiful in the areas where there's a wide variety of vegetation. "Then why did it go to Elkhorn Flat?"

Sayen shifts beside me as she crosses her arms. "Furious makes them mobile. That family was obviously in the wrong place at the wrong time."

My head shakes slowly. I know that makes sense.

But why doesn't it compute?

I take a step forward, my toe nudging the edge of the cliff. "It killed those humans, but they were never a meal..." I suck in a breath, realizing I'd better step back before this revelation launches me over the edge.

My eyes are wide as I turn to Sayen. "I don't think their prey are herbivores."

She pulls back ever so slightly. "What do you mean?"

I pace to the truck and back again, possibilities whirring through my mind. "Every wolf infected with Furious has attacked, or tried to attack, someone." I stop, staring out at Elkhorn Flat. "I think they're looking for humans."

Sayen sucks in a sharp breath.

I slap my palm. "It makes sense! Wolves are usually so scared of humans. They avoid them if they can. But all the infected wolves have almost killed someone." I pause. "Until two days ago. Then they finished the job."

Sayen's arms tighten around her. Whoa. I feel like I just punched her in the gut. "Sayen?"

She swallows, her cream skin looking pale. "They target humans?"

I frown. "That's what I'm thinking."

But like a gust of wind just shot up her back, she straightens. "It's almost karma, isn't it?"

What?

Sayen turns, looking back out over the landscape. "So, which way would the wolf go then?"

Deciding to ignore that comment isn't an easy decision. But I know if I ask, then my relationship with Sayen changes. It becomes based on curiosity. A need to know more.

And I don't need to know any more about Weres.

Mirroring her movement, I scan the countryside. "Well, not back into the reserve, that's for sure."

"If they're seeking more...prey, they'd head the opposite way."

Elkhorn Flat is relatively isolated, which was probably lucky. Who knows what it would've looked like if the wolf found somewhere more populated.

My eyes shoot to the nearest signs of habitation. Then widen.

Wilmot.

A smaller town, only a few miles from Jacksonville.

Sayen's breath exhales. "Surely not."

I turn back to the truck. "Not sure we can afford to hope I'm wrong."

Sayen doesn't object when I take the driver's side. The drive back down is just as quiet, but for some reason, it feels different. It's probably because Sayen isn't sitting still. She crosses and uncrosses her arms, periodically pulls on her seatbelt like it's too tight around her neck. She even winds down the window then jams it back up. Three times, I almost ask.

But that feels way too much like curiosity.

Instead, I focus on business. "There's an information center at the edge of Wilmot. I say we get a map of the local hiking trails and target the ones that head in the direction of Elkhorn Flat."

"Okay."

"So, it's agreed I'm calling the shots from now on?"

She finally looks directly at me. "So did not say that."

I shrug. "You weren't saying much at all, so I figured that was the only logical conclusion."

Clamping my mouth shut, I focus on the road. I was trying to make a joke, but that sounded suspiciously like I was fishing. Hopefully, she won't take the bait and we can stay on course.

Sayen keeps staring at me. "I was just wondering. Maybe that family balanced the loss of wolf lives."

My heart jerks in my chest. "Some sort of eye for an eye?"

She shrugs one shoulder. "Yeah."

The truck keeps driving through the silence. How much have I wondered that myself? Humans kill wolves without thinking of the consequences. Without caring about the ramifications. But even as I entertain it, I reject it. "That's a very old way of thinking, Sayen."

She looks out the window. "It goes all the way back to survival of the fittest, KJ."

Now my heart thumps uncomfortably. This wasn't the can of worms I was expecting. "I agree that it needs to stop. But that's not the way."

That's how the last generation tried to solve this.

"Then how?"

Two words. One question.

And no freaking answer.

I do what anyone who's found themselves stumped would do. I change the subject. "I'm going to pull in and get gas."

"Sure."

Sheesh. Could she draw that word out any longer?

As I fill up the truck, I decide it's time to stop thinking about what Sayen just said. That crap is exactly why I don't like Weres. It's why I'm heading back to Evelyn Island the minute I get some answers about Furious.

A bulky Range Rover pulls into the bay beside me and the barely-there glance I throw it fast turns into a double take.

We're not far from Wilmot. Why didn't I consider that when I pulled in here? I glare at Sayen, who's cluelessly rifling through the glove compartment.

A woman climbs out, flashing red hair catching the light. She steps to the back window and leans in. "Luna, if you don't stop wiping that on your sister, I'm going to— Belinda! I hated Mr. Puddles when my little sister had him. Don't think I won't get your father to build him a box to live in."

The only response she gets is a round of giggles.

Grabbing the pump, she mutters to herself. "Then I'll send that son of a biscuit to Mexico." She sees me staring, pauses, then smiles. "Want to buy a stuffed duck?"

Another wave of giggles tinkle from the vehicle.

Glancing away sharply, I try to get my pulse under control. It's like a freaking freight train has been let loose in my veins. I tug my beanie down. "Ah, no thanks."

That duck has got to be looking the worse for wear twenty years down the track.

The red-haired woman doesn't lose her smile as she shrugs. "One day someone will say yes."

She starts pumping gas just as mine stops with a *clank*. Good. Time to get the hell out of here.

The passenger side door of the truck opens and Sayen jumps out, waving a fuel card from the center. "I'll pay." Then she stops as she registers the woman I'm pretending isn't there. "Oh, hey, Tara."

You've got to be kidding me.

Tara's face lights up with another smile. "Hey, Sayen. Great to see you." She glances from Sayen to me then back again, now clearly wondering who I am. I preferred remaining as some anonymous tourist.

"Tara, this is KJ. He's here from Evelyn Island to help out in the lab."

Tara's smile fades. "Thank you for your help. It's important more than ever that we work together."

I nod, too many emotions assaulting me to speak. Anger. Sadness. Bitterness. Envy. All of the above and then some.

But ultimately, one wins. Acceptance. Acceptance that it was her father who started all this. Because although Tara bonded with a Phelan, she's the firstborn daughter of Kurt Channon. The Were who tried to use our strength and power to dominate humans.

I know Tara is Josh's mother, and Josh is a good guy. But it was Kurt who stood for everything I hate in Weres.

When the silence stretches straight into awkward, Sayen glances at me. I still don't respond. The secret that defines me is one I'll never tell her.

Sayen turns back to Tara, pulling up a bright smile. "Well, we'd better get back to it. I might see you at the next pack barbecue."

Tara smiles back. "I certainly hope so. I don't think anyone has ever managed to keep the twins out of trouble for as long as you did." She angles her head. "What are you two doing out this way? I thought the lab was where you cool kids hung out nowadays."

Sayen turns to me, eyebrows raised. That question I'm definitely answering. It's time to wrap this little chit chat up.

"Sayen wanted to show me the area. Said something about not wanting to become vitamin D deficient." Grabbing the fuel card from her hand, I head straight into the gas station.

Straining to hear if Sayen tells Tara the truth, I'm relieved when she heads to the minivan instead. I hear something about Mr. Puddles needing water as the sliding doors shut behind me.

It's not a coincidence that the time taken in the toilet is just the right amount of time it takes for Tara to pay and leave. When I head out, Sayen is back in the driver's seat. I figure it's payment for making her wait.

I open the map I bought as Sayen pulls out, scanning the green and brown wavy lines. With that over and done with, it's time to get back to business. "Looking at this, I say we check out this hiking trail first."

Sayen's glance is brief before she focuses on the road again. "Looks like the most direct route between Elkhorn Flat and here."

I release the breath I'd been holding, sending a silent thank you to her for not asking. "If the wolf is tracking humans, it makes sense this is the way it'd go. We'll see if we can find anything."

Sayen indicates left as we head off the highway. It's only about half an hour's drive.

"So..."

I tense, not liking the tone in that single word.

"Tara is the Channon Alpha. She's bonded to Noah's twin."

"I know." Maybe if I keep my answers short, Sayen will get the hint I don't want to talk about this.

"She's a Were."

"Yup."

"So they're just as invested in saving the wolves as we are."

My monosyllabic answer trickles into silence. Sayen will figure out that I don't want to talk about this, but I also won't.

Her fingers flex on the steering wheel. "I'm wondering why you didn't tell her about your theory."

I still don't reply. I'll spend the rest of this car trip a mute if I need to. Not only is Sayen pushing too far, she's also sounding too curious for my liking.

Sayen sighs and I recognize the sound of defeat. But just as she settles back into the seat, she throws out one last statement.

"Seeing as Wilmot is this pack's home ground."

22

HUNTER

A va didn't come home last night, and I know because I didn't sleep.

And I didn't need coffee to keep me awake.

The piercing pain in my chest did a damned good job of that.

As I enter Resolve at the crack of dawn the following day, I pause half-way through the door. If Ava didn't come home, then she stayed here last night. That's certainly what I told Mom when she asked where Ava was. It was a relief that Mom had been too preoccupied to question any further. Everyone has a lot to carry at the moment.

The door shuts with a thud behind me. The sound seems to ricochet through my hollow chest. My body feels like a shell, a cave that's been plundered by the truth.

What am I going to say to Ava?

There's nothing I can change. I made my choices because of who I am. I even tried to warn her.

It's telling that to the puncture wound in my rib cage that I can't seem to do.

The control room is empty, but I expected that. Josh and

Riley are probably still asleep on the lounges in the back room. To be honest, I hoped it would be.

For the first time since this place opened, I don't head to the coffee machine at the back. I couldn't stomach it today. Instead, I head to the bank of screens.

The images out on the tundra show what they usually do—a peaceful landscape sinking into winter. Scanning the ones inside Resolve, I discover my hunch was right. Riley is curled up on a sofa like a snug cat, while Josh is squashed into the other one like a concertinaed giraffe.

The captive wolves are nowhere to be seen, but that's also to be expected. With the nights getting colder, most of them retire to their dens for the night. For those not in isolation like Achak and Sakari, they have the benefit of shared body warmth in their little man-made caves.

Scanning again, my tight muscles tighten even further. I haven't seen Ava anywhere.

What will our conversation be like? There's no future for her with someone like me. She's seen that now.

But I love her enough that despite the pain of knowing this, the thought of not seeing her at all hurts even more. It'll be my job to make this as painless as possible for her. I caused this hurt, I need to do what I can.

When nothing moves on the screens, I head back out. The sinkhole in my chest knows I'm out looking for Ava far more than checking up on the wolves, but I still go through the motions. A tail is sticking out of the den that houses the three remaining wolves apart from Sakari. I'd smile if I didn't think that part of my face was broken.

Achak's enclosure is silent. He's probably curled up deep in his den. I move past quietly, not wanting to wake him. The minute he's awake he'll start pacing the fence line again. He's already created a compacted perimeter inside his cage, the soil hard and rutted. His feet are going to start looking the same if he doesn't give up soon.

Sakari's pen is the last and closest to the building. My feet slow, then stop. If I was going to find Ava anywhere, this would be it. The hole in my chest seems to grow and shrink at the same time. It knows there's only one person who can fill it.

It also knows that person deserves better than having to plug that hole.

But the pen is empty. I glance around, thinking maybe Ava ducked inside for something. There's nothing, no scent that she's been here recently, no sense that she's close. My whole body freezes into a frown. It hadn't occurred to me I wouldn't go through the painful process of seeing Ava this morning.

There's a rustle of movement from the den. Sakari's nose comes out from the gloom, sniffing the air. I hold still, letting her scent my presence. She starts a little when she recognizes me and I wait for her to bound out like she usually does.

It never stops to amaze me how much love this wolf has to give.

Except her nose just stays there. After a second, her head slowly extends out, followed by the rest of her body.

I gasp, hands gripping the fence.

Sakari moves like she's riddled with arthritis. Her fur hangs like a sack, her bones some sort of angular clothes hanger. She looks like she did before Ava healed her. No. She looks worse.

She takes a few steps out into the pale morning before collapsing.

I'm by her side before she's pulled in a breath. Kneeling, I reach out a trembling hand, not sure where to touch. Her head looks so fragile, her body gaunt. The only part that looks full of life is her belly. As she lies on her side, it rises like a hill from her emaciated body.

"Sakari," I choke. "I'm so sorry."

She pulls in a breath, even that looking like hard work. Breathing out looks like a relief she doesn't have to hold up her ribcage any more.

I move in close, stroking her body. Her breathing evens out as her eyes stay closed. Grabbing my cell, I frantically press the keypad.

It rings once before KJ picks up. "If you've run out of coffee, I can't help you."

"Sakari's sick again."

"What?" There's a rustle, probably as KJ hauls himself out of bed. "But Ava healed her, like, yesterday."

"I know. But I just came out to check on her. She looks worse."

"Gimme a sec. I'll get the video feed up." More rustling then tapping carries through my cell. "Aw, jeez."

I don't bother to look up at the camera pointing down on us. "What's going on, KJ? This isn't normal."

"You don't think I would've told you if I knew?"

KJ's testiness actually makes me feel better. It means he understands the seriousness of what's happening. I wait. We need to know what's going on.

"The pups have been growing fast. Too fast."

Like a Were, but I don't say it. We already know this.

"And her body's feeding the babies before her. But we've upped her supplements, haven't we?"

I nod. "Doubled her calories and her nutrients."

"Maybe we triple it then?"

Which will mean another roadkill run, but that's the least of my worries. "She needs to give birth soon, KJ."

KJ sighs. "Yeah. By the looks of her, that's not too far away." He pauses, probably studying the emaciated body I'm stroking. "What did Ava say after she healed her?"

The hole in my chest swells. "That the pups are strong. That something didn't align between the pups and Sakari."

"Right." KJ pauses for some reason. "She's going to have to heal her again."

I close my eyes as the pain grows. "I don't know where she is."

"As in, she's ducked into town for more coffee and I'm unsure of her exact location?" KJ's voice is cautious, like he can sense this is bigger than that.

"She figured something was up, KJ. She asked me."

"Oh." KJ breathes the word out.

"So, I told her." I squeeze my eyes with my fingers, hoping it will keep in the torture. "We haven't spoken since."

"Hunter."

Of all the words he could have used, he had to use my name in that devastated tone. I hope it wasn't a question, because my jaw is wound too tight to speak right now.

"She loves you, Hunter. She won't turn away from this."

From me.

Well, KJ didn't see her face. Didn't feel her pain. And he doesn't know that Ava believed I was more.

"Despite all that, you're going to have to find her. She needs to heal Sakari."

I finally relax enough to open my eyes. "Okay."

"You've got this."

I pull in a breath, hold it, then let it out. "Sure."

Sakari opens her eyes as she lifts her head up. She nudges me, her calm canine pools drawing me in. Although the pain doesn't recede, the tension does. I drop my head till our foreheads touch. Just like Ava, there's nothing I won't do for this animal. "I'm going to get you some help."

"Nice. So you listen to her." I can practically hear the eye roll.

Striding to the gate, I wave to KJ as I hang up. I have food and supplements to find. And an Ava to face.

Back in the control room, I'm relieved to find Josh and Riley there.

That is, until I see their faces. They both carry an unhealthy mix of stricken and spent. But I don't want to know about another Furious attack. Or humans calling to arms in retaliation. Or Weres telling us we need to stop it.

Sakari needs Ava.

"Riley, I need you to give Sakari the last of the meat." Riley opens her mouth to speak, but I hold up my hand. "Josh, Sakari needs her supplements. Can we do them intravenously?"

"But—"

"We don't have time for explanations. Sakari's sick again. Really sick." I head back to the door. "Has anyone seen Ava?"

Josh clears his throat. "That's what we've been trying to tell you."

Something in his tone has me slowing, not wanting to turn around. It has ice shooting down my spine. But then I'm spinning, striding back. Has Ava been hurt? Have I let her down again?

I finally register Riley's eyes, that golden color that we share, are glistening. "Achak is gone." She swallows. "And so is Ava."

23

HUNTER

Ava's gone.

The tracks from Achak's cage show human footsteps leading him out, but within a mile of Resolve, Ava shifts. It's two wolves, one so much larger than the other, that head out to the tundra.

It's one girl who has taken my heart with her.

My guess, and Josh agrees, is that she's going to take Achak back to the mainland. She'll probably contact her pack once she reaches civilization to find a way to get them both back to Jacksonville.

As much as my heart screams for it, I don't follow her. Ava's let me know how she feels about what I've done.

And I don't blame her. She should have run weeks ago.

I grimace as I take a sip of my cold coffee. It's all my hollow body can stomach right now. I haven't slept much, but to be honest, I'm not sure I'm awake. The days now stretch out in one blurry mockery of what could've been. It's not something I want to be conscious for.

Riley enters the control room cautiously, glancing around to confirm I'm alone. I know they've been avoiding me, and if I could feel, I'd be grateful. I'm not good company right now.

She comes to stand beside me as I stare at the bank of screens. We've moved Sakari to the observation pen, and it's her image that takes up the center screen. Like me, she hasn't moved since I got here.

Riley reaches out, pauses, then drops her hand. "Hey."

I take another sip, wishing the coffee could be even more bitter. "Hey."

Riley moves to my side, watching the screens beside me. "She's stable. And still eating."

"Good."

Is this how life is going to be for me? Not sleeping, never feeling awake.

Sleepwalking.

"Hunter..."

The cup hitting the desk is louder than I expected. Louder than Riley expected too, seeing as she jumps a little. "I'm heading out soon. We need to keep up Sakari's food."

"Maybe I could come with you?"

I finally look at her, and just like I knew they would, the memories come. Everywhere I go, Resolve is entrenched with memories of Ava. Even my sister. Their morning banter. The bonding over Mocha Munch. I hate that my relationship with my sister has been tainted by my pain. "I'm good."

I think I can see some of my pain mirrored in Riley's eyes. I wish I could fix it for her. She pushes her fringe back, holding her hand in her hair. "I think it's better—"

"I'd prefer to go on my own."

Riley bites her lip. "Okay." Her voice is almost a whisper, but I still don't move. Man, I'd love to find a way out of this horrible dream, but Ava will always haunt me. To be honest, I wouldn't choose to have it any other way.

The door opens again, and this time Josh rushes in. "Guys, we have visitors."

My sluggish muscles try to slip into high alert, but it's like they don't want to wake up. "Who?"

I get my answer when Josh steps out of the way and several people file in. The first is Gareth, and I quickly recognize the rest of our pack members.

Gareth nods. "Alpha. We'd like a word."

I blink. "Of course."

There's four of them, all Weres wanting a say in everything that's going on. Do they know Ava's gone? Do they even realize what sort of leader I am?

I indicate to some chairs, and everyone takes a seat. There aren't many Rendells, in fact, most of us are here. Riley takes a seat beside me.

I straighten, even though my shoulders feel too heavy. "How can I help?"

Gareth clears his throat. "Have you seen the news?"

"Not this morning."

The last I heard, the wolf with Furious was still at large, with humans clueless that Weres were hunting it just as intensely as they are. The funeral date has been set for the murdered family, and a memorial of flowers and cards had already filled half of Elkhorn Flat.

My world was broken in more ways than one.

Gareth nods, unsurprised. "It only just came out. It's the humans."

The humans. Interesting how they've labeled them so distinctly. So separately.

Thomas, a grizzled old Inuit, grunts. "Not a surprise though."

Olivia is Gareth's sister. Although younger, she seems to have aged faster. Her dark hair is streaked with far more grey, and her sharp eyes seem to have seen more of the world. "They're calling for a nationwide cull."

Thomas crosses his arms. "It's only a matter of time before it's a worldwide cull."

I narrow my eyes. "They've been culling for years."

Gareth's eyes are grave. "There are protests. They want wolf numbers reduced even further. They're saying it's a matter of national safety."

My hands twist into fists. "There won't be any left."

Thomas slams his palm into his hand. "That's their bloody plan. Don't you see?"

Olivia is shaking her head sadly. "I think you're right, Thomas."

Thomas has always been the doomsayer in our pack. He was the biggest voice opposing captive breeding, Dad's biggest supporter, which is saying something considering the backing he got from Gareth. It worries me that the world's becoming somewhere he could be right.

Gareth sighs. "And that's not all."

Great. There's more.

"Two captive breeding programs have been attacked overnight."

Alarm spears down my spine. "Which ones?"

Gareth glances at Riley and then back at me. "The one in Mexico, and Jacksonville." He holds his hands up before we can respond. "No one was hurt. They lit fires, but just like here, they've had twenty-four-hour watches there for weeks. We smelled them long before they could do any damage."

Ava's center was set alight? I don't know which hits me harder. Knowing she could be in danger, or knowing I have no ability to do anything about it. I'm no longer a part of her life. The only thing that's a thin band-aid on the wound where my heart used to be is the knowledge her family will keep her safe. Ava is well loved by many more than just me.

Olivia looks at everyone in turn. There are seven Weres here. All angry. All hurting. "We need to do something about this."

Which is exactly how every other Were is going to be feeling. These conversations are probably happening all over the continent. Sitting back and watching as humans try to exterminate wolves like dangerous vermin won't be something they can do. "What are you suggesting?"

Charlotte, a quiet Were, looks up at me. She's holding hands with Quinn, her mate, showing they're in this together. "We're not sure. How do we stop this, Alpha?"

I blink. How do I answer that when the title no longer feels like it fits? How do I even pretend I can solve this considering the mess I've made with the most important person in my life?

Thomas' chair scrapes as he leans forwards. "Yes, we bloody well know what we need to do. We scare them off."

Scare them off? Gareth doesn't look surprised, which means he already knows what Thomas is talking about. I wait, bracing myself.

Gareth sighs, the process of breathing in and out seeming to settle him. "We make poaching too dangerous for them to continue."

Every molecule of air freezes in my lungs. "You're talking of hurting them. Maybe killing them?"

Thomas is almost out of his chair now. "Just like they have the wolves." He pierces me with his brown eyes. "And our pack."

Just like they killed Dad.

I'm already shaking my head. "They'll just up the ante."

Gareth shrugs. "So do we."

Shit. I look around. Riley is wide eyed beside me, the others are all resolute. Their expressions all show how far they'll go to protect wolves.

But don't they see? They do this, and they threaten the secret of Weres' existence.

They do this, and all humans will do is work harder to exterminate wolves. And then...

I reel back. "This could start a war."

A war between humans and Were.

Thomas finally leans back. "Not if humans know what's good for them. They have no idea what they'd be up against."

Gareth looks from Riley to me. "How else do you suggest we do this? You've shown you're willing to make the tough decisions to save our wolves, Hunter. We can't let them go extinct."

My chest sucks in and out, in and out. The hole where my heart was, now aches with an intensity I wish I didn't feel. I hadn't realized how sure having Ava made me.

It's like I was almost starting to believe...

I shake my head. This is how it's meant to be. Her gone. Me here. "We're not making that sort of decision today. This takes some thought. We need to consider our options." I look around. "How do the Fae feel about this?"

Gareth and Thomas look at each other. Gareth shrugs again. "You can have that talk. We already know what needs to be done."

Something flickers at the edge of my vision. After two years at Resolve, keeping the screens in my peripheral has become second nature. Angling slightly, I try to see what caught my attention without anyone noticing.

There's a flash of movement on one of the screens. A flash of movement that shouldn't be there. I stand, pacing towards them, making a show of thinking as I look a little closer.

Bloody hell.

Turning, I stand before the screen so no-one else can register what I just did. "Like I said, no decisions are going to be made today. Thank you for bringing this to me. I'm going to think

about it, maybe talk to Dawn." I head to the door. "Until then, I
have to get more food for our wolves."

Riley pushes upright. "You're going? Now?"

I turn at the door. "Yep. We have four beautiful wolves we
have a responsibility to."

I shut it behind me, closing off four shocked faces. Let them
stew. What they've suggested is too close to how this whole
legacy started. Weres showing humans who is the most powerful. If you take this scenario one step further, you'd have Weres
controlling humans with our brute strength.

But since when did we protect just wolves?

Knowing this will all be waiting for me when I get back, I
push it away. Right now, we have an intruder stalking the
boundary of Resolve.

And the last person we want near our wolves is that bastard
poacher, Kyle.

Grabbing a quad, I make a beeline for where I saw Kyle. It
doesn't matter if there's ditches or jagged jumps along the way,
I'm like an arrow. Who knows what's going to happen next, but
my pack doesn't need to see a poacher loitering around the
remaining arctic wolves.

It doesn't take me long to reach him, which isn't a good
thing. Kyle shouldn't be this close to Resolve. I spot him easily in
the distance even though he's lying on the ground. Lips tight, I
accelerate. There's a voice in my head suggesting I use him as a
speed hump.

Kyle glances up when he hears me but then returns to whatever he was doing. As I get closer, I see he's belly down behind a
scrubby bush, binoculars trained to his eyes.

Binoculars that are trained on Resolve.

I leave the quad back a bit, seeing as the temptation to follow
through on that is too strong. Plus, striding those last few feet

might shave off some of the anger simmering through my muscles.

I stand over him, hands on my hips. "What the hell are you doing here?"

Kyle smiles up at me from his ground level position. "Sightseeing."

Nope. The walk over didn't dial down the anger one bit. I plant my feet into the ground. I want to kick this schmuck right where he lays. "Let's skip the smart-ass routine. Why are you watching Resolve?"

Kyle sighs, then pushes himself up. He takes his sweet time dusting off his jacket and pants. When he finally looks up, he flicks his tongue across his pale lips. "So, you've got yourselves some wolves, huh?"

My shoulders bunch as his words hit me in the solar plexus. "How long have you been here, Kyle?"

Kyle shrugs, looping the binoculars over his shoulder. "Long enough to see you have three beautiful wolves all in one convenient spot."

So, he hasn't seen Sakari. Or Achak. "It's none of your business."

"In my line of business, it kinda is..."

As a poacher. A paid one.

Anger, fueled by fear, powers through my muscles. The remaining arctic wolves are housed in one place. Now that Kyle knows about them, there's a possibility captivity just became as dangerous as being out in the wild.

I step into his personal space. "You touch those wolves and you have no idea what you'll be unleashing."

Kyle pushes forward on his toes, shoving his face close to mine. "With the money I'll get, I'll be so long gone, I won't care."

I'm just drawing in a breath, trying to cool the rage that's flared up, when my body instinctively pulls in harder. As the scent draws deep in my lungs, a roaring starts deep in my chest. It's an echo of the sound that ripped through me when my father was shot. I know why the fury is so out of control with Kyle.

It's not just the fact that he wants wolves dead.

It's not just that he seems to know about Weres.

It's not even his controlled movements, his cold calculations.

It's his smell.

Kyle is the poacher who killed my father.

Kyle never sees the punch coming, but this is one I've been imagining for a long time. He staggers back, the flash of pain quickly replaced by anger. "That wasn't a smart move."

I shrug. "Felt good though."

"Nor is it going to stop me."

"Two years ago." I'm breathing heavy, like I'm dredging something from the deep. "You shot a white wolf."

"Probably."

"He was big. He was standing on the top of a ridge."

Kyle's eyes flare with recognition. "That wolf was a trophy kill. The proof that I ultimately won." Then narrow with fury. "I never found his body."

"And you never will." There's no satisfaction in the words. In the confirmation of what my senses already knew.

But there will be satisfaction in Kyle knowing justice.

This time when I launch myself at him, Kyle is already moving in. Fists raised, faces twisted with black fury, we crash. I'm already pummeling as we head for the hard ground, my fists trying to find any chunk of flesh they can. Vaguely, I can feel Kyle inflicting his own damage, but it seems far away. Disconnected.

A particularly strong blow to my jaw pierces the numbness, and I pause. Kyle is beneath me, his face bloodied, his eyes wild with rage. I know I should stop. Kyle will quickly find out he's no match for my Were strength. But the anger has too much momentum. All the decisions I've had to make snowball. All the lives I've had to see end will always compound it.

I've finally run into a wall I can't break down. A hurdle I can't conquer.

And that's because it's me.

The next punch snaps Kyle's head back into the rocky ground. Of course, he's scared. He knows what I know.

I'm not planning on stopping.

Except Kyle isn't looking at me. He's staring in horror over my shoulder. Keeping my hands on his shirt, I quickly glance back, knowing it's probably a trick this coward would have up his sleeve.

Then I see it.

How could I have not heard it? Smelled it?

The polar bear behind us rears onto his back legs, towering over us only feet away. He's white and massive and rippling with fury.

We both scramble to our feet only to find ourselves frozen where we stand. Never have I felt smaller. Never have I seen the power that nature can wield in one single animal.

The bear roars, his head rolling from side to side as he trumpets his rage. He shouldn't be this close to civilization. But everything has been messed up since wolves have been hunted. It looks like this is the new order humans have created.

And now he's either telling us to back off...or he's found his next meal.

Our best bet is to hope it's the first, and to slowly step back. He needs to learn we're not a threat.

I reach out to Kyle, planning on guiding him out of the bear's personal space, but Kyle shoves me and as I stumble, he runs. Behind us is the quad, and he's obviously trying to make a run for it.

The bear looks at me, but something must tell him that I'm no normal human. That our fight would be far more equal than he's looking for.

Kyle trips once but he never loses momentum. His hands reach out and he scrabbles across the ground for several desperate steps before righting himself. When he glances back his eyes almost swallow his face.

He hadn't banked on the bear choosing him over the prostate guy he left behind.

The bear drops to all fours and starts powering after him. His alabaster body ripples as each paw pounds the ground.

Yanking myself upright, I watch as the bear makes short work of the distance between him and Kyle. There's no way Kyle is going to make it to the quad.

He's about to get the death he deserves. A death that won't have to be at my hands.

Kyle screams in panic, the knowledge of what's coming next stamped across his petrified face. Even if I wanted to, I couldn't stop this.

Not without shifting. Not without killing the polar bear.

And Kyle's life isn't worth our secret or the life of an animal he'd shoot in a heartbeat.

When Kyle trips, I know it will be his last sensation of soil beneath him. He rolls onto his back, desperately scrabbling backward. He pushes his hands out, like his arms will have any ability to hold back the almost half a ton of raging animal about to crash down on him.

My chest bursts with pain and I gasp. For some reason, it reminds me of what I saw when Ava was healing Sakari and her hand grasped mine. But this moment is nothing like that one. In that slice of time, I saw the potential, the essence of what we are.

Right now, I'm watching the death of everything we shouldn't be.

I'm watching a thread be severed.

Without knowing I've made a decision, I start running forward. Kyle's desperate eyes watch me approach, and I close my eyes as I know what I have to do next.

Shifting takes barely a second. Reaching the bear only takes a couple more. Barreling into the mass of muscle feels like slow motion.

The polar bear is driven back by my momentum, and I land on top of him. My jaws are on his throat before his massive paws can push me away.

Taking his life is far quicker than it should be. I clamp down, hating the coppery flow of blood that hits my mouth. It flows down my neck and over my chest, the bear's heart steadily pumping out his life force.

When he collapses, I release him.

Stepping back, it hurts to take in the devastation. The great body, unmoving. The pure white, stained by congealing red. The same red I can taste in my mouth and feel splashed across my body. It makes me want to vomit.

But there's no time to figure out what the hell just happened. Kyle is watching, and who knows what he's thinking. A quick glance over my shoulder finds him pushed up on one elbow, his whole face slack in shock, and that's enough for me.

Heading north, seeking the isolation of the deep tundra, I surge forward. I need to get away from this all.

As my paws eat the miles, two facts set up a rolling rhythm to accompany me. A drumroll that's heralding the truth I'm going to have to face.

Kyle was the man who shot my father.

And despite the consequences, I couldn't watch him die.

24

SAYEN

"It's been two days, KJ."

KJ hikes the backpack up a little further as we trek through the pine forest. "Thank you for the time stamp, Sayen. I did tell you to stay back at the lab, you know."

I ignore the last statement. KJ didn't put up much of an argument when I insisted on coming. I attribute the little zing of pleasure that knowledge gives me to the fact I'm fulfilling my mission. The pack decided we need to keep an eye on KJ's whereabouts now that he's decided to follow through on this theory.

He's learning stuff about Furious faster than we are, and we need to make sure if he's going to be so damned nosy, that he chooses the right side.

I fall in behind him like I have each day we've done these treks. It's created more hours than I'd like to notice those shoulders carrying the bursting backpack. Too much time to be curious as to why it seems so full. Too much time to wonder why a Were wears a beanie. And way too much time to wonder why I'm curious.

Because this is important, I tell myself. It was inevitable that

I'd get a little emotionally invested considering how much time we've spent together. KJ could be a valuable player in the war that's coming.

"So, same as usual today?" I ask.

KJ doesn't glance back. "Yep. Looks like the wolf didn't want to take the most direct hiking trails to Wilmot."

We've walked miles down each one, my heart thumping each time we passed a hiker. They'd smiled, tried to chat. But neither KJ or I were interested in being social.

"And what exactly are we looking for?"

This time KJ looks back, his hazel eyes unimpressed. "Tracks. Scats. Any sign it's been this way."

I arch a brow at him. "And you can track, can you?"

KJ points to a tuft of grass we're walking past. "See the chewed edges?"

I nod. Something has definitely had a nibble there.

"Forty-five-degree cut means a rodent. Probably a deer mouse."

KJ keeps walking and I narrow my eyes at his back. "Where did a guy who loves the lab learn to track?"

The tension in his muscles is subtle, but I've been watching this back for two days. It means I don't miss the tightening of his shoulders, the straightening of his spine.

"Of course, tracking that prey animal isn't going to help us on this little expedition."

Because KJ is convinced that wolves infected with Furious target humans.

The poacher who picked up the drop was supposed to take it deep into the reserve, but he said wolves are getting harder and harder to find. Or he just shot it into the first wolf he came across...

I grit my teeth, jamming my jaw down hard. This is exactly what we wanted.

It was always part of the plan. It's why Furious was created.

I just hadn't planned on it being this soon. On the sense of responsibility.

Or the guilt.

Or how overwhelming those feelings would be during the late night hours when sleep refuses to come...

KJ stops so suddenly that I almost walk into him. "Wha—?"

But then I smell it. Blood. Wolf blood.

We're both running, side by side, as we come around the bend. Like we've both hit a barricade, we stop the moment we see it.

Not it. Them.

This hiking trail winds through miles of pine forest. It's quiet, almost monotonous walking over dry pine needles, through armies of trunks, under tangled arms of shade. I knew it wouldn't be a popular hiking trail for humans, which is why I figured KJ must be getting desperate to check it out.

It's also why wolves would be comfortable coming here.

This pack, I count four lifeless bodies lying around us, must've figured it was safe to traverse.

KJ drops to his knees beside the one closest to us. A charcoal female, the single bullet wound to her head creating a sticky halo of blood. The next is a male, a young one judging by his size, his body reaching away like he was trying to escape.

"Oh, no." KJ runs to the wolf furthest from us. He's already scrabbling off his backpack, knocking his beanie askew as he brings it around to his front.

Oh no. This one's still alive.

I collapse on the other side, coming around to stroke the animal's head. The female's eyes are unfocused, filled with pain. She pants, tongue lolling onto the pine littered ground.

KJ has a gauze out and is pressing it to her chest wound, but I've seen enough wolf deaths to know it's too late.

This girl is dying.

Like my thought had been a premonition, the wolf pulls in a breath, releases it, and her whole body goes still.

"Dammit!" KJ's voice is raw with anger and pain.

It fuels the feeling that started the moment we found this battlefield.

The humans who killed these animals don't know they've just added fuel to the fire. A fire that will become a war.

KJ's shoulders drop, helpless with the knowledge there's nothing we can do.

There's no one to tell. There's no one to champion these animals, to fight for the injustice of their deaths.

Except for Weres.

I push myself upright. Who needs hatred when you have this sort of rage fueling you?

KJ, on the other hand, flops to his butt. Leaning back against a tree trunk, he rights his beanie as he looks around. "They haven't been skinned."

Ah, yes. The payment scheme. "These were revenge killings."

His head flops back onto the tree behind him. "Yes, they were."

When will he realize that dejection isn't an emotion we can afford? That sort of apathy got us where we are today. "They're not going to stop, KJ."

"Of course, they're not. Furious has—"

"This was happening way before Furious! Humans were killing wolves long before we were born." I have to consciously unwind the muscles in my fists and modulate my tone. "And Weres have failed to stop them."

KJ pushes himself upright, adjusting his beanie again. What the hell is with that thing?

He glances down at the dead wolf. "You were the ones who contributed to the hatred of wolves."

Anger explodes like a grenade and my arms fling out wide. "You're one of us too, KJ! And you're worse than the ones who turn away from what we could do to fix this. You won't even acknowledge your heritage."

KJ stalks forward, hazel eyes boring into mine. "Being a Were isn't something to be proud of."

My breath stalls when he comes to stand right before me. So much emotion is pouring off him, it's a hurricane around me. The anger buffets me, the bitterness hits me in the solar plexus. But it's the sorrow, the regret, that I don't expect. It seems to slice right through me, touching a place where the same emotions live.

Pine is replaced by KJ in my lungs. My vision sees no one but him.

Those hazel eyes, shifting, slowing...His lips, parting ever so slightly, then holding there.

The wisp of red hair that's escaped the wool permanently perched on his head.

I step back because I don't understand where this is going. I step back because I've just realized something.

KJ knew this area well enough to know where Lovers Lookout was.

KJ, who has been so passionate about saving the wolves, clammed up the moment he saw Tara Channon.

KJ's beanie was hiding a shot of red hair.

Probably any other Were in our generation wouldn't make the connection.

But there was a small group of Tates who knew Kurt Channon. Who believed in him. Who keep his mission alive.

And they're the Weres who raised me after Noah Phelan killed my father.

Looking away, I take a breath in. "We need to get back. Someone will need to return so we can bury these guys."

KJ is already collecting his backpack and heading back the way we came.

I'm happy to take my back seat. For now.

KJ.

Kurt Junior.

This intelligent, complicated, tortured guy is the firstborn son of Kurt Channon.

Helix was right. He's everything we need.

25

AVA

Watching the plane come in to land at Evelyn Island airport, I know it will be the same one that takes me away. It'll need time to refuel and restock, then I'll be gone.

I pinch the bridge of my nose. I made sure I stayed out on the tundra until my well of tears ran dry. I wanted to come in, book my flight, and fly into oblivion. No fuss. No mess.

A tear slips past my lame defenses. Who am I kidding? There's one almighty mess where my heart used to be.

I look around. It feels like the whole world is a mess right now. The only other people in the airport are an elderly Inuit couple. They're tucked in close, chuckling over something on a cell phone. Their thread is a thick one, deep and abiding. I stare hard at the ceiling, willing the tears away again. Envy isn't something I've experienced with such ferocity before.

Telling myself to get a grip, I take out my own cell phone. I won't have photos to smile at, but those two are probably smarter than I am. My guess is they've figured out you should never assume that you'll have time. That the moments you're experiencing can become more than just your past.

That they'll be more than memories.

Biting my lip, I dial the same number I've dialed three times today. I don't know why I can't get hold of my parents, but their cells keep going to message bank. It worries me. Usually, this means they're out in the reserve somewhere and don't have reception, it's just that the reserve is becoming a dangerous place to be.

But this time someone answers my call.

"Hello?"

It's not the voice I was looking for, but I recognize it nonetheless. "Hi, Dawn."

"Ava," her voice fills with a smile. "How are you?"

How am I? Broken hearted. Lost. Alone. "I'm okay. I was just wondering if Mom or Dad were there?"

"Sorry, I haven't seen them today. They said something about having some errands to run. Is everything okay? Is it Sakari?"

My stomach clenches as I ride the wave of pain. Sakari and her genetically engineered pups.

The ones Hunter didn't trust me enough to tell me about.

"The last time I checked, Sakari and the pups were doing fine." I clear my throat. My voice sounds husky and raw. "Did Mom and Dad say what time they'd be back?"

"I don't think they mentioned it. Are you sure everything's okay?" Dawn's voice is low with worry.

Gritting my teeth, I hunch down in the furthest seat at the back of the room. "I'm fine," I lie. "I think the strain of all the stuff going on is getting to me."

"Oh, honey. I know. So many people are very angry. We had an arson attempt here at the center."

"What?"

"Everyone's fine. They didn't take into account that Weres can smell smoke a mile away. But it just shows you that everything is ramping up."

I slump, pulling down the beanie I used to cover my hair. "That's good."

I wonder if this is why KJ wears these things—there's a sense of comfort that comes from anonymity. I don't want anyone recognizing me and trying to stop me from leaving.

"Don't forget you're not alone out there, Ava. We're all here for you, even Achak."

The smile in Dawn's voice tells me she's trying to lighten the mood. But I feel like I'm bleeding from the inside out. "Thanks, Dawn. Can you ask Mom or Dad to give me a call when you see them?"

"Sure—"

"Thanks. Sorry, gotta go."

I hang up and fold in on myself. I can't cry here like I did out on the tundra. There's no silence to swallow the noise. No expanse to absorb the waterfall. Instead, I tighten everything up. This is how I'm going to have to hold myself together. I can't depend on others to do that for me. I'm the child of this darned legacy.

And I no longer even have Achak.

When I first released him, his joy had been a beautiful thing to see, even through my tear-filled eyes. He leaped and bound, straight away heading for the tundra. I'd been happy to follow, having already decided on my plan.

Running with him had given me time to think. As a wolf, the wind slicing around me, my legs pulling me away from Resolve as fast as possible, I'd reminded myself I can't afford to fall apart. So much is depending on me. And yes, I'd been arrogant enough to believe I wouldn't be doing it on my own.

But maybe this was what the legacy had always been about. About me proving that, somehow, I must show the power of one.

Achak refusing to leave the tundra had only given weight to that theory.

We'd come to the point where we needed to turn south. I was going to call my parents and organize a way to transport him home. But as I'd turned, Achak had stopped. I'd taken a few more steps in the new direction, but he hadn't moved.

I even shifted back to human, trying to show him what I meant. Achak had simply taken several steps to the north, clearly communicating that's where he was heading. Covering the distance between us, I'd sunk to my knees and rested my forehead against his.

"You're not leaving, are you?"

He'd licked my cheek in response.

A part of me wanted to go with him. Things were simpler out on the tundra. Less painful.

Instead, I'd stood and watched him lope away, having no idea whether I was doing the right thing or not. Was Achak safer at Resolve? Or was his happiness what really mattered? That sense of surety that's always been my foundation disintegrated when Hunter told me the truth about Sakari.

People trickle through the gates, but I barely notice it. All it means is that the time to board is coming closer.

It feels so wrong to go. Is this how Achak felt? That he was tied too tightly to this place to leave?

But I can't go back.

Because I don't have Hunter either.

You can't work as a team when one half is determined to go solo. No matter how much you want it. No matter how much you believed the other person would see it.

The worst part is I know why. Hunter believes he isn't good enough. Would he have thought that if I wasn't the child of the Prophecy? The irony is like a battering ram to my chest. It's a cruel twist of fate that connecting with Hunter meant I could finally feel like we'll fulfill this legacy...only to have it be the thing that pushed him away.

The first boarding call tumbles down from the speaker above me and I shudder. I know this isn't going to be easy. I hear the Inuit couple stand and shuffle over to the gate. As far as I can tell, there's no one else leaving.

When someone walks in, something about his stride familiar, I tug my beanie down. I don't want anyone to recognize me. This is hard enough as it is. Hunched, I watch from the corner of my eye, waiting for the chance to slip by. Maybe having to shoot past and through the gate as quickly as possible will make this easier.

The man approaches another who's standing to the side. He must've arrived on the incoming flight. They shake hands, nodding but not smiling. Their demeanor speaks of a business meeting, but their clothing—shirts, cargo pants, and boots—don't fit that conclusion. I turn away. Whatever it is, it's no longer my concern.

I'm leaving.

"Welcome to Evelyn Island, Chase. You're about to become very rich."

I have to clamp my lips shut to stop the gasp escaping. I know that voice! I resist the urge to turn around. I don't need to see to know it's Kyle. His voice admitting why he kills wolves is something I'll never forget.

But why is he at the airport?

I keep my head low, pretending to be absorbed in my phone.

"Good to be here. Any news?"

There's a pause, and I'm guessing Kyle is making sure they can't be overheard. "We can talk more at the campsite." There's another pause and I hold my breath. A human couldn't hear this conversation from this distance across the airport. "But yes, there's news."

Kyle must've reached the same conclusion.

"I don't want to be wasting my time, Kyle." The man sounds older, gruff. I could imagine him leading a platoon somewhere.

"Believe me, sir. That won't be the case." Kyle's voice drops to a murmur. "I've confirmed three wolves."

Sweet saints! They're talking about Resolve!

"White wolves."

There's a low chuckle. "Nice. More buck for your bang with the white ones."

The final boarding call intrudes on my shock. The men walk past, and I bury myself deeper in my phone.

"It'll be a night sting." Kyle's voice is starting to fade. "But nothing we haven't done before. And there's some unbelievable stuff going down there..."

The sliding door opens then shuts off the rest of the conversation. I sit in the hard plastic chair, curved over like an old crone, trying to digest what I just heard.

Resolve needs to know that Kyle has recruited and is planning on attacking the wolves. I grab my phone. All it would take is a quick phone call to Josh. The Rendells' lives are dedicated to protecting those wolves.

A young guy wearing the airport uniform smiles politely at me as he approaches. "Ma'am, the plane is ready to leave."

I shoot upright, feeling scattered and confused. "I just need to make a quick phone call."

The smile takes on a harried edge. "You're the last person to board, ma'am..." He walks back to the gate, pointedly watching me.

My thumb is trembling as it hovers over the keypad. All I need to do is make one phone call, tell Josh what I've heard, and I've done my bit. I can leave with a clear conscience. I'm not needed here anymore.

Then why am I standing here, thumb no longer quivering because it's now frozen?

Because it feels like giving up.

I frown hard. I didn't give up. Hunter did.

He'd already decided for both of us how this would turn out.

Except by leaving, I prove him right.

26

AVA

W hy am I back here?
Resolve looks exactly the same as it did just a few days ago. A squat cement building built to withstand the harsh climate of the arctic circle. There are several cars in the parking lot that have me pausing.

I should've just made the phone call.

Which brings me back to the question. Why am I here?

I told myself I wouldn't return unless Hunter asked me. Unless Hunter made some show that he was willing to work together. Not side by side. Not together most of the time.

But to step up and be totally, irrevocably committed. With no more secrets between us.

I know that essentially means I'm asking for a Bonding. I can't think of any other statement that would show me, and the Were world, that we are one.

My eyes fill with moisture and I angrily wipe it away. I've had enough of the tears. Yes, Hunter is bonded to my heart and soul in all the ways that count. But he needs to see that.

Surely, I'm not stupid enough to still hope...that some small glimmer in me still believes...?

It's that moment I feel him. There's a franticness to his energy, a yearning. I wait in the middle of the parking lot, surrounded by the white that no longer melts. Wanting.

Hoping.

My heart kicks over into a rapid rhythm, like it's calling him, urging him to come faster. Please let this hope be true...

The door rips open and he's there, dark head scanning one way then the other. When his copper eyes find me, my world tilts, adjusts, and realigns. My chest swells, life breathing back into it.

This is my mate.

I wish I could move, but I know I can't. I never intended to come back here, and I'm not sure what it says about me that I have. I wait. This is Hunter's decision.

Hunter slowly walks toward me, his eyes never leaving mine. I take him in like I haven't seen him for a lifetime. Dark hair, disheveled and unkempt. His shirt, wrinkled and worn, hugging the shoulders I loved to cling to. His natural, wild grace as he steadily approaches.

Damn it. I'm here because I'm still hoping. Still believing that somehow this is possible. I'm not sure I'll be able to recover from the fall if I'm wrong...again.

Hunter stops inches in front of me, his copper eyes devouring me. There's so much emotion in those shifting pools —disbelief, joy, love.

What I need is honesty and commitment.

He opens his mouth, then closes it. "You came back."

I swallow. "There's something I need to tell you."

Hunter raises his hand. "Me first."

Closing my mouth, I wait. My heart is hammering at my ribs, my mind is wondering if I'm about to be crushed completely.

"You were right, Ava. You were right all along."

His words hit me like a force of nature. I'm almost proud that I don't flinch, let alone crumple like a twig. I don't reply. I can't. My whole body is hurting too much.

"I've put you through so much." His eyes fill with pain. "Too much."

I'm such a fool. An idiot. The worst part, is that I came here. Like a loyal puppy. A stupid, lovesick puppy.

I shake my head. I can't hear any more. "Kyle knows of the wolves," I choke. "He's assembled some others, they're planning to attack Resolve."

Hunter's eyes widen. "He's brought others?"

I finally find the ability to move. It takes focus, concentrating on unlocking muscles so they can get me the hell out of here, but it gives me something to do...other than be hit with the knowledge of my stupidity all over again.

Hunter's hand shoots out, but stops. "That doesn't matter right now. I already knew Kyle was coming. We've been preparing."

I frown, confused. "You knew? You've been preparing?"

Hunter's lips relax, almost curving into a smile. "It's why I couldn't come after you."

The frown intensifies. "You didn't know where I went."

"I would have found you, Ava. Even if you went to the other side of the galaxy."

My breath whooshes out. It's true. Hunter may not see our thread, but he feels our connection as deeply as I do. It will always be a magical trail of golden motes leading us back to each other.

Hunter pulls in a deep breath. "Kyle is the poacher who killed my father."

I gasp, but Hunter lifts his hand up. I wait, knowing whatever he has to say is important.

"He admitted to it."

My hand flies to my throat. "You wanted him dead."

Hunter looks away. "I did. It couldn't be okay with a world where my father's murderer walked free."

But I just saw Kyle at the airport. "You didn't kill him."

Hunter rubs the back of his head. His golden gaze turns rueful. "I almost did. I wanted to."

But he didn't. Waiting, I know I need to hear him say it.

"And the polar bear almost did the dirty work for me."

Polar bear? I step forward in alarm, but stop myself. I still haven't heard him say it.

Hunter's arm falls to his side, his gaze becoming somber and serious. "I couldn't let Kyle die, Ava. It meant I had to kill the bear to save him."

My world freezes. Snowflakes flutter, feeling like they're in slow motion. Hunter is as still as I am. Neither of us blinks. Neither of us breathes.

Hunter is the first to move. He pulls in a breath as his eyes fill with vulnerability. "You were right."

Sweet saints, I want to touch him. But... "I need to hear it, Hunter."

I know I'm asking for so much. I'm not asking for Hunter to believe in me. Or even us.

I'm asking for him to believe in himself.

I don't expect the light of humor that sparks in his copper eyes, or the slight tilt of his lips. If this was any other time, I'd expect Hunter to shake his head. Instead, he takes a small step, the distance between us now just a hairbreadth.

"Ava. I've loved you for a long time. You were literally my dream come true. What we have, it's done what I thought was impossible. I know now there's nothing stronger than this." His arms wave to indicate the two of us.

With each word my heart heals. My soul lifts. The world becomes somewhere I can't wait to be part of.

Hunter stills, and I know his words are a promise. "We'll beat this. We'll win."

Except there's no way I'm letting him off this easy. "Because..."

This time the smile blooms, fast becoming a grin. He shakes his head. "I can't believe I find this tenaciousness sexy." His head leans down, his lips hovering above mine. "Because we are the legacy."

Although Hunter is only millimeters from me, I leap. I launch myself with such abandon the force bowls him backward. I mold over his hard chest, my lips finding what they've been missing.

This kiss is one we've never had before. Not in the two years of dreams. Not in the months of reality.

This kiss is two halves, two equals, rejoicing in becoming one. This kiss is the ending of something that was beautiful but flawed, and the beginning of something infinite and true. It's Hunter and me and love and passion and potential.

It's a kiss I never want to end.

It's a kiss that promises so much more...

My heart is pulsing through my whole body, my mind is mush, when the sound of gravel crunching filters into my consciousness. I ignore it. Hunter and I kissing is nothing anyone at Resolve hasn't seen before. They're welcome to add this mind-blowing experience to their viewing tally.

But the voice that spears through the passion has me reeling back. It's not a voice I would ever have expected to hear on Evelyn Island.

I spin in shock, arms clinging to Hunter. I have to blink a few times to prove I'm not hallucinating.

My parents stand beside a car, the one I didn't hear arrive.

Mom, Eden Phelan, the Queen of the Fae, is misty-eyed and smiling.

Dad, on the other hand, the one and only Noah Phelan, Prime Alpha, has his arms crossed as he frowns at us. "This must be Hunter. I was looking forward to meeting him in person."

27

KJ

This is the last hiking trail. The last thread of evidence that my theory is correct. If it comes up a dead end, then I'm back to square one.

No one wants to go back to square one. Ever.

Heck. I don't even want to go back to square eighty-five, which is why I'm powering over this trail like the hounds of my past are on my tail. Even despite the climb.

Today's hike started with a hill. More of a mini-mountain, really. I use the steady uphill climb to punish my muscles.

"This would go quicker if we shifted, you know."

I ignore the suggestion, just like I have every other time Sayen has put it forward.

"We'd cover more ground. Just saying..."

I stop and spin around. "You're wasting your breath. You know I don't shift."

Sayen's been different since yesterday. Less quiet. More cocky. I'll admit I like it, but it has me wary. I don't want to like it.

She angles her head, which only brings my attention to her lips. "There's a lot of strength in you, KJ. I like that strength. That strength is your Were side."

Spinning right back, I start walking again. Correction. I stride. My past is no longer hot on my heels, a tempting Were is. I'm not sure which is worse.

I talk to the trail in front of me. "My strength comes from deciding what's right."

Sayen's response is quiet, almost a whisper. "Mine too."

I stop again, even though I know I shouldn't. This girl is layers on layers of mystery. Guarded and defensive, yet vulnerable. Proud and sure, yet wondering what she stands for. If we didn't have so many parallels, I could probably turn away.

Instead, I stop and face her. "And what's right, Sayen? What have you got all figured out."

Sayen stares at me, nibbling the edge of her lip. I'm breathing a little heavily as I wait to see if she'll pick up the gauntlet. If she wants honesty, then she's going to have to dole some out.

"I know Weres will have to be the ones who decide how this ends."

I snort. "Nice sidestep."

She narrows her eyes. "I know our strength will be in our unity."

I roll my eyes. "Did you read that somewhere?"

Something blazes in Sayen's dark eyes. It has me sucking in my breath, and I don't know if I'm scared or excited.

Stepping forward, she jerks off my beanie. "I also know that the son of the one Were who was willing to stand for what needs to be done should be part of this."

I reel back, the sun a strange heat beating down on my head. I don't know what to process first. Sayen knowing who I am, or Sayen talking about my father like that.

Like...like a leader.

I'm shaking my head before I realize it, rejecting everything Sayen has just brought into the harsh light of day. I hate my father and everything he stands for. Kurt Channon wanted Weres to use our strength and power to dominate humans.

And he was willing to kill to do it.

At the same time, I've spent years searching for a different answer. Dedicating my life to trying to undo what he did.

And standing here, most of the way up the side of mountain chasing a hunch, I have to admit it. I've gone nowhere but backward.

Sayen stands there, her gaze unblinking. What do I do in the face of such unflinching challenge? I do what any self-respecting non-Were would do. I run.

I sprint for the top of the hill like I'm trying to launch myself off the top of it.

I know it's pointless, and I know Sayen is behind me the whole way up, but I go through the motions anyway. It's like I have to go through some weird metaphor for my life—running away, always hoping I'm running toward something.

Except this time, I'm trying to explode my lungs.

When I hit the top, I fold over, leaning my arms on my legs. Sucking in great lungfuls of air as Sayen breaks beside me, panting just as hard.

Straightening, I take in her flushed face. "How do you know Kurt?" I refuse to call him my father.

"I never met him, but he knew my father."

Her father? I cast my mind back twenty years. It was before I was born, but I've lived the legacy of those years my whole life. I know everything that happened.

Kurt had a handful of supporters. Some Channons, a few Tates. I look at Sayen in shock. "You're a Tate."

She nods, no longer hiding. "My father was Daniel Tate."

Kurt's right hand man. The one who tried to expose Weres. "He was banished."

Anger flashes across Sayen's face. "And then he was killed."

I frown. There are details there, at the edge of my memory. There's something about Daniel's death that...

Sayen lifts her hands to her hips. "Noah Phelan killed my father, and left three of our pack as human. He thought that was where it ended..."

My breathing has just gotten back to normal when it hitches again. "What are you saying? It did end there, Sayen."

She shakes her head. "Some of us haven't forgotten. My dad died for a cause that our kind were too cowardly to follow." She points at me, a kind of fever in her eyes. "And look where it got us—a trail of dead wolves leading nowhere but extinction."

Sayen has been hinting at this the whole time. I knew there would have to be Weres that still thought like Kurt. But they were closer to home than I realized.

And their anger runs deeper than I realized.

"All Kurt wanted was power. Not peace."

"No!" Sayen's hand slices through the air. "He knew peace would come at a cost." She stares me down, unflinching in her belief. "Your father knew that Weres had the strength to make that sacrifice."

I step back. I have to. Sayen's intensity is hitting me in waves. It feels like it could push me right off the edge of this hilltop. I even look around, just to make sure I'm not near an edge or something. Not to mention looking away breaks the spell Sayen's words were weaving.

She's so sure. What would it be like to have that sort of certainty...?

Turning my back, I jam my fingers through my hair. This is the first time in years I've been outside without my beanie on. Hunter called it my tea-cozy security blanket. He was right. I feel naked without it.

As I scan the forest, I decide I'm going to count Douglas fir. It's just the kind of illogical, outcome-based activity I need to do right now. It means not thinking of anything deeper than integers.

"KJ..."

Sayen's voice, quiet and almost sweet, reaches over my shoulder, but I ignore it. Douglas fir can be easily mixed up with pinyon pine, and I don't want my sample to be compromised. Instead, I focus on the path as it winds back down the hill and through the trees. That was the path I imagined I'd be trekking down this afternoon, tracking a wolf with Furious. Was I wrong about that theory too?

"K—"

I hold up my hand. "I'm counting Douglas fir. Don't ask why and don't interrupt."

There's a rustle and I'm pretty sure Sayen just crossed her arms. Well, I don't think my heart rate will ever be the same again after the revelations she threw at me today. She's going to have to wait.

"Oh, crap." Suddenly, my chest feels like it's being beaten from the inside out as my heart discovers a rhythm faster than I've ever experienced.

"What? You lost count?"

I grab Sayen's arm, pulling her beside me as I point. She gasps as she sees what is undeniably down on the path. "It's him."

I nod. "It's him."

The wolf powering through the trees below is undoubtedly a male, and judging by the speed, he's our wolf. The wolf with Furious.

Spinning around, I take stock of what's around us. All I need is a— "That'll do it."

Slipping off my backpack, I head to a tree beside the path we just came up. A Douglas fir, ironically. When I packed the cable three days ago, I didn't think I'd actually use it.

Heart thumping, I start setting up the snare.

"You're going to trap it?" Sayen's voice is full of alarm.

I carefully lay the loop in the center of the trail. "You want to hold it for me while I get a blood sample?"

"And here I thought you were a smart guy, KJ. This is insane."

I focus on scattering some bracken fern over the wire. "Is he close?"

Sayen's back before I've finished the final check. "He's not far. I think he's picked up the pace."

Pushing upright, I dust my hands on my jeans. "He's probably smelled us." I grab her hand. "I need to get in position. I doubt we have much time."

Glancing back at the snare, I swallow. I'm putting a lot of faith in that length of cable. Pulling Sayen back to where we came, I tighten the hold on her hand. "Now, I need you to go back to the information center. Call Dawn."

"What? That's your plan? To send me away?"

"Of course, that's my plan. This guy ain't gonna be happy to be tied to a tree." Sayen is actually smart enough to look scared. Good. She needs to appreciate what we're about to face. "This is a wolf who's killed people, Sayen."

Except my words have the exact opposite I was hoping they would. I watch as Sayen buries that fear so efficiently and so completely that I swear she's done it before. Squaring her shoulders, she grasps my hand tightly. "I'm not going anywhere." Looking around, she seems to almost be talking to herself. "This is how I make it okay."

There's no time to analyze what that means because a rustle explodes from the other side of the hilltop. We spin around to see the wolf skid to a halt.

This is the longest we know that a wolf has lived with Furious, and you can tell. His eyes are red-rimmed and bloodshot.

The froth thanks to his partially paralyzed throat looks like a soda has overflowed down his black chest. He snarls, and the sound ripples down his body.

Slowly, I step backward, trying to tuck Sayen behind me but she won't budge. She stays staunchly at my side. Man, and I thought I was crazy.

The wolf watches our movements with his hot eyes. Growling, he flashes his saliva-streaked teeth.

With a sense of surety that slams fear straight down my spine, I realize I miscalculated. This wolf won't be stalking, step by step, toward his prey. He won't even be running at us. As if to confirm my theory, he crouches, bunching his muscles like a coil.

This wolf is planning on attacking with one leap. Which means he'll jump straight over the snare.

I turn to Sayen. "Run!" She looks up at me, realization dawning across her face. "Shift and get the hell out of here, Sayen."

Sayen releases my hand and I allow myself a small burst of relief. At least I won't have to feel responsible for her death, too.

I don't realize what she's done until I've hit the ground. Using her Were strength, Sayen rams me off the path.

She stands in the center, alone, as the rabid wolf latches his blood-shot eyes on her. Unafraid, and deeply terrified, she looks at me rather than the wolf. "Get your sample, okay?"

I wait for her to shift, but she doesn't. Oh no. She knows its human blood this wolf wants. She knows we need this wolf alive to get a sample from him. She's sacrificing herself?

Over my dead and decaying body.

Like a wave erupting, the wolf leaps, spittle spraying behind him. Sayen uses the moment to run forward. Straight at him.

Holy shit. She's going to try and get him in the snare.

There's no time to think. All I know is Sayen isn't dying today.

Shifting is more painful than I expected. Muscles that thought they'd always be human feel like they're shredding. Bones splinter, lengthen, and struggle to reform. Lava explodes across my skin as it stretches and grows. I hold in the scream at the godawful change my body is fighting.

As the metamorphosis occurs, the wolf sails through the air. Sayen maintains her forward trajectory, her shoulders hunched and her head tucked in like she's about to slam through a wall.

The wolf's trajectory and speed topple Sayen like a leaf. She's propelled backward, hitting the ground hard. The frenzied wolf pins her down, snapping at her. Her arms hold him back, shaking with the strain, but even with Were strength, she'll never stand a chance.

With a roar that's far more animal than human, I run. I jump. And I barrel into him.

His size is no match for mine. His fury could never compete with the raging torrent of emotion that's now my fuel.

I'm a battering ram as my body collides with his. The momentum lifts the wolf, sending us both spearing through the air. Maybe I can get him back near the snare. I risk that cutting length being my noose, but it's the only way this scenario can end well.

Except losing his prey only enrages the wolf further. Before we've hit the ground, his jaws are snapping, trying to find any piece of flesh he can. We crash into the unforgiving rock as he clamps onto my shoulder. There's no surprise when his teeth puncture deep into my muscle—this wolf's poisoned mind is hungering for death.

My death.

Then Sayen's.

Ignoring the tearing pain that's trying to blindside me, I try to get the upper hand. And fail miserably. Even though he's smaller, he's had a lot longer living in his canine skin. He's had practice in killing. Without letting go of my shoulder, he twists and I find myself underneath. His chest heaves, his breath hot and riddled with the stench of old blood. I can't tell if it's the pain or the smell that makes me want to gag.

I struggle, and he clamps down harder. Agony explodes through my shoulder and down my arm. I mean my leg.

Think, KJ. You don't have strength, but you do have brains.

This bastard is going to have to let go eventually, then he's going to go for my throat. Which only gives me a split second...I try to get a sense of my surroundings. I won't be winning this with my ability to fight.

The pain flares again when his jaws pull back, serrating the skin like jagged knives. The world darkens and blurs at the edges, and I hold onto consciousness with all I have. As his head rears back, my throat his target, I bunch everything in. Four legs. The last of my strength.

And push.

The wolf catapults into the air, the intent to return already etched in his furious face.

But he hasn't registered what I have.

Our tumble brought us close to the edge of the hill. This wolf won't be landing on his feet, ready to attack again.

His eyes finally flash with fear when he doesn't find terra firma like he expected. His body losing its sense of balance as his center of gravity disappears, triggering frantic scrabbling. But it's too late. His claws scrape the edge but never gain traction as he tumbles backward. His face, grimy with my blood, is the last thing I see as he drops. The sound of his body crashing past trees and rocks tells me we just lost our chance at getting what this whole thing had been all about.

Shifting back to human is a relief, but I don't get up straight away. Sharp pebbles dig into my back as I stare at the blue sky. Man, my shoulder feels like it's been through a shredder.

"KJ!" Sayen crumples beside me, dark eyes frantic. "Are you—"

I hold up my good hand. "I'm fine."

Sayen grasps it as she glances at my shoulder. "You're really not. We need to get you back."

"I like that idea." I go to sit up only to have a grenade detonate down my arm. "Maybe in a sec."

Sayen pulls off her jacket and slips it under my head. She sits there, looking at me. There's an expression of wonder on her face I've never seen before. "You shifted."

I try to glare through the pain. "You didn't."

The talk as to why Sayen decided that she'd face the wolf with Furious is one we're going to have. Soon. Right now, though, her lips seemed to have caught my attention...again...

"Why would you do that?"

Sayen is watching me closely, and I know I have to be honest with my answer. I could be glib and tell her I would've done the same for anyone, which is the truth. I could point out that the only way I can convince her she's wrong about Kurt is if she's alive. Also the truth.

But there are levels to truth. Layers in honesty. And near-death experiences mean you tend to cut to the chase.

"Because I think you've shown me...hope."

I'm not sure if I pull her down or if Sayen folds into me, but our lips touch, brush, then touch again. They're softer than I let myself imagine. It's more amazing than I could've dreamed.

As I kiss her, I don't know who I'm kissing—Sayen, the mysterious girl who welcomed death? Or Sayen, the one who lives for everything I've rejected? I pull back, uncertainty undermining the most unforgettable kiss I've ever experienced. Was this the right thing to do, no matter how much my heart thought so?

Her hand comes down to caress my cheek, sending a shiver down my spine. "You've been bitten by a rabid wolf, KJ."

Holy crap. Suddenly, the pain in my shoulder intensifies. I've been bitten by a wolf with Furious. Oh no. The virus is traveling through my bloodstream as we speak.

Sayen's fingers slip back into my hair. "You're going to be fine. Furious can't transfer to humans."

Dammit.

Kissing her was the wrong thing to do.

HUNTER

"Now that's impressive."

My sister turns to me wide-eyed as we watch Ava. I nod, conscious that Noah and Eden are behind us. What are they thinking as they watch their daughter work her magic on Sakari? What would they think if they knew why Sakari was so unwell?

Ava knows. She pointed out that things were desperate. That the decision was made with the best of intentions.

To save the wolves. To try and stop them from going extinct.

Now I have to develop the faith that Ava has, that it will all work out okay. Somehow...

Ava sits back, shoulders sagging. She's finished, and although she won't admit it, she's tired. This is the second day in a row she's had to heal Sakari. The pups are progressively sucking the life out of her. I never thought I'd think it, but I hope these pups come soon. I don't think Sakari has much time left.

And moving the wolves only added to her stress.

The warehouse we're in is industrial and cavernous. We're all here—my family, my pack, Eden's parents, and Josh—and it feels like we're standing in a massive metal cave. The wolves, each in their own crate, are lined up against the back wall.

This is where they'll stay till tomorrow morning...when we fly them out to Jacksonville.

Riley brushes my arm. "I'm going to miss them."

I nod and sigh simultaneously. "I hate that we had to do it."

Eden comes to stand on my other side. Her green eyes, so much like Ava's, are warm as she looks at me. "They'll be well looked after. You made the right call."

Faith, Hunter. All you need is Faith. "It's the only way we can keep them safe."

Ava told us everything she heard at the airport. Knowing the poachers are coming has given us the upper hand. I wouldn't mind seeing Kyle's face after he goes to the effort of getting into Resolve only to find it empty of wolves. It's the only positive out of this whole mess.

Moving Sakari, despite the late stage of her pregnancy, wasn't an easy call. Ava and Eden had used their Fae skills to make the move as smooth as possible. It was touching to see the bond between mother and daughter as they stayed tight by Sakari's side.

Like she knew I was already missing her, Ava walks over. She's beside me, hand tucked in mine, before I can wonder how she feels about her parents being here. Seeing what she can do. Seeing her with me. I pull in a breath to settle my heart. It feels good to know she wants to stake a claim.

She looks at me, then the others. "The pups are strong. Sakari is doing fine."

Everyone nods, but stays quiet. Despite all the space around us, the warehouse feels oppressive with the amount of tension in here.

Noah steps up beside me. "Shall we do a last run through? They could come as early as tonight."

I nod, noticing that despite his rank and age, he's letting me take the lead. It fills me with a sense of responsibility at the same time as being deeply intimidating. I turn back to the crates. "The wolves are secure?"

Gareth nods. "Being cooped up isn't going to be fun, but at least they'll be alive."

"Good. And everyone knows when they're on the roster? Even though there won't be any wolves at Resolve, we need to make it look like there is. It's going to have to be guarded twenty-four-seven."

Everyone nods, their faces resolute.

Noah crosses his arms. "Kyle said they'll be doing this under the cover of darkness. We have three doors coming into Resolve, which we'll not only patrol, but have cameras trained on them. They should never get beyond them."

Eden joins her husband. "If they try to get in, they'll fail, never realizing it's a waste of their time."

A collection of nods ripples around me.

I can feel Ava's tension and it matches mine. Maybe it's the tension of everyone around me. We have to plan for an attack on Resolve, act like we're protecting what's inside.

As we ship the wolves away from everything they've known.

Ava smiles, probably the only person who could at a time like this. "Our wolves stay safe until we solve this."

Solve Furious. Solve the tension building between humans and wolves. I look around. And now Weres.

I look down at the girl who makes me believe the impossible.

Challenge. Accepted.

Turing back to everyone, I pull in a breath. Everything we've discussed up until now has been familiar. But I brought everyone in here for more than a recap. It's time to make sure everyone is clear. "And if the worst happens, and they get through...no one shifts." I look around, hating that I have to say this. "No one gets hurt."

It doesn't surprise me that Thomas doesn't like that. "Then what are we supposed to do if they get in? They won't like us trying to stop them from getting any further. Do we ask them politely to leave?"

I pick up one of the two tranquilizer guns sitting on a crate. "If worse comes to worst and they try to get physical, you use one of these."

Thomas' face clouds in a way I've seen before. He's about to point out there are only two guns and several of them. If he's really thought it through, then he'll point out that tranquilizers take time to act. If someone's coming at you, they aren't going to be much help.

A part of me wishes I could be there tonight. Kyle isn't likely to strike the first day his friends arrived, but the amount of anger being held by Weres makes me nervous. Even without wolves to protect at Resolve, if they get pushed too far, their anger could overflow.

So how do I explain that this is what we stand for? That he's going to have to trust me? Trust Ava?

I hide my shock when I feel a hand rest on my arm. Eden smiles at me as she holds it there. Noah comes around to stand beside Ava. Whoa. They're giving their Prime Alpha tick of approval.

Josh and Riley smile. Gareth arches an impressed brow. Mom looks like she's going to faint with pride. Thomas looks like he just had a shot of apple cider vinegar. The others seem to take a collective breath, as if they're coming to terms with it.

For now, I'll take it. "Tomorrow these guys fly out to a center with a whole lot more manpower. After that, they can have a guest tour if they like."

One night. That's all we need to get through.

Everyone begins to disperse. It's late afternoon and we all have jobs to do.

Riley hugs me goodbye. "I wish I could stay with you guys. The wolves are going to be unsettled by this all."

I ruffle her fringe, knowing how much she hates it. "Resolve needs to look as normal as possible. Plus, once the wolves go to sleep, this place is going be a dead zone."

It'll just be Ava and me, alone...

"Fine then. But I want updates. I'm not going to be sleeping anyway."

We watch them all leave. Ava hugs her parents goodbye, the affection obvious between them. I can see where she got her quiet strength from. Noah and Eden exude a calmness and confidence that's impressive, even when the way forward is so obviously murky.

Faith. That's what they radiate. They're like the freaking sun with the stuff. I'm glad they'll be there at Resolve tonight. The wolves may not be there, but those most important to me will be.

The moment they're all gone, Ava is back in my arms. I breathe in her scent, still awed that she's here. "I'm glad you came back."

Her wintergreen eyes twinkle. "I wasn't going to."

"You shouldn't have. This was my bridge to build." I brush a strand of gossamer hair back. "I was coming, you know. After Kyle, after I realized." Ava's eyes warm and my chest does the same. I'm glad I'm telling her. "Except I couldn't."

"Because Kyle is here."

I shake my head. That irony was something I could've done without. "Saving him made me see what you'd been saying, but I couldn't leave Resolve."

Ava doesn't respond, but her face says it all. It softens with tenderness, it glows with love.

"So, like I said. I'm glad you came back."

Her hand comes up to cup my cheek. "To be honest, I'm not sure I had it in me to get on that plane. It felt like I was giving up on you. On us."

Humbled by this girl, my forehead comes down to touch hers. "I love you."

She pushes up, her lips so close I can feel her breath. "Our love began before we were even sure the other existed. I've always loved you, Hunter."

Our kiss is slow. Deliberate. Deep.

We take the time to reconnect and reaffirm. Our touch, from our lips to our hearts, is a pact and a pledge.

I pull back before it turns to more. It's inevitable with this much emotion and so much hanging over us. I'm not sure what tonight will bring, but I do know that long hours are about to stretch out in front of us, and last time we had that, pulling away was the hardest thing I've ever done. Could this be the time to ask?

"Ava."

Her eyes flutter open, so full of passion that I almost forget what I was about to say.

"You're my heart, Ava. My sun. The other half of my soul. One day..."

Ava tenses, and my heart hitches. Does she know what I'm trying to say?

But the word Bonding has never been mentioned. Is it too soon?

I clear my throat. "I know this is happening so fast. I know the world feels like a pressure cooker at the moment. But I'm wondering..."

Jeez, this is taking some time to get to the point.

But Ava's face is slowly blooming a smile. Her eyes devour me as she waits. Man, this girl has patience patented.

A quick breath and I know the words are ready. They're more than ready.

"Ava. I want forever—"

My phone rings loudly through the warehouse. Dammit. This isn't a time I can ignore it.

Ava shakes her head. "Grab it. We need to make sure everything's okay."

Frowning, I pull it out of my pocket. "If this is Riley wanting to know if any of the wolves have sneezed, I'm going to..."

Except Josh's name lights up the screen. I jab the cell, lifting it to my ear.

"Hunter."

My shoulders whip back as I straighten. The frown in Josh's voice is obvious. "Is everything okay?"

"It's the screens. The cameras are all down."

Ava's by my side in a second as I put it on speaker phone. "What? How?"

The sound of Josh rapping on a keyboard filters through. "I don't know. They just...died."

This isn't good. It's barely twilight outside. "Get KJ on the phone. See what he can do from his end, maybe he can walk you through how to fix this."

"Will do."

The line goes dead as Ava and I stare at each other. There are no wolves to monitor at Resolve, but the poachers don't know that. What it does mean, is that Josh and the others won't be able to see the poachers coming. They'll be a bunch of sitting ducks. Worse, they'll be a bunch of blind sitting ducks.

I tuck my phone in my pocket. My first instinct is to go over there, but then I stop.

Ava is looking at me, biting her lip.

I grasp her hand. "We need to figure out our next move."

Ava nods. "You want to go to Resolve."

Damn, this girl is a mind reader. "But you can't leave the wolves."

She shakes her head.

Which makes the decision easy. "Then we stay here."

Ava tries to hide the surprise, but she doesn't quite manage it. "Okay."

I arch a brow at her, wondering how I can consider smiling at a time like this. "I haven't learned how to clone myself yet."

Her own eyes twinkle. "Was I supposed to try and convince you to go?"

I pull her in, fitting her against me. "Let's see if they can get the surveillance back up. Your parents are there, Gareth's there. I'm pretty sure I'm redundant anyway."

Ava's arms are tight around my waist. "I need you."

My own arms are like a vice around her. "Ditto."

The desire to make this girl mine is almost overwhelming. As much as it makes me nervous, it's inevitable that I'll talk of our future tonight. I want the world to know we belong together.

We're on the trajectory for the inevitable next kiss when a soft *clang* sounds outside the warehouse. We pause, then pull back. Holding still, we wait.

The sound was quiet enough that a human probably wouldn't have heard it, so it's probably the wind or something. There's no way the poachers could know we're here. We went to great lengths to load the wolves up within the compound, not using the trucks with an open back, spreading out the transport over the entire day, unloading them only once the warehouse doors were shut.

When I can't hear anything else I start to slowly unwind. It's going to be a long night.

My arms are just relaxing when Sakari growls deep in her crate. I'm instantly on high alert, back to holding Ava tight.

Simultaneously, we move closer to the crates. It's probably nothing...

The door at the other end opens with a *bang* and my heart leaps in my chest. Anyone from Resolve would have rung or knocked. I press dial on my phone and then mute it, hoping I'm overreacting.

When Kyle separates from the shadows I narrow my eyes. His three cronies appear in a triangular formation behind him.

Shit.

Ava comes to stand on my right, her hand twisting tightly through mine.

Kyle stops a few feet away, and I already hate the smile on his face. "Vacant warehouse, huh? Romantic."

"Leave. Now."

He chuckles. "Or what?"

Dammit. Kyle knows I can shift, and he's brought an audience.

Turkey looks like he's bouncing on his toes. "There are four crates, Kyle. Four!"

Kyle surveys the enclosed cages behind us like a predator at a banquet. "Nice little bonus, isn't it?"

Stall. That's all I've got, and hope to hell Josh has realized what's going on. Cutting the cameras at Resolve was a decoy.

I can feel Ava's fear tightly encased in an armor of determination. She stares hard at Kyle. "These are the last of the arctic wolves. You can't kill them."

Kyle rubs his chin in thought. "The last ones, huh? I'll make sure I mention that to Helix. Should bump up the price."

Brick rubs his hands together behind him. The other guy hasn't moved, which tells me I need to watch them even more closely.

"Kyle, please. One of them is pregnant."

Kyle's lip curls as he takes a step forward. "I need the money now."

Taking their cue, the others move out. We're trapped. The wolves behind us. The poachers in front of us. I do the math—four of them. Two of us.

Kyle's dark gaze zeroes in on me. His eyes are hot with hatred. "Turn."

"I don't know what you're talking about."

"You know exactly what I'm talking about. A lifetime of searching is about to pay off."

The others pause around him, and I'm guessing this wasn't part of the plan.

"I saved your life, Kyle." It's the only reason he knows Weres exist.

He smiles again. "Thought it would make a difference, did you?"

I don't answer. Of course, I did. Kyle now knows the wolf he shot wasn't just a wolf. It was human. But it doesn't seem to matter. Whatever his drive is, it's stronger.

Shit.

Ava straightens as she pulls in a breath. "You need to stop. We won't let you hurt these animals."

"That's what I'm hoping."

If we shift, Kyle has proof Weres exist. He has three witnesses. And a pelt he's desperate for.

If we don't, we're outnumbered and leave the wolves vulnerable. I leave Ava vulnerable.

Rage and fear are pumping through my veins. I channel them, focus them. All we need to do is keep these guys occupied until the others arrive.

Please let them get here in time...

I lower my head, determination tensing my body. "You're not going to get what you're looking for Kyle."

Kyle's hand comes up, and two flicks of his fingers is all it takes.

Two men rush at me as one rushes at Ava. I step in front of her, meaning they dovetail straight at me. Surprise hits Turkey as my fist collides with his jaw. He arches backward through the air, taking out the guy behind him.

Brick powers at me like a battering ram. I don't have time to get a punch lined up, so all I can do is brace myself. His head hits me in the chest, slamming the air straight out of me. But oxygen can wait. This prick isn't getting to Ava or the wolves.

I shove him backward and he stumbles. I've just raised my fist when a voice, high and frantic, sends shards of ice down my spine.

"Hunter!"

The new guy has Ava. His face is unmoving as she struggles against the hold he has on her arms. With a sharp movement, he yanks her in, slamming her back into him. One arm is around her waist, the other on her throat, and all I can do it watch.

"Don't shift, Ava!"

Ava pauses, helplessness flashing through the anger in her eyes. I take a step toward her, but she grimaces as the man's hands tighten in warning.

"Did you hear that?" Kyle sweeps around, pointing at me in victory. "That's what I was talking about?"

I straighten, breathing hard not because of the fight, but because fear is a hurricane in my chest. "I don't want her to move, Kyle. You're crazy."

We need time.

I need to get Ava away from that bastard.

The wolves are barking and snarling in their crates. I entertain letting them out for the briefest of seconds, but we don't need more deaths at the hands of wolves. I hate how tied my hands feel.

"Your girl's caught, Hunter. The wolves are ours for the taking." Kyle angles his head, his eyes full of challenge. "What are you going to do about it?"

"I can't believe I saved your life, your worthless piece of—"

Kyle jerks his wrist and a knife flicks out. "The girl first."

I roar my denial, but as I leap forward, Ava cries out. The guy smiles as his muscles bunch, and his whole body acts like a vice. Ava's scream is cut short.

Like I've hit an invisible wall, I jerk still. "You will not hurt her!"

"You know how to fix this, Hunter. I'm not sure why you're fighting the inevitable."

There's no doubt in my mind Kyle has a gun on him. There's no way he'd be baiting me knowing what I can become. Which means I'd have to be quick.

Which means if I shift, I become the killer I tried so hard not to be.

Ava is shaking her head, tears creating two wet streaks down her face. "No," she mouths.

Kyle stalks forward, his eyes hot with victory. "I'm close. We both know you could end this in an instant."

I could end him in an instant.

Another couple of steps and Kyle's scent fills my nostrils. The scent forever associated with my father's death. The scent that for some reason I let live.

There's another scuffle as Ava begins to struggle again. "You don't know what you're doing, Kyle. You don't understand who he is."

Kyle's eyes never leave mine. "I know exactly what he is."

But Kyle doesn't know who or what Ava is.

What we are.

I straighten. Back-up won't be here in time. Maybe they weren't coming at all. A decision has to be made.

Taking a step forward, I come toe to toe with Kyle. Determination is a blaze burning through my body. "My promise to keep Ava and the wolves safe is my reason to breathe." Triumph is an ugly flare across Kyle's face, but as I say that truth, another one is right there beside it. "What you haven't figured out yet, is that same vow extends to humans."

Kyle, spins away, just like I thought he would. I already know I'll do everything I can to stop any of them from hurting Ava.

I don't expect him to twist back, face contorted with violence. There's no time to react to the blade that slices through the air.

Pain screams through me as the knife plunges into my side. The warm gush of blood is instantaneous and Kyle grimaces in satisfaction as he jerks it in deeper. "All you had to do was change, Hunter."

I try not to cry out, but a strangled groan filters through my clenched teeth.

I hit the ground hard. The knife clatters on the concrete beside me.

Ava screams, but I can't get to her.

It feels like the knife is still in there, piercing deeper and twisting further with each beat of my heart. I grab my side, feeling the flow of blood, wondering how the hell I'm going to stop it.

"Hold on, Hunter." Ava's by my side, her voice trembling and I know she's crying. "I'll heal you."

I fight the blackness. I can't afford to lose consciousness.

"Ava." Crap, my voice is nothing but a hoarse whisper. "Sakari. The wolves."

My vision narrows to Ava's frantic face above me.

My knowledge whittles down to one fact.

If I'm dead I can't protect them.

29

AVA

There's so much blood.

It pools on the concrete, a puddle steadily spreading. It coats Hunter's hands. It's slick and sticky against my own.

I try to get the wracking sobs under control—I don't have much time.

Kyle stands over me, but I ignore him. Hunter's thread is hemorrhaging along with his body. Feet run past, and I try to do the same with them. If they hurt me, then Hunter dies, and if that happens, then this isn't a world I want to live in.

The man who held me strides past. "Ignore her. Get the wolves."

No! The wolves! "Stop! Can't you see he's dying?"

Kyle curls his lip as he turns away. "Yes. It was a waste, wasn't it?"

The wolves barking and growling become a roar of noise as the men move in. Every cage except Sakari's. No...Sakari doesn't have the strength to cope with this. Sweet saints, we can't lose her now. Not after everything she's survived...

Kyle pulls out a gun as two others expose the long blades of their knives. "We need to be quick."

The knowledge I can't save them all spears me in the chest. I cry out, but the sound just echoes off the metal walls. The poachers close around the first crate.

Sakari's crate.

Hunter's face is the palest I've ever seen it. His skin looks like a shade of the concrete he lies on, his lips are almost colorless. I can feel him fading.

I know I have to save him first. Without Hunter I'm nothing.

I drop my head, closing off what feels so inevitable around me. I find Hunter's thread, so achingly frail, and pour myself into it. The motes rush through, finding him, flaring bright as they flow into him.

I know within a heartbeat that it's not enough. It's like I haven't turned the tap on hard enough, or his essence is leaving faster than I can recharge it.

A sob escapes me, and it feels like my chest is rupturing. This can't be happening. I can't be too late.

I can't lose Hunter.

In desperation, I find my thread, I find theirs. I find the wolves'. Then I find the intersections and connections and junctions. There's mine to Hunter and to everybody in this room. There's Hunter's, so fragile, but still the lifeline I need it to be. I find the ones that the poachers don't even know connect them to the wolves. To us.

And I breathe into them, flare the energy.

Inject into them all the hope and heart that I can.

All of a sudden, the motes feel like they've been injected with electricity. They spill from me to Hunter, but then surge out like they can't be contained. Like some power plant just exploded, the golden streams arch out, creating a magnificent web between every living being within the warehouse.

It's glorious. It's the most beautiful thing I've ever been a part of.

And it quickly becomes the most terrifying.

My head swims, nausea surges in my gut. Pain swells and I don't know if it's mine or Hunter's or something else.

Hunter's body arches and I gasp. I don't know if I'm helping or hurting, whether his energy is being replenished or depleted. I grab him, not knowing what to do, but knowing I won't let him go.

Like a switch has been flipped, the web disappears. It's gone so completely, that I wonder whether I just imagined it all. Hunter collapses back onto the concrete, and I fold over him.

Please, please...

He's breathing! Hope blooms through my chest. Holding my breath, I watch and wait as reality tries to intrude.

"Sweet lord, what have we done?"

A knife clatters to the ground. A door slams. Silence swallows the room.

Hunter's eyes flutter open. He looks up at me, face slack with wonder. I have no idea what just happened, but I don't care.

Hunter is undeniably, beautifully alive.

With that knowledge, I stop fighting the blackness and let it take me.

Hunter's going to be okay.

WHEN CONSCIOUSNESS FINDS ME AGAIN, it brings confusion with it. I'm in a bed, nothing but a sense of comfort and safety enveloping me. As I pull myself from the depths, I register my surroundings in stages. The pillow, the scent I now associate with home. Quietness giving way to the sound of someone else breathing.

A rhythm I know. A rhythm that's familiar.

I open my eyes, searching for him, panic shooting down my nerves.

The poachers.

The wolves.

Hunter!

And then he's there, face close, eyes warm. "Hey, it's okay. I'm fine."

I flop back into the pillows, recognizing I'm in his bedroom. "What...?"

Hunter brushes back my hair, his copper eyes so full of tenderness it makes my eyes sting. "Everyone's fine. Just take it easy. You've been out for a solid twenty-four hours."

A whole day! "But they were going to—"

"Sh, I'll explain it all, I promise. Everything's fine."

Seeing as that's the third time he's said that, I finally allow myself to relax. Taking him in, I let myself appreciate that maybe he's telling the truth. Apart from some seriously mussed up hair, Hunter looks...amazing.

Grabbing his hand, I bring it to my cheek. It's warm and strong. With my other hand, I brush his lips, feeling the moist breath brush my fingers.

"Ava."

Gosh, I love it when he says my name like that. It's something I'll never tire of. Possibly because it usually precedes a kiss.

But he pulls back, gazing at me. "You were really out of it. You scared me there for a while."

I jerk my head back. "I scared you?" My voice peaks with incredulity.

From outside the door, there's a scuffle. "She's awake!"

A second later, it flings open and Riley rushes in. "She's definitely awake!"

Behind her comes Josh, who I figured wasn't far away, but

then Lauren, and finally my parents. Mom rushes in next to Hunter, anxious eyes searching my face.

I grasp her hand. "I'm fine, Mom. I swear."

Dad's behind her, his hand on her shoulder and I swallow when I see his eyes are as misty as hers. His jaw works and for the first time in my life, I realize he's speechless.

I smile up at him. "Love you too, Dad."

He nods sharply. "Always will."

I look around at the smiling faces, enjoying the love that fills the room, a little uncomfortable at being the center of attention. "Can someone fill me in on what happened?"

Riley plops herself on the end of the bed. "The wolves left this morning. They'd be in Jacksonville by now."

"Oh." I wanted to be there for them.

Josh nudges Riley over. "They did fine. It was smooth sailing —" He grins at me, "Flying the whole way."

I relax a little. "Well, that's good news." I frown. "But the poachers, they were..."

Hunter clasps my hand, squeezing it. "They didn't. The wolves were never hurt."

I look around the room, confused by Hunter's words, but even more so by the mix of expressions around the room. Mom and Dad have some weird blend of surprise and pride. Josh and Riley are staring at me with awe.

Only Hunter seems to have taken whatever happened in his stride. I focus on him. "And?"

Except then he blushes. I push myself upright a little more. "Tell me."

"Well, after you...ah, healed me, the poachers seemed to see the world differently."

"Differently?" None of this is making sense.

Hunter pulls in a sigh, then levels his gaze at me. "They can't see the threads, but now they can feel them."

What? I stare at Hunter, mouth slack with shock.

Josh nods. "We arrived just after. They were shell-shocked, Ava. They kept looking at you and Hunter and the wolves, trying to get their head around it."

Riley grins. "One was crying."

They can feel what I see? "But that—"

"Means they can feel their pain." Hunter finishes for me. "They won't be hurting any more wolves."

I'm glad I'm sitting down. My brain is so focused on trying to assimilate this, there's no way I could do something like stay upright right now.

Hunter frowns. "Although Kyle was long gone before anyone even realized."

I flop backward, suddenly exhausted, but trying to understand what this is going to mean.

Mom leans over to kiss me on the forehead. "We can think this through later, honey. You need to rest."

"Mom. I've been out for twenty-four hours. I don't need to—" Except I'm interrupted by my own traitorous body as I yawn.

Dad arches a brow at me before heading to the door. "Everyone out. My daughter isn't going to have a nap because she isn't tired."

Josh and Riley are grinning and holding hands as they head out. Mom graces me with another kiss before following them. Dad looks at Hunter, but Hunter doesn't move. "I'll wait here."

"Like you have from the moment she fainted?"

Hunter's lips twitch. "Basically."

Dad nods, glancing over at me. "You got yourself a good one."

I grin. "Damn straight I did."

With a chuckle, Dad pulls the door closed. Suddenly, it feels like they took all of my energy with them.

Hunter pulls up the duvet, his face now stern. "You heard your parents. Rest."

Too tired to argue, I snuggle down but then shuffle over. I don't want to be away from Hunter any more than he does me. "Join me?"

Hunter opens his mouth and I can see the no already forming on his lips. Mr. Protective is here, huh?

I blink up at him. I doubt Hunter's slept since this all happened. "You'd argue with a sick girl?"

Hunter's grin is immediate and so is the flash of joy in my chest. Gingerly, he climbs in and settles down. I wait till he's finished before firmly tucking myself around him. When my head settles on his chest, I let out a sigh. This is where I belong.

Hunter's chuckle is soft but I glory in the sound and sensation. "You're the strongest person I know, Ava."

I place a kiss on his body beside me. "I love you too, Hunter."

Just as sleep is about to pull me down, I start. Holy cow, how could I forget? "Hunter—"

Hunter's eyes glow as he looks down on me. "Sakari had her pups in the warehouse, while you were..." He waves his hand as if casting a spell.

That's why she was quiet. Poor Sakari, having to give birth in a crate, all alone. Holy heck, her pups! I look up at Hunter, eyes wide. "And?"

"They're beautiful, healthy arctic wolves."

As I sink back onto his chest, I smile.

Who knows what tomorrow's going to bring. The problems that sparked the war that almost broke out in the warehouse still exist. There's no way changing the views of a handful of poachers is going to make enough of a difference.

But Hunter and I have started something.

Something good.

30

SAYEN

"I couldn't do it."

As the words spill out, shame fills me. Like hot acid, it burns through my insides and I have to clutch my stomach. I wait, the cell pressed hard against my ear, for the voice on the other end to respond.

"That's disappointing."

I close my eyes, wincing. The task was straightforward, and this mission was important. Every step of this plan is needed for us to execute it. We can't afford for anyone to be weak.

But as I'd stood over the pups, their little white bodies curled in sleep, I couldn't do it.

There's a sigh. "Actually, I'm glad."

I frown, confused. "You're glad?"

The laugh on the end of the line is a soft one. A familiar one. It's the laugh that I got when I was five and demanded to know why I'd been brought to the Tate ranch. That was the day I discovered I was an orphan.

"Seems it was meant to be. I have a new plan for those pups."

I don't bother asking. I won't be told until I need to know. I hang my head. "I'm sorry. I failed you."

"We've all tasted failure, Sayen. Ultimately, it makes you stronger the next time you'll be faced with a decision like this."

I straighten my shoulders. We all know where this is heading —there'll be times I'll be making this decision again. "It won't happen next time."

"I know it won't." I pull myself up another inch at the edge of steel in the voice. It's the uncompromising strength that I clung to as a child. It turned me from a lost little girl to someone my father would be proud of. "And how is our friend, KJ?"

KJ. The first person to kiss me. "Just as determined to find out what he can about Furious."

The laugh, part chuckle, part exhale, creeps into my ear again. "I love his determination."

I'm not so sure. It was KJ's face that flashed in my mind as I'd stood beside the pups, a syringe full of green liquid in my hand. Images of him leaning over a microscope telling me he's not hungry, scanning reams of data for hours on end. KJ focusing on my lips...

A giant russet wolf saving my life.

KJ's determination has had an uncomfortable side effect I don't like.

"Well, the wolf we were tracking died. We weren't able to get a sample."

"Poor KJ. I'm wondering if it's time for Kurt's son to get what he wants."

I frown, confused. "We're going to give him a sample of Furious?"

This time the laugh is louder, actually full of humor. "It's time for you to show your willingness to right your wrong, Sayen."

I harden every muscle in my body. "I'm ready." I won't let Helix down again.

"Good. I'm thinking it's time for KJ to join us."

31

AVA

R esolve without wolves is like school on summer break. The halls feel empty. The building feels like it's redundant. Anyone walking into it wonders when it'll come back to life again.

Hunter is staring at the screens, a habit I doubt he'll ever break. I slip under his arm, hoping I never get tired of the warmth that comes with him wrapping it around me. "I'm going to miss this place."

Hunter's sigh is low and long. "Yeah. I know. And I never thought I'd say that."

I've only been here for a few short months. This has been Hunter's life for over two years. And it's not just Resolve he's leaving...

I rest my head on his shoulder, breathing his wild scent in. "I hope you like Jacksonville."

Can Hunter be happy away from the tundra?

The brush of a kiss on my head is sweet and light. "My heart is with you, and the wolves. The only way it can be happy is when I'm with them."

I squeeze him tight. This guy always knows the right thing to say.

Hunter tenses and I pull back. Has he suddenly realized exactly what he's leaving behind? His family. His pack. Everything that defines him.

"Someone's coming."

The camera aimed at the parking lot shows a truck pulling in, and it's not a truck we know.

I frown. "There's nothing here to see."

Hunter releases me and steps closer to the screen. "Son of a..."

As three doors open and three bodies climb out, I gasp. It's the poachers. We haven't seen or heard from them since the night at the warehouse four days ago. The night that Kyle tried to kill Hunter.

But also the night that Hunter believes they discovered exactly how connected we all are.

I grasp his hand. "Let's see what they want."

Hunter's frown is the biggest I've seen in the past few days. Recovering from my little fainting episode took longer than I expected. Waves of weakness kept hitting me even if I was sitting around watching TV.

Hunter had been there to anticipate anything I could need. A sandwich. A drink. A laugh and a kiss. There'd been a sweetness and lightness about him that had taken my breath away on a daily basis. I didn't think it was possible, but I fell even deeper in love with this guy over the past few days. It cemented the idea that blossomed when I learned we're going home tomorrow. Although maybe idea isn't the best term. It's more of a hope.

Which is why the storm clouds darkening his face frustrate me. Hunter's had so few opportunities to be nothing but loved and in love and that was going to end when we returned to the mainland. But now these guys have cut that short.

Hunter pauses, pulling us to a stop. "Are you up for this? It's probably nothing we want to hear anyway."

I plant a quick kiss on his lips. "I've had the most amazing guy nursing me back to health. I couldn't be better."

He frowns even deeper. "Well, if they undo all my good work, then I'm not going to be nice."

I tug him toward the door, working hard not to smile. "Neither will I."

We meet the poachers outside of Resolve. Even without the wolves in there, we don't want them familiar with the layout of the building. The door shuts behind us and we pull up a few feet away. My muscles knot with tension. Although we joked about this, who knows what this showdown is going to look like.

I resist glancing at the camera behind us. There's nothing Hunter and I can't face, but it's comforting knowing that KJ might be watching.

Standing side by side, we watch them approach. The guy Hunter calls Brick is at the forefront, the other two on either side. Kyle isn't among them and I don't know what that means.

They stop a few feet away, maintaining a healthy distance. Neither Hunter or I speak. Why they're here has yet to be revealed.

Brick clears his throat. "Ah, we just wanted to...ah..."

Seeing Brick nervous is almost entertaining. It's also intriguing.

The tall guy that I saw at the airport steps up, assessing Hunter. "So, you're completely healed."

Hunter crosses his arms. "Yep."

He nods slowly. "We're here to apologize."

I feel Hunter's surprise flash alongside mine. Apologize?

Brick nods too. "What happened at the warehouse...we didn't realize."

The one Hunter named Turkey hangs his head. "We've done so much wrong."

The pain in his voice clenches my heart so hard it makes my eyes sting. As a collective, these three men are full of shame and remorse. Now it's their turn to wait, and I feel like we're now their judges.

I shake my head. "Like you said, you didn't know."

Hunter finally unwinds his arms, his hand coming down to clasp mine. "It's the choices you make now that count."

They all glance at each other, and the tall guy straightens, owning his full height. "That's why we're here. We want to help."

This time Hunter's shock is far stronger than mine. They want to help? We glance at each other, both totally speechless.

Turkey's hands are wringing each other so tightly I feel sorry for them. "We feel it now. We need to right our wrongs."

I open my mouth to respond but then stop. Maybe Hunter and I need to talk about this. These men worked with Kyle. They wanted to kill our wolves.

Hunter's hand squeezes mine. "Who is Helix?"

The tall guy shakes his head. "We don't know."

Hunter starts to move, obviously ready to walk away, but Brick steps forward, his hand outstretched. "We're telling the truth!"

"We've only spoken on the phone," says tall guy. "And he uses voice modulation technology." He shrugs. "All we can tell you is that Helix is willing to pay a lot of money for wolf pelts."

I look up at Hunter—they're telling the truth.

Hunter seems to come to a decision, and I somehow know it's the right one. "The wolves are no longer here. We sent them to the mainland."

Turkey and Brick look surprised, possibly disappointed, but their new spokesperson simply nods, eyes assessing. "Makes sense. They'll be safer there." He turns on his heel, and his two friends glance at each other, confused. "That's where we'll head. We'll offer our help at the reserve in Jacksonville."

Turkey and Brick grin. They look like two children who just got what they secretly asked Santa for Christmas. Turkey actually waves, while Brick gives a jaunty salute.

With that, they climb back into their truck and drive away.

I look up at Hunter, not surprised to find him just as bemused looking as I feel. "What just happened there?"

"I think we just saw one of the first products of our little Legacy."

"Actually," I say as I reach up to clasp his beautiful face. "This is."

I pull down on his head, pressing my lips to his. His warm, soft mouth touches mine, and I open myself to it. This is what the legacy created.

Us.

When mouths tangle and collide, I get a taste of how much more we can be. How much more I want us to be.

Looking up into his gorgeous copper eyes, I take the last leap of faith. "Before we leave, can we go for one last run?"

Hunter studies me and I have to work hard not to blush. On the surface, it's not a big ask so there's no reason for me to struggle to hold his gaze as heat floods my cheeks.

With a quizzical frown, Hunter grabs my hand and heads for the door. "Your wish. My command."

32

HUNTER

"This is where it all started, huh?"

Ava is turning around in a circle. It's completely white now, so similar to the day she appeared as a golden wolf... which feels like a lifetime ago. Man, I was so sure I was dreaming that night, desperately wishing I wasn't.

She smiles at me, eyes luminescent. "I love this place."

I brush a strand of hair from her face. "We've been through a lot, haven't we?"

"We certainly have."

"And it only made us stronger."

Her smile grows. "In the words of Hunter Rendell, damn straight."

Which is probably a good thing, considering what we've got to deal with when we get to Jacksonville. "It seems we make a pretty good team."

She rolls her eyes. "Which is what I've been trying to tell you. Sakari's pups are beautiful and healthy. We now have three ex-poachers wanting to help." She steps in closer. "Most importantly, nothing can tear us apart now."

Possessiveness swells in my chest. My heart knows Ava is mine. So does my soul.

One day everyone else will too.

I grin. "Damn straight."

I kiss her, knowing that somehow this is the end and the beginning all in one. For some reason, it means the desire seems to explode in a nanosecond. Ava's hands are on me, mine on her, as it sweeps us away.

I pull away before this goes too far, wondering how the snow around us hasn't melted. It's been harder and harder to not follow the trail that our passion blazes. It's a primal call that's almost impossible to resist. But we're not bonded, and I won't do that to Ava. And even though I already know this love is forever, we haven't even spoken about it. I tried in the warehouse, but we were interrupted, and now we're heading to Jacksonville. It's fine. I'm willing to wait.

I smile at her, loving the look of her just-kissed face. "You ready to run?" Who knows how long before we're back here, able to do this again.

If we're back here...

"Almost."

I look around. "What's left to do?"

All of a sudden, that shy look steals across Ava's face. It has me wanting to frown. One thing Ava has never been is shy, which makes me nervous. Instead, I wait. Ava knows she can ask me anything.

"Hunter. Back in the warehouse, you asked about forever...."

"Always, Ava. You have my heart for as long as you want it."

"I want you to know that it's a yes."

My whole body smiles. "I think I'm starting to figure that out."

Ava pulls in a breath. "Which is why I think we should Bond."

I blink. Then blink again. "You're sure?"

Her returning look is the most amazing mix of adoring and exasperated I've ever seen. "Yes, I'm sure."

My heart is dancing so hard I don't know how it's stayed in my chest. "Give me the date and time and I'm there."

"I was thinking of now and here."

Every molecule of air is punched from my lungs. "But... here?" Bondings are public events, to be celebrated with your family and friends.

"I don't need witnesses, Hunter. I just need you."

I swallow. "Now?"

"I want to go back to Jacksonville as bonded mates. You're mine and I'm yours, Hunter. This will cement it, for everyone." She bites her lip as she looks away. "I'm sorry. I'm being pushy. I'm happy to wait if that's what you want."

I tilt her chin up so she can see my eyes as I say my next words. "Ava. For the second time in my life, you've just made all my dreams come true."

Her smile parallels the sensation blooming in my chest. Big and wide and indescribable.

I pull in a steadying breath. I've wished for this moment. I've dreamed of it. But I'm not sure I ever thought it would happen. Every time it played in my mind, there wasn't a crowd—we were out on the tundra. There wasn't pomp and ceremony—there was just...us.

She's right. Here. Now.

It's perfect.

She steps back, creating a breath of distance between us. Face expectant, eyes glowing, she looks at me and waits.

All we need to do is say the words. To be honest, there's never been a bunch of words I wanted to say more. They feel like they've been trying to escape my chest since the moment I saw this girl.

With a conviction born of love, I start. I hold out my hand, palm up and open. "In your hands..."

Ava's face blooms with love as she places her own in it. "I place my trust."

Man, she's beautiful.

Her free hand comes up to tenderly stroke my cheek. "In your eyes..."

"I found my home." I place my palm over her heart, the undeniable flutter beneath connecting somewhere deep within me. "In your heart..."

"I found my love." Ava's voice is so sure, so confident. Her hand comes up to mirror mine, resting on my chest. "In your spirit..."

My chest expands, never wanting to lose the sensation of her touch. "I found my mate."

Together, our eyes locked, our hearts clasped beneath each other's palm, we say the words that will make this binding. Absolute. Forever.

"I give you my body, so that two become one.

I give you my soul, till our life shall be done."

As we stand there, the words a foundation between us, neither of us wanting to so much as blink, something happens. Something blooms. It starts between us, then grows and multiplies until it can't be contained. The warmth doesn't surprise me, it's always been there with Ava.

The color does.

It's a labyrinth of gold sparking from our center. It's a pulsing river of gossamer weaving beneath us. It's a shimmer of energy that seems to rain down on us.

Ava's smile must match mine. Full of wonder, brimming with reverence. She throws back her arms as the threads wind around us. Grabbing her, we're both laughing as I lift her and spin us around. We become the center in this whirlpool of gold. We're surrounded by love and everything it promises.

Hope.

We slow, and the energy seems to dissipate. The golden hue begins to wane.

We simultaneously pull in a breath, staring at each other. At this Bonding, there won't be any music, any dancing. But we don't need it. I can feel our hearts singing, our souls spin and weave in a waltz that's old as the earth we stand on.

This is Ava.

And me.

This is us.

33

KJ

With a click of the mouse, I stop the recording. Who knew that my remote access to the cameras would mean I'd be able to see this. I sincerely doubt Hunter or Ava remembered the camera they set up when they decided to Bond out on the arctic tundra. I even meant to look away when I realized what was happening.

But when I saw their movements, I couldn't look away. It's like trying to look away from a birth or something. You know it's private, but something new and amazing is being created, and deep down, you secretly want to be a part of it.

I couldn't hear the words, but their movements had been full of meaning. I'd leaned in closer when something seemed to shift. Some sort of energy had sucked in like a backdraft. You couldn't see it, but even down the line, you could *feel* it.

When they hugged and spun around, that's when it got real. Like a golden supernova had exploded, a wildfire of energy had burst out. It was a kaleidoscope of only one color—beginning with the not-quite-normal marmalade of Hunter's eyes, and ending with the sunfire gold that could only be Ava.

Then the camera went black. In fact, they short-circuited the entire system even back at Resolve.

It's probably a good thing. No one needs to see what's going to happen next with those two. I have no idea how they've lasted as long as they have. And without the wolves at the center, then I've got plenty of time to get the cameras back up and running.

And despite the unintended invasion, Hunter and Ava now have proof of their Bonding. If they choose to share those glorious moments, no one can contest that they belong to each other.

And what they are going to mean.

To be honest, it's the first ray of hope I've seen since I arrived at Evelyn Island.

And that was over ten years ago. When my mother saw how determined I was, she knew I couldn't grow up under the shadow of my father. It took a few tries to find somewhere I could be anonymous. Somewhere I could have a fresh start, and she had to go as far north as the arctic circle.

But when I moved in with my aunt, I knew that's where I was going to stay. Between Hunter and the barren tundra, it was a no-brainer. I was so sure I'd found the place I could discover redemption.

When Mom died, and I doubt stepping in front of that truck was an accident, I knew I was staying.

Man, I wish I'd never left it. Flicking to the last tab on my screen, I click the cancel button on my flight.

I was looking forward to going home, even though I don't have a sample of Furious. Despite access to all the right equipment, I'm no closer to figuring out what it is, where it came from, and how the hell we're going to nuke it.

Except one person has the answers I'm looking for. The last person I want to be around.

Because I'm drawn to Sayen. I didn't think I'd develop feelings for anyone, let alone a Were.

I've not only done that, I've fallen for a Were who believes in everything my father ever stood for. One who's somehow involved with the darker side of all this. What does that say about me? How do I know which part of Sayen I'm drawn to?

I reach up to pull my beanie down only to remember it's not there. I hate that its loss is probably some metaphor for the change I can feel coming. To be honest, I don't want to know if everything I've been running away from has been a waste of time.

That maybe I can't escape being the legacy of Kurt Channon.

Pushing away from the desk, I freeze as the door opens. Somehow, I know it's her even before I see her striking features. I seem to have memorized everything about this girl.

Her smile is small, possibly a little nervous. "I think we need to talk."

I swallow. "I think you're right."

She doesn't look happy that I agree. She shoves her hands in her pockets, suddenly avoiding eye contact. "Maybe we can talk outside? Get away from the lab for a sec?"

Did not see that coming. The lab is where Sayen and I have spent most of our time. I look around. "It's pretty private. Dawn said something about going out, and no one else comes here at this time of the afternoon."

Sayen closes her eyes for a brief moment, and I frown. Something's not right.

When she opens them, her eyes are the Sayen I used to know. Closed. Unreadable. "I just thought it would be a nice change, that's all."

I shrug, deciding it doesn't really matter. Sayen obviously has something big she wants to talk about it, and so do I. If she wants to talk outside, then we can talk outside. "Fine, lead the way."

Sayen almost looks disappointed, but I'm pretty sure I'm

losing it. Too many hours spent staring at things spinning in the centrifuge machine from the looks of things. I'm probably reading Sayen all wrong.

I follow her down the hall and out the door. Outside, the air is cool with the promise of winter. I focus on looking forward to seeing Hunter again. On the relief that Sakari's pups look like any other arctic wolf pups.

Sayen pauses out front, right beside the plaque that captures where this all started.

United we conquer.

My dad decided that meant we had to unite Weres. Give them a common goal.

Was he right?

Sayen turns, and I'm instantly frowning when I see the shimmer of tears in her eyes.

"Sayen?"

She shakes her head and takes a step back. "I'm sorry," she whispers.

My mouth opens to ask what she's talking about, but a sharp pain stabs my shoulder.

I spin, trying to source the pain, but the world twists further than it should. Nausea blinds me. Darkness closes in, and the world around me narrows to a pinpoint down a tunnel.

I turn back to Sayen.

What the—

THE END

Ready for the next installment of the Prime Prophecy series?
Check out LEGACY FULFILLED!

THE EPIC FINALE TO AN UNFORGETTABLE LOVE STORY

Fighting the power of darkness,
their love will be the light.

Wolf numbers are dangerously low, and with fear of this endangered species spiraling out of control, extinction is a real possibility. Hunter and Ava know the future of all arctic wolves hinges on the survival of three pups. They know they are the legacy everyone is waiting for. And they know their love is strong.

But they're about to face what should be impossible...

Relentless poaching, the deadly virus known as *Furious,* and the faceless threat of Helix have combined to create a monster that will threaten them all. Weres, Fae, and humans are about to face an unstoppable wave of fury.

Ava's destiny is to be the solution. Hunter's promise is to protect at all costs. As the answer become clear, they're going to have to reconcile their responsibilities...and hope their love is powerful enough to alter the choice that seems inevitable.

An epic finale to an unforgettable love story from USA Today Best-Selling author, Tamar Sloan.

CLICK HERE to grab your copy now.

I'D LOVE TO CONNECT!

Don't miss out on notifications and tasters of my upcoming books (I might be biased, but there's some awesome stories in the pipeline)! Subscribe to be the first to know and to make the most of any deals I have on offer.

SIGN UP HERE

Every couple of weeks you'll get exclusive tasters of upcoming books, awesome offers and bargain reads, and an opportunity to connect (personally, I reckon that's the best bit).

There's also some cool freebies coming your way...

I'd love to see you over there.

Tamar :)

ALSO BY TAMAR SLOAN

KEEPERS OF THE LIGHT

Angels and demons have battled for millennia.

Their inevitable war has begun.

Hidden Angel

Chosen Angel

Marked Angel

Forbidden Angel

Rogue Angel

Cursed Angel

Blood Angel

KEEPERS OF THE CHALICE

A vampire. A huntress.

A cure that will change everything.

Vampire Unleashed

Vampire Unveiled

Vampire Undone

Vampire Undefeated

Vampire United

KEEPERS OF THE GRAIL

Seven Gates of Hell. Seven Deadly Sins.

One impossible choice.

Gates of Demons

Gates of Chaos

Gates of Greed

Gates of Wrath

Gates of Secrets

Gates of Hell

THE SOVEREIGN CODE

Humans saved bees from extinction...and created the deadliest threat we've seen yet.

Harvest Day

Hive Mind

Queen Hunt

Venom Rising

Sting Wars

THE THAW CHRONICLES

Only the chosen shall breed.

Burning

Rising

Breaking

Falling

ZODIAC GUARDIANS

Twelve teens. One task. Save the Universe.

DESCENDANTS OF THE GODS

Demigods as you've never seen before.

Child of Crossroads

Daughter of Time

Secret of Fate

Son of Poseidon

Blood of Medusa

ABOUT THE AUTHOR

Tamar really struggled writing this bio, in part because it's in third person, but mostly because she hasn't decided whether she's primarily a psychologist who loves writing, or a writer with a lifelong fascination with psychology.

She must have been someone pretty awesome in a previous life (past life regression indicated a Care Bear), because she gets to do both. Beginning her career as a youth worker, then a secondary school teacher, before becoming a psychologist, Tamar helps children and teens to live and thrive despite life's hurdles like loss, relationship difficulties, mental health issues, and trauma.

As lover of reading, inspired by books that sparked beautiful movies in her head, Tamar loves to write young adult romance. To be honest, it was probably inevitable that her knowledge and love of literature would translate into writing emotion driven stories of finding life and love beyond our comfort zones. You can find out more about Tamar's books at www.tamarsloan.com

A lifetime consumer of knowledge, Tamar holds degrees in Applied Science, Education and Psychology. When not reading, writing or working with teens, Tamar can be found with her husband and two children enjoying country life on their small slice of the Australian bush.

The driving force for all of Tamar's writing is sharing and connecting. In truth, connecting with others is why she writes.

She loves to hear from readers and fellow writers. Find her on all the usual social media channels or her website.